To The One.
You know who you are. XOXOXO

St. Louis Sisters:

A 1970s Retelling of Little Women

by Carly Berg

St Louis Sisters is a work of fiction. Unless
otherwise indicated, all the names, characters,
businesses, places, events and incidents in this book
are either the product of the author's imagination or
used in a fictitious manner. Any resemblance to
actual persons, living or dead, or actual events is
purely coincidental

Part One

December 23, 1976
Black Jack, Missouri

Black Jack, Missouri is about twenty miles north of St. Louis. It was named for three unusually large blackjack oak trees located at the intersection of what is now Old Halls Ferry Road and Parker Road. In the 1840s and thereabouts, this clump of trees provided a shady rest stop for farmers who were hauling their goods to market.

Chapter 1

We've just sat down to our supper of eggs, scrambled with potato, onion and delicious, shameful government cheese, when Mooms makes one of her announcements. She says, "Girls. Don't expect any Christmas presents this year. We don't have money for extras. And we shouldn't be thinking about ourselves now anyway."

Amy rushes out of the dining room, startling the cat, who dashes upstairs. Beth's face blooms into color, like she's about to cry.

It breaks my heart. Granted, Amy's a brat and everything, but she's still only twelve. And Beth might be fourteen, age-wise, but the girl still plays with dolls, for glob's sake.

Besides, if I'd known earlier that Mooms wasn't getting me anything for Christmas, I'd have had the option of not getting her anything, either. I'm more upset about Amy and Beth at the moment, though. I say, "But can't you get a couple cheapie things for the little girls, at least, just from Venture or something? Heck, Zayre or even Grandpa Pidgeons would do. Just a few small things. You know, like candy, barrettes, hand cream, playing cards, socks, just little stuff?" Even Miss Hannah, our unwanted live-in maid, keeps hinting about what she got us all for Christmas. And she's, like, the poorest person in the whole world.

Mooms says, "We'll have a nice Christmas dinner, which is more than Daddy and the other men over there fighting in the Viet Cong will get. We already have our gift. Our gift is being here, safe, fed and together in a free country, Jo." She says "Jo" like my name is a reprimand.

Meg, whose real name is Margaret, just like Mooms's, thinks she is the second Mooms. Meg kicks me under the table. She says we can't argue with Mooms because Mooms is Not Herself, ever since we lost the house and everything. Meg says that Everything Mooms Has Been Put Through made her neurotic, which is liable to cross the line into psychotic city at any time if we aren't careful.

But the rest of us are going through it all too, not just Mooms. We girls had to leave our house, our friends, our schools and everything. And we miss Daddy, too. I shut up though, because who'd want to make their own mother get hauled off by the men in white coats.

Meg pulls Beth into the living room, where Amy's run off to, and gets both little girls settled down. Then, they all come back to the table together and we finish our supper. Well, the rest of them do, anyway. I went ahead and ate mine while it was hot.

Miss Hannah and Beth start clearing the table. Meg, AKA Mooms Junior, pulls me aside in the living room. She says, "Let's get more presents for the little girls, so they'll have a decent Christmas. How about if we each spend at least ten more bucks total, five more on each of them?"

"Okay. I guess so," I say, looking down at my ratty black Converse tennis shoes. I'll never get a pair of the cool cowboy boots I have my eye on. Every time I get close to having enough money saved, something else comes up.

It's dark out now. Meg shuts the Venetian blinds and turns on the Christmas tree lights. The tree is artificial and its branches are bent out of shape from our black cat, Party. He likes to sit on the tree's fake limbs, when he's not busy knocking off ornaments and batting them around the living room. Party usually knocks the whole tree over at least once a day during the Christmas season.

Our tree reminds me of the pitiful one on *A Charlie Brown Christmas*. When we still had our house in west county, it was the tree we'd put up in the basement rumpus room. We'd go out as a family every year after Thanksgiving, to pick out a real tree for the living room.

My gifts are already bought and wrapped in funnies pages from the *Post-Dispatch*. Meg and I chipped in on just about everything. She picked it all out because I'm not very good at picking out girlie stuff. I wrapped it, though. Here's the list of presents:

Mooms

A pair of good leather pumps from Baker's Shoes. They're as close as we could find to her usual pair, but a size larger and "wide." Mooms had to get a receptionist job at the hospital after everything fell apart. She always comes home complaining that her feet are killing her. Her feet swell up, and then her shoes fit too tight.

Meg

I got Meg a ten-dollar gift certificate from Famous-Barr. Meg's a real clothes horse, so I thought she could put it towards something nice.

Beth and Amy

So far, we got them each a winter sweater, green for Beth and red for Amy. And we got them each a

pair of fun, wild-colored toe socks, and a jumbo
Bonne Bell Lip Smacker apiece.

Aunt March

We got her the Emeraude cologne and dusting
powder set. Meg thought the ads for it were very
elegant. Just right for a snobby and rich old bat like
Aunt March.

Miss Hannah

A red sweatsuit from K-Mart. Miss Hannah
always wears an old, bleached-out pink sweatsuit.
Meg thought getting the new one in red, a
Christmas color, was a nice touch. Pink is sickening
on anyone over about five years old anyway, if you
ask me.

Larry

Larry is my new pal next door. His full name is
Laurence Laurence Laurence, which I didn't believe
until he showed me his birth certificate. I rolled him
two fat joints from my latest nickel bag and tied a
red ribbon around them. Mooms Junior doesn't
need to know about it.

Daddy

Nothing. He doesn't deserve anything, after how
corrupt he's turned out to be and I don't know when
I'll see him again anyway.

We hear people outside, singing "Silent Night."
We get bundled up real quick so we can join them.
It's Meg's idea. Meg sings like an angel. I think
we're all so bored in the house that we don't even

care that the carolers didn't actually invite us to come along.

We girls all go, except Beth. She's always been a little frail, which might be due to her being born prematurely, and a little weird, which is definitely due to the Senior and Junior Moomses babying her, if you ask me.

I've tried to straighten the girl out, I really have. A couple of years ago, at our old house, I pulled Beth's stupid dolls apart and snuck them out to the trash can on trash pickup day, in the sliver of time after Daddy left for work but before Mooms got out of the shower. Anybody would agree that twelve (at the time) is too old to play with dolls. Hell's bells, Amy's twelve now and she makes out with boys. Somebody needs to straighten Amy out too, but it's hard to catch her in the act.

Anyway, that day, Beth woke up and noticed that her dolls were gone, then started mewling. "Mommy, Mommy, Miss Beasley is gone! Chatty Cathy and Chrissy are gone!" She had the brand name dolls from when we lived in west county, her own and the ones passed down from my sisters, too. Of course, the Moomses went all crazy, tearing up the place looking for them. They rescued them out of the trash cans at the street, just as the garbage truck was pulling up, globdammit.

The Moomses patched the dolls up and now they are "patients" in Beth's "doll hospital," which is a folded up old blanket on the floor next to her bed. It's hilarious when Party yanks a patient out of bed by its hair and zooms through the house with it.

Party knows that's sure to get him chased, which he apparently finds thrilling.

I got grounded for a month for throwing the dolls away, if you can believe that shit. The Moomses think Beth's interest in dolls is cute or something. They treat her like she is a delicate baby, then they wonder why she gets picked on at school.

So, Meg, Amy and I go out caroling and Beth stays in the house with Miss Hannah and Mooms Senior. Mooms is fixing Beth a mug of hot chocolate with marshmallows, a reward for being babyish and weird.

I'm happy to find Larry out here. It was so funny, he joined the carolers without being invited, too. His guitar is on a fat strap around his neck. I say, "I'm surprised your fingers haven't frozen right off, boy."

He says, "I can't play with my gloves on. And don't never call a Black man 'boy,' Joseph."

"Oh. Sorry."

He nods, accepting my apology. Larry lives with his rich old gramps, who doesn't like Larry's singing and guitar playing one bit, even though Larry is super good at it. He's so good at it that Beth idolizes him. She even said hello to him once, before turning beet red and running upstairs to hide in her bedroom. Beth's a good guitar player too, for an eighth grader.

Larry's gramps says guitars are for hippies and fags. We were smoking a doobie in Larry's room the other day when he told me the Gramps said that.

Larry added, "He forgot to add "niggers," and we both cracked up laughing, because we were buzzed.

Then I caught myself and worried that Larry might get mad at me for laughing, even though he was laughing too. Then I got the pot paranoia and was sure Larry hated me completely, deep down. Fortunately, Larry said he had the munchies and went downstairs to get some Charles Chips and French onion dip and then everything was okay again.

I'm surprised the Gramps let Larry in the house in the first place though, since Larry is half Black. People I know, if they don't like homosexuals, they won't like Blacks, either.

We're in front of some old couple's house down the street now, singing "The Little Drummer Boy." I decide not to make a joke to Larry about the drummer "boy." Meg, who's standing behind me, pokes me in the back. Whenever we're singing, Meg lets me know that I can't sing and therefore need to attempt to sing much more softly. I sing louder and step back onto her foot. Her voice goes higher on impact, like "Pah-rum-pum-PUUUM-pum." Ha!

I don't ask Larry nosy questions. I just let him tell me about his life when he feels like it. My Aunt March knows Larry's gramps from way back, though. She said the Gramps took Larry in a few years ago, after Larry's parents died. They drove off the road and into a tree somewhere outside of Los Angeles, both stoned out of their heads.

Aunt March said Larry's mother was Mr. Vaughn's, AKA the Gramps's, daughter. She used to sing and play the guitar. She fell in love with a Black bass player and got pregnant with Larry. Mixed race marriage was still illegal in Missouri then. And then there was the social disapproval, which was still very dangerous back then. So, the two of them took off to California together.

There, they got married, had Larry, and tried to make it in the music business. Their band was called "American Zebra." Supposedly, they were starting to get well known out there, before they died. Aunt March said it's no wonder Larry likes music, it's in his blood. She said it's also no wonder Vincent Vaughn doesn't approve of Larry's interest in music, all things considered.

Indiana is known as "The Hoosier State, "a title that's carried with pride there, though it's not known for sure where the term came from. One likelihood is that it originated in the early 1800s, from the custom of standing at a distance and yelling "Who's here?" before approaching a homestead on the frontier.

However, in the greater St. Louis area, "hoosier" has a unique meaning. Here, a "hoosier" is a low class, ignorant person (with no connection to people from Indiana, these days, at least).
The origin of "hoosier" being used as a slur isn't clear. But the animosity may have come from the clashes between early St. Louis union members, and outsiders brought in from Indiana to replace strikers at that time.

Chapter 2

It's Christmas Eve day. I have to go out in the last-minute rush because of Mooms. The bus driver yells at me for standing in the aisle while the bus is moving, which is unfair when the only reason I'm standing is because nobody will let me sit.

People will put their purse or newspaper on the seat next to them, then act like they don't see you trying to find a seat. I finally say, "Excuse me," loudly to some hoosier who's wearing a baseball cap with a pair of stuffed felt antlers sticking out of it. He moves his backpack off the seat, but I still have to stumble over his legs.

I bet he'd move his ignorant horn-head self out of the way if it was the gorgeous Meg who wanted to sit down, or maybe even pretty little Amy. Amy thinks her nose is too flat for prettiness, but really the only thing wrong with Amy is that she is too conceited and horny for a child.

Apparently, it's not necessary for horn-head hoosier males to be courteous to plain-looking girls like me. My waist-length hair is the only thing pretty about me. It's my girl disguise.

We finally get to Jamestown Mall, and as I'm going through the entrance doors, some other hoosier with poor home training says, "Move it!" and shoves an old, hunched over lady out of his way. Shoves her! It makes me so mad I push through the crowd after him without even thinking. I shove him back, yelling, "No, you move, jack-ass. You. Move."

He stands there looking stupid for a sec, then screws up his beard-stubbled, pockmarked face and growls, "Dyke."

I yell, "Dick," right back in his ugly face, and give the creepy bastard another good hard shove.

That time he shoves me back, so I shove him again, even harder. We're both knocking into other people, since it's so crowded here at the entrance.

A security guard blows his whistle. He's talking into his walkie-talkie as he rushes over. He grabs the guy and hustles him out of the mall.

I hurry away, in case they decide to kick me out, too.

A half hour later, I'm sitting in Orange Julius, enjoying a fruity beverage and feeling pretty globdamn terrific. I wish someone I knew had seen me go after the dick, though.

A bag on the table in front of me holds two turquoise pendants on silver chains, each in its own little white box. The saleslady said they're very popular with young girls. I hope so. Meg told me to get the girls jewelry, since she was going to give them some other stuff, and jewelry would balance out their gifts or something. Meg had to go to her babysitting job today though, so I'm on my own with it.

Now I just have to find a set of guitar strings for Beth and a set of drawing pencils for Amy. The turquoise necklaces were already five bucks apiece but I don't want this to be the hard candy Christmas that Amy and Beth still remember when they're grown. It's not their fault they're used to more.

All four of us March girls have an artsy streak, as Mooms likes to say. Meg sings, just like Mooms Senior, naturally. Beth plays the guitar. Amy is the artist of the family and I write stories.

When I get home, there's a pot of chili on the stove for supper tonight and two apple pies baking in the oven for tomorrow. The house smells luscious. Beth is playing "I Saw Mommy Kissing Santa Claus" on her guitar. It's a pretty sad song, considering our circumstances, really, but everyone's happily singing along. Meg's and Mooms's clear, rich voices stand out above the rest. Party is perched in the brightly lit Christmas tree, posing in the branches like he is on assignment from the Barbizon School of Modeling. It's a fine scene for a man to come home to.

Miraculous birth stories exist across many cultures, such as the Christian Mary's virgin birth of Jesus, on what was to become Christmas day.

There have also been rare and scattered reports of self-fertilized births among intersexed humans. Though this appears to be possible in theory, none have been medically verified, thus far.

Chapter 3

I made the attic mine as soon as we moved in here because a garret seems the right sort of place for a writer. Mooms has a bedroom of course, and the little girls share a room. And then we had to give Miss Hannah a room since she's old and doesn't have anywhere else to go. The fourth bedroom is Meg's. I'd have to share her room, if I slept on the second floor with everyone else.

These century-old farmhouse bedrooms aren't like the ones in our old house, either. The bedrooms here are small and don't even have closets. They're barely big enough for one person. So, I'm way up here by myself. Which is why I didn't hear all the hubbub going on two floors below.

I'm the last one to come downstairs on Christmas morning. I've got the presents from me and Meg in a big cardboard box and I can't wait to see the looks on everyone's faces when they open them.

But downstairs, nobody's paying any attention to the presents. They're piled up under the tree, undisturbed. Even with Mooms not getting us anything, I'm happy to see that there are still quite a few packages.

My three sisters surround Miss Hannah, who's sitting in Mooms's rocking chair. Miss Hannah is holding something. When I push my way through, I see that it's a baby, wrapped up in one of our bath towels. Miss Hannah sees me, and says, all crazy-eyed, "It's a Christmas miracle, Jo."

The baby is very small and pink, a newborn. I say, "What is a Christmas miracle? And whose kid is that?"

Miss Hannah says, "This here is the Christmas miracle. This here is the new baby Jesus."

I just say, "Oh." I start arranging my presents under the tree while I wait for somebody to make sense. My family isn't really religious, aside from the Junior and Senior Mooms's on again, off again interest in the New Age gobbledygook. We all just nod and sort of act like we agree whenever Miss Hannah starts her Christian talk, so we don't hurt her feelings.

Meg says, "Mooms went to the hospital for Pampers and formula. The stores are all closed today, but she said she can get the basics from her work."

Amy holds out her finger. The baby grasps it and holds onto it like a little monkey. Amy says, "It's a Christmas miracle, Jo."

"Yeah, I remember hearing that somewhere. What the fuck is going on?"

Mooms Junior says, "Language."

"Don't tell me what to do." Meg is only two years older than me. That's nowhere near enough age difference for her to think she can boss me around.

She says, "Don't talk back."

Don't talk back? Okay, now I'm furious. I say, "Keep it up and I'll kerplop you, bitch." A "kerplop" is when you kick a girl between the legs. I think we March girls made the word up somewhere along the line but I'm not a hundred percent sure. Kerploppings are only threatened though, never actually performed. That would be weird as hell.

Beth says, "You guys? It's Christmas." She says it in such a sweet little voice that we stop bickering immediately.

Amy says, "I got to help give him a bath."

"Nice," I say. "Now, will somebody tell me whose baby that is and why it's here?"

Meg says, "We don't know. When Mooms and I came down this morning, he was under the Christmas tree. In that baby carrier over there."

I pick up the baby carrier, check under its cushiony part, then turn it upside down, looking for clues but not finding any. "Is it a joke?"

Nobody answers me. It would be a pretty weird joke. "What should we do? Call the cops or something, I guess?"

Meg says, "Mooms said not to do anything until she gets back."

The tiny creature starts to cry. It turns red and twists its little face up and goes, "Meh. Meh." Adorable, really.

Miss Hannah puts the baby up on her shoulder and pats his back. Beth picks up the big plastic doll she's holding, the one with "scars" where its arm was "operated on." Beth copies Miss Hannah's motions, holds the doll up on her shoulder and pats it.

It makes me mad. A fourteen-year-old girl with titties, still playing with dolls. I'm the only one around here who cares if Beth looks demented.

Mooms comes bustling in, swoops up the baby and puts an itty-bitty Pamper on him. His bellybutton has what looks like a folded-up Kleenex taped over it. Miss Hannah gets up, and Mooms rocks the baby in the rocking chair while she feeds him from a half-size baby bottle.

We all stand around and gawk at the baby for a while longer. Then I say, "Okay, let's open presents." I turn on the radio and "Rudolph the Red Nose Reindeer" is playing on KSLQ, which gets us back on track.

I glare at Miss Hannah when I see that she made Beth some doll clothes for Christmas. Then I remember again that we have to be nice on Christmas. And Miss Hannah is, like, the nicest person in the world, anyway. I force my mouth to curl into a smile.

I get homemade hair holders from Beth, elastic that she sewed fabric over. They're all in the dark, solid colors I like. Just the basics for when I want to keep my hair out of my face.

Amy gives me little fabric sachet squares that she made, to scent the clothes in my armoire and dresser drawers. The fragrance is fresh pine, nothing flowery. It's nice.

Miss Hannah gives me a box of her amazing homemade fudge.

And from Meg, I get the best gift of all: *Writer's Market 1977,* a book of listings for places to send my stories, to try for publication.

My family gets me, pretty much, at least. They even call me "the man of the house," now that Daddy's gone. I'm the one everybody hollers for when there's a spider to be dealt with or the trash needs to go out or the toilet gets stopped up again.

It's a lot nicer than the treatment Larry gets from the Gramps, at any sign that Larry's acting girly. I've heard the Gramps bark commands like, "Walk straight!" and "Hold your books right!" Larry has a habit of walking with his schoolbooks held up by his chest like the girls do, rather than down at his side like the other guys. That look on Larry's face when the old goat corrects him, like, ugh.

Behind the oohs and aahs and general present-opening cheer, I feel like we're secretly sizing each other up. We're all trying to figure out who had the nerve to plop out a baby in the middle of the night and stick it under the Christmas tree.

It's wintertime though, so everybody wears heavier, baggier, clothes, which could hide extra weight. We even wear jackets or sweaters inside the house a lot of the time, now that we can't afford to just crank up the heat whenever we feel like it. But it still seems like hiding a full pregnancy and the birth would be practically impossible to pull off. This is not that big of a house. Not for six people.

I say, "We need to start keeping these doors locked." I check the front and back doors and they are both unlocked. We never bothered much about locking the doors before. We didn't know somebody might sneak in and drop off a baby.

Chapter 4

Mooms, Miss Hannah and my sisters are all
dolled up, with dresses on and stuff, and the table is
set for Christmas dinner. Aunt March should be here
in half an hour. I hope she's not still mad at me for
scorching the dress she'd planned to wear today. I
work for her on Saturdays and she made me iron it
last week, even though I told her I didn't know how
to iron. Now it has a big burnt triangle right on the
hind-end. Which is kind of funny, when you think
about it.

Mooms is fluttering around, nervous. Aunt
March is Daddy's aunt, so she's really my great
aunt. Her husband died before I was born. He died
of pie. It was at the big family reunion they used to
have every year at another great uncle's farm. There
was a pie-eating contest and he ate glob knows how
much blueberry, cherry, peach and apple pie. Aunt
March said Uncle March was just about to be
declared the winner but instead, he fell over dead
and ruined the whole day.

Aunt March makes Mooms nervous. She makes
the rest of us nervous, too. She will say anything to
anybody, for one thing. And we have to put up with

it, because this farmhouse is one of her rent houses. She lets us live here for free.

It's strange that she goes by Aunt March, too. "March" is her last name, just like it's our last name. I don't even know what her first name is. It doesn't seem very friendly, that's all.

Mooms sets the crystal candle holders on the dining room table, then decides they look too expensive for people who are getting free rent and puts them away. She makes Amy take off the cameo ring she'd let Amy borrow for the day, for the same reason. Then Mooms decides we need to take down the big mirror that's on the wall behind the couch, on an emergency basis, because Aunt March might not like us putting screw holes in the wall.

Taking the big mirror down falls to me, along with filling the screw holes in, which Mooms didn't even think of. I use toothpaste to plug up the holes, an idea I came up with myself. I'm pretty proud of that. You'd never know there were ever any holes there. I go ahead and take down the macrame wall hanging and fill in that hole with toothpaste, too.

Then Mooms notices Party, who is on his back with all four legs windmilling, fighting a long red ribbon that's left over from a Christmas present. Mooms makes Meg shut Party into her bedroom, along with his water and food bowl and litterbox. It's like Mooms was so used to being the homeowner that she just now remembered that she's not in a house that she owns anymore.

I know Aunt March the best out of us girls, since I work for her. She makes me do more personal things than her live-in maid does, for some reason. And she talks about me to her other help like she practically raised me when really, I hardly even know her.

I usually have to give her a manicure and pedicure, roll her hair up in curlers after combing Dippity-Do through it, and give her poodle, Mop, a bath. Then I have to clip a colorful bow onto Mop's head, although he is a boy dog. That one little nonconformity made me like Aunt March more, even if it is only for a dog.

Aunt March is so rich that even her help has help. When she can't think of anything else for me to do, she has me go do whatever her live-in maid needs, for example. And sometimes there's another girl helping the regular maid, too. Every Saturday morning, Aunt March's driver comes to pick me up in Aunt March's powder blue Lincoln Continental. Then he drives me back home in the late afternoon. By then, I'm usually mad about something Aunt March said or did. She's a very rude old bat. But I'll have fifteen bucks in my pocket, which, as Mooms always reminds me, is what counts.

Mooms gives us last minute instructions. She says, "Girls. We're going to say that Miss Hannah here is my friend, who is visiting today, along with her niece's baby. Got it, everybody?"

We all say we understand. Aunt March might not like knowing we have an extra person or a cat living in her house, let alone an unexplained baby. I could just see Aunt March doing that shocked-looking stare of hers and saying that if we can afford to take care of half the town, then we can afford to pay rent. She seems the kind of person who has no idea what it's like to not have enough. It's like she thinks if you're having a hard time, it's your own fault and you deserved it no matter what, even if you're a kid. It's confusing because, at the same time, she's helped us out a ton when she didn't have to.

Mooms said to somebody on the phone way back when that the money came from Daddy's side of the family and that Aunt March grew up so poor that she had a shitter in her backyard. I only learned a couple of years ago that a "shitter" is an outhouse. I always pictured some weirdo pulling down his pants and doing his business in their yard like a dog. And Aunt March's family would say, "Yep, there goes our backyard shitter again. It's a shame we can't afford store-bought fertilizer." Or "It's too bad we can't afford to have the shitter run off." I couldn't ask Mooms to explain, when I wasn't supposed to eavesdrop in the first place.

Aunt March arrives. She doesn't knock. She just opens the door with her key and comes in like she owns the place. She does own the place, but still.

We're soon at the table, eating our Christmas dinner and everything's going along just dandy. Aunt March is chatty and giggly. I've never seen her so happy. Maybe she's lonesome in that giant house with nobody around but hired help. Or else it's the two glasses of red wine she's drunk so far.

She brought a large bag of gifts with her. I wonder what she got me.

Aunt March compliments the roast beef and mashed potatoes.

Mooms has had a couple of glasses of wine, too. She says, "Oh, thank you, Aunt March. I just wish Robert was here to celebrate with us. It doesn't seem right, does it, to enjoy this nice family feast, when Robert and so many other men are over there fighting in the Viet Cong." Mooms stops talking and turns pink, like maybe she knows that she just messed up.

Aunt March drops her fork. It bounces off the wobbly pink Jello salad on her plate, then hits the floor. Taking on her startled and predatory owl face, Aunt March over-pronounces each word, like she's talking to someone who's hard of hearing. She says, "Mar-gar-et. the Viet-nam War ended two years ago. Rob-ert is not in Viet-nam. Robert is in pris-on for se-cur-ities fraud."

Holy shit. We do not talk about that in front of Mooms.

Meg squeaks, "Who wants another dinner roll?"

Mooms says, "Hmmm. Hmmm," sounding like a motor that's trying to start up but failing. She bobs her head longer than seems sensible.

Beth brings Aunt March a clean fork from the kitchen. We finish the meal in silence.

The genes that cause cats to be black are linked to their sex and eye color. Black cats are more often male than female (up to 75% of them are male, by some reports). Also, black cats most often have yellow/golden eyes.

The Cat Fanciers' Association recognizes 22 breeds of black cats but only one of them, the Bombay cat, is always black.

Chapter 5

The next night, Mooms comes home from work carrying a bolt of heavy black fabric. As soon as supper's over, she has me help lug her old Singer sewing machine in its antique cabinet, out into the living room. She starts making something large with the black material. I say, "What's that, Mooms, curtains?"

Meg says, "A bedspread?"

"A beanbag chair for me and Beth's room?" Amy adds, hopefully.

"A tent," Mooms mumbles, around the straight pins sticking out of her mouth.

"Cool. I'd love to go camping after it warms up outside," I say, but Mooms shakes her head.

She takes the pins out of her mouth and steps away from her sewing project. "Girls," she says, taking the baby from Miss Hannah. "I've… I've got some terrible news."

Amy sets her sketch pad down. Beth sets her doll aside, the one with the mismatched button eyes. (It had to be given a "prosthetic" eye after losing one in an "accident.")

Mooms says, "Girls. Your father is dead."

The little girls start wailing.

Mooms says, "He died on the battlefield. On Christmas Day, while we were here enjoying a fancy meal and opening presents. He was very brave."

Meg, Miss Hannah and I exchange looks.

Meg comforts the little girls, who aren't that little anymore, when you think about it. I mean, Beth and Amy know Daddy's true whereabouts as well as the rest of us do, so I don't know what their problem is. I start upstairs to get Larry's Christmas joints that I haven't had a chance to give him yet. I want to go over there. It's getting too loony here.

"Girls!" Mooms shrieks. I freeze in place. "Girls. Come here. Sit down."

We girls sit down on the big old couch, lined up by age. Miss Hannah stands between the dining room and the living room, wringing a dishtowel.

Mooms paces around the room with little Robbie. She says, "Also. I've made a decision about the baby."

Amy stops mid-wail to plead with Mooms to keep him. Beth joins in. They're jumping up and down. "Please, can we keep him, Mooms? We'll help take care of him. Pretty please, oh pleasey."

I've never heard of anyone getting a surprise mystery baby before, except on the Sunday morning cartoons. The cartoon baby would always be left in a basket on the porch. I don't remember what would happen to it after that. But in real life, this just doesn't sound right.

Everybody's acting like the baby is a stray puppy. And even if it was a stray puppy, wouldn't you still have to try to find its owner? I mean, what if someone stole someone else's puppy or baby and dumped it, for revenge or something? I remember finding a pocket knife in the woods behind our old house when I was six or seven, when Mooms took us on a walk through the trails there. I was so excited about that knife that I could hardly even breathe. But my parents made a big deal out of making me put an ad in the lost and found section of the newspaper first, to try to find the owner. Nobody claimed it and I got to keep it in the end, but I had to at least try. And that was only a pocket knife.

I've already said more than once that we should call the cops. But Mooms gets mad and Miss Hannah starts going on about how miracles aren't subject to man's rules. And then Mooms Junior gives me her warning look, like *Do you really want to push our mother over the edge? Really?*

Mooms holds up her hand. "Yes. We are keeping the baby."

After the cheering from Beth and Amy dies down, Mooms says, "Your father, the old Robert, is gone, unfortunately. But the universe has blessed us with his reincarnation. Your new brother will be named after him, Robert Earl March Junior."

Amy and Beth start whooping it up again. Then Beth gets hiccups, probably from being so sad, then so happy right on top of it.

Meg, Miss Hannah and I exchange another look. I guess none of us know what to say.

Mooms says, "I start my maternity leave tomorrow. Oh, that reminds me. I'll have to file for a birth certificate."

Meg says, "He's *yours*? But we came downstairs at the same time."

Miss Hannah says, "Miracles can't be explained." It's often hard to tell whose side Miss Hannah is on.

I remember something that I had forgotten all about before. It flashes through my mind like a streak of light.

Mooms clears her throat. We all wait with rapt attention for her next words. But she just holds her finger up in the air and says, "Hush." Then she goes back to her sewing.

What I've remembered is walking in on Mooms in the bathroom, on the day before Thanksgiving. I remember because we were just about to make the Thanksgiving pumpkin pies, and I was going to help, when I hardly ever help in the kitchen. Mooms was stepping out of the shower. That kind of thing happens when you have one bathroom for six people and nobody bothers to lock doors.

So, I didn't give it much thought at the time, aside from being grossed out, as anybody would be when seeing one of their parents naked. Anyway, if Mooms had a baby on Christmas Eve, she'd have to be heavily pregnant when I walked in on her the day before Thanksgiving. She'd have been about eight months along. Mooms is thin, so that would have to be noticeable, unclothed. Her stomach was a little stretched out, after all, she'd had four babies. But it hung down, extra skin, no fullness.

So that eliminates Mooms from this whodunnit, regardless of her hints otherwise. Miss Hannah is too old and Amy is surely too young. Well, I did catch Amy necking with boys twice at our other house. But that's a far cry from real sex. Oh, and she only started her period, like, three months ago. No way it's Amy's. And I know it's not mine.

That only leaves Meg and Beth from our house. I seriously doubt it was either of them. And yet, the baby is a fact. He's here, and somebody had to have given birth to him.

My family reminds me of a house in a subdivision a couple of miles from here. Amy came home on her bike, all excited, telling us that a girl's family at her school had to move out of their house because it was falling apart.

Amy always knows what's going on because she's allowed to be out riding her bike for hours, unsupervised. Meg and I would never have been allowed to do that. Amy didn't even get in trouble when Mooms caught her riding her bike with the neighborhood kids, in the thick fog of mosquito killer smoke from the bug truck last summer. Man, Meg and I would have been grounded for weeks for that. Once I asked Moom why we were treated differently and she said kids who are born later just get more tired parents. So, we get our neighborhood news from little Miss free bird Amy. We girls (except for Beth, of course) walked over to that falling down house three different times, to check out the progress of the catastrophe.

The first time, the house was roped off and had "Keep Out" signs all over the place. There wasn't much to see. But on our next visit, a couple of weeks later, the house was clearly cracking open. You could see part of the inside walls and, in places, you could even some junk that the owners left behind. The third time we checked, the whole damn house had split wide open and half of it had tumbled down the hill and into the creek. It was the talk of the town. I even started writing a story about it, titled "A Broken Home," though I'll have to change it because it's a cliché'.

When I finally escape over to Larry's, he seems happy to get the Christmas joints. He shares so much weed with me that giving him a little back seems stupid, in a way. But I don't have anywhere near the money he does. So, I figure it's the thought that counts.

In his bedroom up on the third floor, he cracks the window open and lights up one of the joints right away. It would be rude to ask for a toke of the present I just gave him but I gladly accept it when he offers it. I really need a buzz. I'm so worried my stomach hurts. Keeping that baby has got to be illegal. And what happens if Mooms gets caught, and then she gets locked up, too? See, we're at the part where the cracked house is just about to split wide open and tumble down the hill.

Larry startles me out of my thoughts. He says, "Do you know Sally Gardiner? She's a senior like Meg." Larry and I are sophomores.

I'm buzzed and still thinking about my family problems. I mumble, "a broken home."

He looks at me funny. He says, "Sally's parents split up?"

It seems easier to act like I didn't just stupidly talk out of my head. So I say, "Uh, Meg probably knows who Sally is, especially if she's popular. Why?"

"Sally's having a New Year's Eve bash. It's open invitation. Last year's was wild. Her parents went away for the night. They were, you know, still together then."

"Wow. Did her parents supply the booze?"

"I don't know who supplied it, but there was a keg. Oh, we're supposed to get dressed up."

"Whoa, what's this "we" you speak of? I don't like parties." I like people well enough, sort of, but only in smaller groups. Once you get beyond the number of people in my family, the number I'm used to being around, half a dozen or so, it gets to be too much for me.

"Boy, you're going," he says, waving his hand like it's all settled.

And it soon is all settled, after Meg finds out about it. Even with Mooms assuming that the parents will be there, she still won't let Meg go unless I go, too. Mooms is still pretty strict, even with her neurosis, when it comes to me and Meg at least. With Meg and Larry both nagging me nonstop about going to the stupid party, I give in.

#

The next night, Mooms finishes sewing her black tent. She says it should really be erected outdoors but that indoors will have to do, since the yard is covered in snow.

She makes us erect the tent underneath the dining room table, with a complicated system of ropes, attached to the top of the tent and tied over the top of the table. After a couple of hushings by Mooms, we stop asking her what in the world she's making us do all this for.

When it's finished, it looks like something a little kid would play in, a little tent under the dinner table. Mooms has Meg lay a blanket down so the tent has a soft floor. I almost say out loud that it would have been a lot easier to just toss some blankets over the top of the dining room table in the first place, but it's too late now.

Mooms says, in the voice she uses when she's making announcements, "Girls. There's way too much worry and fear about death in our culture. We dread it and we treat it as if it's a horrifying thing. But it's actually quite natural and normal. Yes, Daddy was taken from us sooner than we expected. But the fact is, our loved ones will all die. And so will we. It's far more reasonable to get used to death, rather dread it. And that is what we are going to do."

Meg, Miss Hannah and I look at each other, eyebrows raised. We do that a lot lately. Was Mooms going to try to kill us? I go on the alert, ready to pounce on Mooms and restrain her, if necessary.

Mooms says, "We'll go from oldest to youngest. And stop looking so scared, everyone. This is just a consciousness-raising exercise. It's nothing to be afraid of."

It's a New Age thing, then? But Meg looks as confused as I am. If it was new-age-ish, surely Meg would recognize it.

Mooms says, "Miss Hannah is first. Miss Hannah, please go lie down in the tent."

Miss Hannah slinks into the tent. Mooms tells her to curl up so her feet aren't hanging out, then Mooms closes the tent's entry flaps.

"Now girls, pretend Miss Hannah is dead. And Miss Hannah, you close your eyes and you pretend you're dead, too," Mooms says, leaning down to flick the side of the tent, making sure Miss Hannah is paying attention in there.

Party, who never wants to be left out of anything, pushes his way in, under the tent flaps.

Mooms says, "Party is dead, too. Now, you girls think about that. Just think about it. That's all. Miss Hannah and Party are dying, and then they are dead."

We all stand around for a while. Beth silently weeps. Meg holds onto her.

"Time's up!" Mooms says, after a while. Miss Hannah comes out of the tent, looking scarily pleased. She says, "Lord have mercy. It's just like when Jesus arose from the dead!"

"My turn," Mooms says, ignoring Miss Hannah's Christian perspective. Mooms crawls into the tent and shuts the flaps. The tent pokes out on the sides now and then, as Party plays inside.

The rest of us sit down on the dining room floor. One at a time, we take our turns going into the little black death tent under the table, curling up so our feet don't hang out under the flaps, and pretending we're dead, while everyone on the outside pretends we're dead, too.

After everyone else is done, Mooms chases Party out of her tent of death and lays the baby down in it. Now that gets to me, thinking of poor little Robbie dead, especially after he's already been discarded once. I feel ashamed of thinking he was a burden that we didn't need. I guess the little guy is growing on me more than I realized.

After Robbie's turn is up, I think about tossing Beth's stupid hospital dolls into the tent. But the weirdness overdose of today has worn me out as it is, so I just go up to bed.

According to Urban Dictionary, a "snicker-snag" is when you hold someone down and dangle spit near their face, then suck it back up into your mouth again.

Chapter 6

Larry pulls up in the driveway, to take us to Sally Gardiner's New Year's Eve bash, in his sixteenth birthday present, a brand-new red Firebird. It was just there in his driveway one day. I didn't even know he'd had his sixteenth birthday until it was past. Sometimes I feel like I'm closer to Larry than Larry is to me. Anyway, I've been in three fights over this stupid party so far. I'm surprised nobody ended up in Mooms's death tent for real.

The first fight started when Mooms Junior said none of my clothes would do, as if what I wear is any of her globdamn business. She had the nerve to go into my garret and get the ruffly, colorful dress out of my armoire, the one Aunt March disappointed me with on Christmas. Some gift that was. Aunt March nags at me to be more lady-like. Meg said, "This is cute. Wear this to the party."

I said, "No way. It looks like Minnie Pearl vomited flowers all over the Hee Haw stage."

Meg said, "Well, I think it's cute. If you don't like it, I'll take it."

"Please do. You can have it." Meg wasted no time rushing the ridiculous dress to her bedroom, like she was afraid I might change my mind and snatch it back.

Then the Moomses decided that Mooms Senior should make me a dress out of the black death tent fabric. I liked that idea. Though, of course, it was still none of Meg's globdamn business. I said, "I'll go get it." Somehow, the black tent had ended up in my garret, a pile of creepiness dumped in the corner. I didn't like the grim reaper vibe it brought to my cozy retreat, so I was pretty happy at the chance to get rid of it. I headed for the stairs, still trying to get along with the Mooms Mafia.

But Mooms Senior said, "No, Jo. I mean I'll make you a dress from the leftover fabric, not from the tent itself."

I didn't argue with Mooms, even though she'd picked up this way of saying my name like it was an insult or something. It sounded like "Go Jo yourself." Or "You can go straight to Jo. But it did make me realize that, duh, I could just put the tent on a shelf in the garage. I made a mental note to do it, when no one was looking, and get it out of my life.

I said, "Okay then. But I want a suit, not a dress." A suit made from leftover death tent fabric would express my feelings about the stupid party perfectly.

But Mooms Junior started whining. I guess she forgot that she's the one who always says we are not supposed to argue with Mooms. Meg said, "No way. No suit. I'll be ruined before I even get started, if I show up at the party as weirdo's sister."

By "getting started," Meg meant sucking up to the alleged cool kids, excuse me, *rich* kids, until they accepted her into their stupid teen-town clique. By "weirdo," she meant me, of course, the one who had so super graciously agreed to go to the stupid party just so Mooms would let her go to it. I'd just about had it with Meg.

After mutual kerplopping threats, Mooms stepped in. She said, "That'll do, girls. I have an idea for something that's in between a dress and a suit, and I don't want to hear any more about it."

That was lucky for Meg because I was just about to tell Mooms that the party would lack adult supervision, which would make Mooms call the whole thing off. Meg has got a lot of damn nerve. My sisters, besides Beth, can be stunningly ungrateful. I hate to say it but they are both exactly like Daddy turned out to be. It's like they're 90% good, so you forget they have that other ten percent that's pure evil.

Mooms made me a jumpsuit, I guess you could call it. It's like a top and bottom but all in one piece. It's not bad. At least it's plain black with no frills.

Meg is wearing a sparkly new red dress from Famous-Barr. I went with her to spend the Christmas gift certificate I gave her. And of course, a trip to Famous always includes stopping by the little restaurant in the store that has the most amazing French onion soup in the universe so that was a good day. Meg looks like a million bucks. It's a shame about her personality.

The second fight was also with Meg, after she had the nerve to tell me that she'd check up on me at the party. She said she'd smile at me if I was acting right and raise her eyebrows if I wasn't. Mooms Senior nodded along, like she agreed that I needed etiquette tips. I didn't. And I double dog didn't need them from the rudest creature on the planet.

But Meg saying that, and getting Mooms to side with her, that was the end. When I got Mooms Junior alone in her room, I wrestled her to the bed and held her down. Then I made a long slurp of spit dangle out of my mouth, right over her face. I kept sucking it back up again, then letting it drool back down again. It was a drool yo-yo. Move over, Duncan haha.

Mooms Junior just laid there, with her big mouth shut for a change. If she'd had anything to say right then, her prissy face would have been saliva city and she knew it. And the cool thing was, I just thought of it, spur-of-the-moment. I didn't even know it was possible. So, you learn something every day. I couldn't wait to tell Larry. And I couldn't imagine what a holy terror Meg would be if it wasn't for me keeping her in line.

So, when Larry drives up, I push Meg out of my way and get in the front seat, my etiquette reminder to her that she is not the damn queen bee, at least not when her mommy isn't present.

Meg sulks sexily in the back seat now, next to Amy, another beauty in the making. Yes, Amy is in the car too, which is the issue that started the third fight. Little Miss Tag-Along wanted to come to the party too, and she just would not accept "no." The younger March girls don't understand the concept of age. Beth thinks she's five and Amy thinks she is twenty-five.

At first, Mooms agreed that a high school party was no place for a twelve-year-old. Then she decided that it would actually be a fine idea to send our little sister along to spy and snitch on us.

After getting over the irritation of having to take Amy along, Meg decided it would be fun to doll Amy up. So, Amy is wearing one of Meg's low-cut dresses, a pair of Meg's high heels with pantyhose, and has her hair and nails done, along with a face full of cosmetics. Meg has taught a hot-to-trot twelve-year-old how to make herself look old enough to get served in a bar. I told Meg it was not a good idea but she wouldn't listen.

On the way out the door, I was already super annoyed. And then I spotted Beth, sitting at the dining room table with Mooms. Beth was in her bunny pajamas, at seven p.m. on New Year's Eve, drinking a glass of pink strawberry milk with one of those loopy crazy straws that are for small children.

I'm surprised Mooms didn't just give her one of Robbie's bottles. Beth is two years older than Amy but no one even considered bringing Beth to the party, least of all Beth herself.

We all needed to start treating Beth like a regular teenager, before it was too late. I decided to treat her the same way I'd treat Meg or Amy if they were getting on my nerves. I whispered in Beth's ear, "You better watch it, bitch. Don't even think I won't kerplop you."

I felt a little sorry for her when her face reddened up, but it was for her own good.

#

Oh, my glob. Old Halls Ferry Road is lined with cars on both sides and Black Sabbath's playing so loud inside that it's even loud out here at the street. Sally's house is a big old Victorian, like Larry's Gramp's place. It has a huge yard with no nearby neighbors, which probably explains why it hasn't been raided by the cops yet. There are so many people here already that we can barely get through the door. Most of the girls are in dresses and heels, but most of the guys have on Levi's and flannel shirts. There's a beer keg in the corner. I get a disposable cup off the stack of cups and fill it.

When I get back, my sisters are gone and a half dozen flirty girls surround Larry. He plays along but his eyes dart about like he's trying to find the nearest exit. He went from not being noticed at all to very popular with the girls, when he started pulling into the school parking lot in his cool new ride. In west county, more teenagers had new or new-ish cars so it didn't cause the big rise in status that it seems to bring on around here.

Then a pair of black girls come over and the first group of girls, who are all white, move on. Larry explains stuff like this to me, little things between blacks and whites that I never noticed before. Before I met Larry, I'd have just figured it was a coincidence but now I wonder if I'm missing something. I'll have to remember to ask him later.

During one of our talks up in Larry's room, he told me that his father would always tell him to never trust white people. Larry, who was just a little kid at the time, said it confused him because his mother, who was also his father's wife, was white. So, he worried about if he should trust his mom. But Larry said he makes an exception for me, regardless. I've gotten a couple of hard, scary glares out in public with Larry, from male hoosiers who looked like they needed a bath and a globdamn job. It's not the "nice" kind of prejudice that most of the grown-ups I know do. With the grown-ups I know, whenever race or homosexuality comes up, their comments usually start with "I'm not prejudice, but." What I'm talking about here is some full-grown man who I don't even know, staring me down hard, like I've broken his heart and now he hates me and wants to lock me up in his basement dungeon.

Larry grabs hold of my hand, in front of the girls. He pulls me close in a half-hug and says, "Ready, babe?" He's talking loud over the music. I go along with it. He stops to fill a cup with beer, then pulls me by the hand, into a small sitting room off to the side of the main room. We sit on the loveseat. Larry lights a joint. Then we notice a couple on the floor, on the rug, along the far wall. The guy is laying on top of the girl. They're clothed but going at it hot and heavy. Larry and I look at each other and we both crack up laughing at the look on the other one's face. We're both like, "Eww!" Anything sexual makes me sick. I can't help it. Larry says, "Hey, you wanna go steady with me?"

I'm still going along with the joke, practically shouting so he can hear me over the music. I say, "Hell, yeah. I would love to go steady with you, baby." The music stops just as I say it. It seems like the entire party hears me. A bunch of people cheer, including the couple making out on the floor. My face burns. I'm mortified to be the center of attention like this, without even a warning.

But Larry looks thrilled. Later, I realize what a super idea it really is. We won't have to worry about people of the opposite sex asking us out or people making their little comments about if we're gay anymore, or any of that noise. Larry and I understand each other.

After I recover from the attention attack, I say to Larry, "Of course, I'll be expecting a promise ring soon with a giant diamond, boyfriend."

He says, "Don't push it, Joseph," which cracks me up.

#

Mooms said we had to be home by eleven, thank glob, so I start trying to round up my sisters at 10:30. Meg sits with Sally Gardiner and her circle of popular seniors and maybe even some college-aged people. Meg looks radiant and seems real jazzed, for a change lately. Maybe she's found her new tribe. A wave of happiness runs through me. I'm proud to be the sister of shining social star Meg, and glad now that I came, so that she could come, in spite of all the hassles.

Meg's holding one of the big red disposable beer cups. I look closer and, yes, that is definitely beer in it, I see the foam. Mooms would not like that one bit. Meg never disobeys Mooms, so this is monumental, a crack in the Junior-Senior Mooms Cartel. 1977 could be an interesting year.

I catch Meg's eye and tap my wrist where my watch would be, if I was wearing one, signaling "It's time to go." Then I go looking for Amy, while Meg says her good-byes.

I can't find Amy. I look all over the main floor of the house twice. The upstairs seems too private to just go wandering through without permission.

Panic rises in my throat. I should have kept Amy with me, even if I was fed up with her for pushing her way in where she wasn't wanted. I find Larry, then Meg finds both of us. We all say, practically simultaneously, "Where's Amy?" Meg enlists Sally's help and the two of them rush upstairs, after directing Larry to go check the cellar.

I put on my coat, figuring I'll check for Amy outside. But before I reach the door, Meg yells. I rush back to the stairway, terrified that something horrible has happened to Amy. But no, Meg's slipped and twisted her ankle. She slipped on a puddle, where some asshole spilled beer and didn't bother to wipe it up.

I take charge. "Meg, you sit down right here on the step and I'll get you some ice real quick. Sally, can you go upstairs and look for Amy? And do you have some aspirin for Meg?"

I find some ice and a plastic bag to put it in, then rush back to Meg. Sally comes back down the stairs with a sullen, pouting Amy.

"Where did you find her?" I say.

Sally says, "Um… In the bedroom. I'll be right back with the aspirin." She rushes off.

I say, "Amy, what were you doing up there?"

Amy doesn't answer me. She slumps down and sits, a few steps higher than Meg, looking furious.

Sally comes back with aspirin and water. We get Meg settled for the moment, then I ask Sally what the deal was with Amy. She says, "Okay, I better tell you guys. She was on the bed, making out with Mike, oh, I can't remember his last name. He's a freshman."

"Oh, he's a high school freshman, is he?" I start up the stairs to teach the punk some respect, but Sally says, "Wait. I mean, I don't think it's completely his fault. He seemed horrified when I yelled at him. He thought Amy was even older than he is. People are saying she's been smoking and drinking beer and telling everyone she's a sophomore. She said she lives in Florissant.

Meg reaches over and grabs at Amy, scolding her so rapidly that she sounds like a chattering cartoon chipmunk.

Sally and I break the two of them up. I say, "Meg, stop it. You need to just worry about that ankle right now. We'll deal with Amy later."

Larry comes back. "What's wrong?" he says.

I say, "Well, Amy… Well, Meg slipped and hurt her ankle. Can you help me get her to the car?"

We thank Sally for the hospitality, then Larry and I get on either side of Meg and she hops along between us, out to the car. We get her into the backseat, next to Amy. Meg picks up where she left off yelling at Amy. She says, "Making out in a bed, with a high school boy. And you only in the sixth grade, just a child! That's how you act in front of all these people I've just met. Thanks a lot. Now I get to be the kinder-whore's sister. Oh, just you wait 'til Mooms hears about this."

Aha! I was wondering what Meg was so mad about. I'd guessed Meg was just crabby because her ankle hurt or embarrassed about falling down, but this makes more sense. Amy's behavior made Meg look bad in front of the crowd she wants to be in with. Like, now we're not just poor, we're obviously poor, easy trash. And Meg already told me I make her "weirdo's sister." I feel a tad sorry for Meg, even though she's a snob, or rather, because she's a snob. Getting so upset about what other people might think seems exhausting and painful. She's still a bitch, though. And I hate to tell her but nobody is that interested in her.

I notice Larry snickering behind the wheel, next to me. "Ha ha, kinder-whore," he repeats, unhelpfully.

Amy laughs, too. She's probably too young and dumb to even know it's an insult. She's probably buzzed, too. We probably all are. Amy tells Meg, "Age is only a number. You're not my boss anyway. You can't tell me what to do."

Meg gives her a couple of hard smacks for her trouble.

Amy yells, "My nose! You hit my nose. Now it will be even flatter. Oh my gawd!"

I say, "Meg, you better not tell Mooms. She'll blame us for not watching her. Mooms will never let us out of the house again. And sit still. You're gonna hurt your ankle even worse than it already is." For once, Meg doesn't try to have the last word, so I continue. "Didn't I tell you not to fix her up all womanish? Didn't I tell you she is a very conceited and horny child?"

Larry shrieks, "A conceited and horny child!" He bursts into laughter. The car skids. We nearly go off the road.

But Amy isn't that funny when you consider how we get poor little babies that end up stuffed under strangers' Christmas trees. I think about Robbie's mother a lot, even aside from trying to figure out who she is. I think about the hell she must have gone through. To distract myself from the mopey turn my buzz is taking, I grab the Visine and the Binaca breath spray out of Larry's glove box and focus on straightening everybody up before we get home.

"Want some breath spray?" I say to Meg, who holds her hand out for it, like a partner in crime for once, like a real sister. She sprays it in her mouth, then passes it on to Amy. After I'm done with the Visine, I pass that back there, too. Amy gives the items back to me, after her turn with them. She says, "If you two tell Mooms on me, I'll tell her that you made me get in the car with a drunk driver."

Larry bursts into tears. "I could have hit a tree!" he screeches.

I'm sick of everybody in this globdamn car. I can't wait to get to the silence and sanity of my garret.

I don't make the connection until later, that Larry's parents died by hitting a tree, and they were driving under the influence then, too. That dawns on me at midnight, in the middle of the neighborhood sounds of pot and pan banging, firecrackers and some idiot shooting off a gun.

I hope Larry has a better new year. I hope we all do.

Chapter 7

Larry gives me his signet ring to wear. It's heavy yellow gold, with "3L" engraved on it, in fancy script. I don't understand it, until he says 3L stands for his name, Laurence Laurence Laurence, and then it seems obvious. I roll tape around the back of the ring, so it fits snugly on my wedding ring finger.

Going along with the mainstream definitely has its benefits. For one thing, the girls at school start talking to me. It's nice to no longer be avoided. Larry and I just smoked a doobie in his car and now we're headed to his room and discussing this strange new development.

I say, "I mean, I know they're only talking to me because you're so popular now and they think I'm going out with you. It's like they think popularity is contagious and they all want to catch some." I sit down on the main floor's stairway. I need a break. Going to the third floor is a long haul when you're stoned.

Larry sits next to me. He says, "Nah, I bet those girls thought you were cool from the start. But now that you have a boyfriend, they quit worrying that you might hit on them, that's all."

"Ha! They should be so lucky. But I doubt it. That is a very un-stuck-up perspective though, to *not* think they only want to get close to me because I'm close to you." It is, too. Larry is very un-stuck-up, for a rich kid.

"Thanks. Really though, who knows how girls think."

"You got that right. Hey, what do you think of that, the big portrait of your Gramps?" It's on the wall across the room from where we're sitting, a larger-than-life head and shoulders painting. I notice it every time I come over here. It seems weird to have a giant picture of yourself on the wall.

"I don't know. I don't think about it. It's just there. Why?"

I go over to the portrait so I can point out what I'm talking about, the slightly narrowed eyes and downcurved mouth.

"See the expression on his face? I mean, he could have, like, smiled. Or the artist could have maybe painted him looking like he *didn't* just sniff a prostie's tuna-flower."

There's silence, so I turn around to look at Larry, irritated that he didn't laugh at my hilariousness. I turn around and practically run right into the Gramps.

The Gramps just stands there, with his bushy white eyebrows raised.

There's nothing to do but run. I run all the way home, biting down on my stupid tongue hard enough to really hurt.

Chapter 8

Now that the holidays are over and the Christmas decorations all taken down, we're in the coldest, darkest, suckiest phase of the year. The house is always chilly because Mooms worries about the heating bill.

 We used to go out to dinner as a family every Friday night, and we girls got to pick the restaurant. My favorite was Victoria Station, a cool restaurant built into old train boxcars. They serve the most amazing hot buttered popovers with your steak. Meg usually picked Casa Gallardo, with its colorful Mexican décor and delicious, crispy chimichangas.

Beth and Amy both picked pizza on their turns, either Imo's with their special cheese blend or Shakey's, with the player piano and the big window into the kitchen, where you could watch the workers twirl the pizza dough in the air. Miss Hannah and Beth try, I guess, but spaghetti or Hamburger Helper at home, with your jacket on at the table, is just so dreary and plain, especially when it's already dark out at supper time.

Beth was too much of a lightweight to get her butt out there and get a part-time job like Meg and I had to do. Mooms babies her, as usual. So, Beth's "job" is helping Miss Hannah around the house. And Beth does help with the housework, the laundry and cooking for us all. But the thing is, we don't need a second maid. Hell, we didn't even want the first maid. What we need is more money. But Mooms is always apologizing to Beth because Mooms can't pay Beth more than five bucks a week. Poor old Miss Hannah doesn't get paid anything at all, just food and a roof over her head. Well, if she really needs something, I'm sure Mooms would try to get it for her but still, Miss Hannah is a full-grown adult and she does a lot more around here than Beth does.

Aunt March's driver has just dropped me off. I stopped in at the garage to smoke part of a doobie and I'm thinking about the juicy dollop of gossip I've got to share at the dinner table tonight. That'll be one bright spot on a cold night, anyway. I can't wait to see the looks on everyone's faces.

I come in the back door and yell, in a jokey-but-I-mean-it way, because the globdamn door is unlocked again. The whole baby ordeal made it so real, how easily a stranger can come right into your house. I say, "Are you people trying to get another baby or what? Hell's bells!"

"Language."

"Shut up, Megma smegma," I retort merrily, before I notice that it is not Mooms Junior standing there glowering at me now, but Mooms Senior. The Moomses sound alike. I didn't even know Mooms

Senior was home. When will I learn to look around before I open the toilet that is my mouth?

"What did you say to me?" Mooms says, in the tight, low voice she uses just before she deconstructs you with her wooden spoon.

I apologize. I grovel mightily. Sufficiently, I guess, because after a while, she seems to get bored with me. Following a long, loud sigh, she says, "Go on and set the table, then."

I'm very relieved. That damn spoon hurts, especially if it lands on your head, spine, back of the hand or elbow funny bone. You'd think fifteen is way too old to get smacked around with a wooden spoon, but one never knows around here.

After the table's set, I go into the bathroom. I see the almost-new cake of Ivory soap in the soap dish. That's twice that my dirty mouth has got me in trouble lately. Well, no, if you ask me, my dirty mouth is pretty funny. It's just that I'm too stupid to remember to check out who's around before I open said dirty mouth.

But still. I'm stoned so I don't think it through too much. I pick up the bar of soap and stick it in my mouth. I bite down, hard, a concrete reminder to stop being such a fucking idiot.

It makes my mouth kind of burn and feel... puckery. I rinse and spit cold water about a dozen times, then stuff toilet paper into my mouth because it seems logical, like when you eat something too spicy and dilute the burn by putting bread in your mouth. Yep, lots and lots of toilet paper in my mouth is my best bet, at this point.

To try to distract myself, I go ahead and tear out all the avocado green, mildly urine-scented rug material. It's just nasty. There are two little shag rugs on the floor, and others wrapped around the toilet tank and the toilet lid and even the toilet seat itself. Good Lard. Highly unsanitary.

Then someone's banging on the door, wanting to use the bathroom. Of course it's globdamn Amy. *Knock. Knock. knock-knock-knock.*

I open the door. I mumble, "May I help you?"

"What's wrong with you? What's in your mouth? Eating toilet treats again?" She pushes her little smart-ass self right past me.

"Actually, I was just enjoying some fresh soap and nutritious toilet paper," I say, talking around the wet paper mâché in my mouth. I open my mouth and show her the big wet toilet paper wad in it. Then I point out the bite marks in the soap.

She shows delightful signs of shock. Her eyes get big and her mouth falls open. If she tells anyone, I'll just laugh and say, "Oh my goodness, our little stinkerpot is telling tales again!" Everyone will believe me because everyone knows that Amy is a brat. She'll look like a real weirdo, that's all.

But Amy recovers quickly. She says, "Oh, okay. Well, save some room for supper."

I snatch up the pile of excess bathroom carpetry as the devil child tries to push me out of t the room.

I say, "All right, already. I can't leave when you're blocking the doorway, dummy." I somehow squeeze around her, stopping only to push my nice bundle of nasty toilet rugs into her face, as a lesson to her. She shuts the door behind me. I say, "You need to respect your elders," trying to cover up how super-duper stupid she made me feel.

She shoots back, "You are sentient, but not sapient." I try to go after her but she locked the door. That was a pretty good one though, I have to admit. I'll have to remember to make a note of it, for use in a story, after my mouth situation corrects. Amy is branching out. She usually only searches the dictionary for the dirty words.

We're having baked potatoes for supper, topped with black beans, government cheese, tomato and onion. It's, like, the cheapest supper in the world but it tastes surprisingly damn good. But I can't eat anything tonight anyway, between the burning in my mouth and nausea that's coming on now. Before sitting down at the table, I discreetly put the mouth toilet paper in the trash, then get a couple of aspirin, a couple of Tums and a couple of glasses of ice water. If anyone asks, I'll just say I don't feel good. No one asks, though.

After we're all seated and everyone else is eating, Mooms says she filed for baby Robbie's birth certificate. She listed it as a home birth, with herself and Daddy as the parents. She says it was necessary to be able to get Robbie's baby shots, and to qualify for free formula through the WIC program.

Beth is holding little Robbie now. We pass him around at meals so everybody gets a chance to eat. I say, "Isn't he precious, Beth? Who needs dolls, now that we've got a real live baby doll, right?" My mouth hurts more when I talk.

Beth doesn't answer me but she looks like she might be considering the question, at least.

Somebody knocks at the door. I get up to go handle the ill-mannered dinner interrupter. It's Larry. He's weighted down with a whole baby shower's worth of gifts for Robbie. Boxes are piled up in his arms, plus there are a couple of big boxes beside him on the porch. Their maid is with him, with yet more baby items. There's a swing in a box and a stroller loaded with blankets and sleepers, and some other stuff.

"Fucking hell?" I say by way of greeting, stepping aside so Larry and his half a warehouse of merchandise can enter.

"I told the Gramps about the miracle baby, and he had the maid go buy all this." He points to the young woman standing next to him.

Larry says, "The receipts are taped on to everything, if your Mooms wants to return any of it. Gramps said your Mooms is an angel to take that baby in."

Mooms is at the door now. She claps and twirls around when she sees everything they've brought.

"Oh, my goodness! Come in, son," she says.

Meg has followed, hobbling along on crutches. She says, "*Son?*" She makes a face.

Mooms says, "That'll do, Margaret." Mooms hardly ever corrects Meg, so this is wonderful. I follow Moom's lead after Mooms moves into the living room, clapping and twirling around, too. Meg glares at me.

"That'll do, Margaret," I say, sweetly.

Seeing the Gramps's maid come in carrying baby stuff, it crosses my mind that maybe she's Robbie's mother. But her hair and eyes are dark. She looks Italian, maybe, like Meg and Beth do. They both have Mooms's coloring. Robbie's pale and blond though, with blue eyes. She's a new maid, anyway. But I keep an eye on her anyway, because you never know for sure. She doesn't even look in Robbie's direction, though, and then she leaves.

Mooms and the Gramps both seem thrilled that Larry and I are a couple now. My guess is they just don't want their kids to be gay or whatever. I'm surprised, though, that Mooms doesn't even seem to care that Larry's Black. I was expecting a lecture that started with "I'm not prejudice, but" and ended with her saying I had to break up with him.

Instead, the little talk Mooms has with me is her wanting to know if I want to get on birth control pills. I nearly run screaming from the room. Sex is repulsive. I can't stand hearing about it.

The real situation with me and Larry goes right over Meg's head. She's just jealous that I have a rich boyfriend. She keeps complaining to Mooms that I'm not supposed to be allowed to date until I'm sixteen, as if it's any of her business.

I think Daddy losing his money hurt Meg the most, of us girls. Not that it was easy on any of us, but I'm a pretty simple guy and the little girls don't seem to notice quite as much. Meg had that higher-up lifestyle longer as a teenager though, so she was more used to it. She loved the Saturday shopping trips to Plaza Frontenac, with its high-end stores, and Mooms's credit card in her purse. She also had her own horse and she was expecting her own car. She loved the name brand clothes and I'd hear her bragging about our family vacations to Acapulco and Maui, and stuff like that.

But Meg's biggest thing, if you ask me, was her snooty west county friend group. And as soon as Daddy lost his money, Meg's so-called friends dropped her like the hot potato that's all she's getting for supper tonight. See, to me, that would be proof that they were never friends in the first place. But now Meg just seems desperate to be in with the rich kids here instead. She didn't learn a thing.

So, it's like Meg is afraid I'll be considered more worthy than her or something, now that I supposedly have a rich boyfriend. She just can't stand it. She rolls her eyes whenever Larry's name comes up, and she calls him "Harry" or "Leroy," pretending she can't even remember his name.

And Mooms always sticks up for Larry, so that's another crack in the Junior-Senior Mooms Syndicate. I'm glad about that, of course. When one child is loved more, then other children are loved less, and it hurts like hell to be one of them.

Miss Hannah fills a plate for Larry. I'm not snobby like Meg but our peasant supper embarrasses me now. I've had dinner at Larry's twice. The maid served chicken cordon bleu one time and seafood cioppino the other time. Our whole meal here would only have been one of several side dishes over there. Larry has good manners, though. He acts like he is overjoyed to get a stupid potato.

Mooms is too busy pawing through all the baby gifts to bother with her supper anymore. There are adorable stuffed animals and rattles and tiny clothes. Baby stuff is cuter than hell. Larry says, "Oh, Gramps said to tell you the crib will be delivered tomorrow." Robbie's been sleeping in a drawer Mooms pulled out of her dresser and padded with folded up towels.

Tears fill Mooms's eyes. She's so happy she practically seems drunk. But it's kind of giving me a swirly feeling. My mind is still trying to catch up with the scene in front of me. But the Gramps is just the old guy next door and someone Aunt March knows. He's not really even a friend of ours. So it seems like way too much. I forget all about the piece of gossip I was going to tell, even though it has to do with Larry's Gramps.

Now I'm trying to think of what connection the Gramps could have to little Robbie. I can't think of anything at all.

After the excitement dies down and supper's over, we move to the living room for after-dinner coffee and cocoa, since we have company (Larry). I get another glass of ice water for my poor, soap-burned mouth, then take a turn holding my baby brother, or whatever he is besides the most precious creature on earth.

#

Meg starts ranting about her babysitting job the minute Larry leaves, like she's been holding it in all night. I'm sure her pride wouldn't let her spill her poor person problems in front of Larry. She forgets that he didn't have it so good himself until a few years ago. Larry didn't live in nice places for most of his life, before his parents' car wreck. He didn't benefit from having a rich grandfather then. Before his parents died, he had never even met the Gramps.

Meg says, "Oh, I'm so tired of that Annie Moffat and her braggy friends, all wearing the latest styles, driving around in new cars and jabbering on about the next big fancy party or rock concert or fashion show. They go to absolutely everything. They always get the best seats in the house, too."

Meg's babysits for the wealthy Moffat family on Saturdays and some other times, too. Annie Moffat's mother has little boys by her second husband. Annie, who's Meg's age, and Annie's brother Edward, who's a couple of years older, go about their privileged teenage lives while Meg takes care of their little half-brothers.

Meg says, "It know it's not Annie Moffat's fault that she's spoiled and has rich parents. But today, the witch pulled one of her stunts again. She made me fix and serve lunch to her and her two friends, like I was her darn personal maid, rather than a babysitter who works for her parents, *not* her. And I was stupid enough to do it, as usual, just to try to get along. Here I'm hopping along on crutches, waiting on Annie Moffat and her snotty friends when it's not even part of my job. That's the part that really makes me mad, that I never stood up for myself. I always just did whatever she said."

I could definitely see Meg being eager to please, too eager to please, thinking that would make those girls like her. She'd think then they might want to include her in their friend group.

She says, "So, I made grilled cheese sandwiches and a fruit tray and served everybody, the little kids and the big kids, the best I could anyway, on crutches and everything. I wasn't all that mad about it. But then, Annie snaps her fingers at me, and says, "More iced tea." "No please, no thank you. She just snapped her fingers at me and barked an order at me, like I was a doggone dog.""

Oh, I know this type of girl. I don't say anything but I could easily see Meg and her old girlfriends in west county doing exactly this kind of catty thing to the domestic help.

Miss Hannah says, "Lord have mercy. That ain't nice at all."

Meg says, "Thank you. So, I get through that. And then, the witch gives me a bag of her old wrinkled clothes, like I'm some kind of beggar on the street. I mean, they weren't even clean. She does it in front of her friends, of course, showing off some more at my expense. She always has to act like she's lady of the manor or something. Then her witchy friends put on these fakey nasty-nice smiles and start telling me what a lucky girl I am, and that they hope I'm grateful."

Now I'm getting mad too, on Meg's behalf.

Meg says, "So I hand the bag of clothes back. I go, "Oh thanks, but these clothes are *way* too big for me.""

I crack up laughing. So does Amy. Beth looks worried.

Meg says, "You guys know I've put up with so much from that girl, ordering me to "go fetch" her cigarettes or her purse, so her friends think she's hot doo-doo with her own personal servant. She also likes to complain to them about "hired help these days," right in front of me. It was the last very, very, very last straw. I went in the bathroom and cried.

Then I told Annie to watch the boys for a minute because I had to go do something. She called after me, real rude, that it wasn't her job to watch the boys for a minute and to just wait until her mother heard about it. But I walked out the door and just kept going, crutches and all, until I was home."

"Yeehaw!" I say. I hand the baby to Mooms, then pull Meg up out of her chair and hold one of her arms up like she's a boxing champion. Amy holds up her other arm. We forget about her sprained ankle and nearly topple her over. "Whoopie," we yell. "Way to go."

We girls and Miss Hannah keep cheering at Meg, until she goes from being mad to giggling. Meg walking out feels like a win for all three of us who do personal servant type work and know the humiliation that can come with it. Well, Miss Hannah does her servant type work for us, and not for much, either, which I don't think about right then.

Mooms changes Robbie into his brand-new dinosaur pajamas and lays him down on the sofa next to her. She says, "You know, Meg, the bills still come due."

Meg and I each have to chip in fifteen bucks a month to the household, along with paying for most of our own stuff.

I say, "There are some help wanted ads at the laundromat, on the bulletin board."

Meg says she'll check those out tomorrow, which seems to satisfy Mooms for now.

There's a knock at the door. It's past ten p.m., but I'm thinking Larry probably just forgot something.

I get to the door and am pleased to note that it is actually locked this time. I open it and a St. Louis County police officer is standing there.

Mooms is behind me. She kind of pushes me to the side.

The cop says, "Yes, ma'am. We've had a report that some jewelry is missing from the, let's see, the Moffat residence? Your daughter, Margaret March, was babysitting there today and left quickly, after some kind of disagreement with the Moffat's daughter?"

"Margaret!" Mooms calls. Meg hobbles to the door.

There's some talk back and forth. I hear Meg say there were also a lot of other people in and out of that house today, not just her. And Mooms says she's sure it's a misunderstanding, that Meg is a straight A student and has never given her a minute of trouble. After the door is closed again, I make sure to lock it.

"What a day," Mooms says, coming back to the living room.

Meg's face is drained of color. My mind is busy. That Moffat bitch is gonna get it.

I decide to think about that later though, and try to cheer everybody up with my delicious gossip now. I say, "Who wants to guess what happened at Aunt March's today?"

No one wants to guess, so I say, "Do youse promise not to tell?" I'm still trying to ramp up the suspense, so I make each person individually promise not to tell: Miss Hannah, Mooms, Meg, Beth and Amy. I hold little Robbie's right hand up and make him swear not to tell too, just to be goofy.

I say, "Alrighty, then. So, Larry's Gramps was over at Aunt March's when I was there today, okay? I had just finished plucking the dead leaves off the houseplants for Aunt March's real maid. Then the real maid told me to go into the kitchen and re-fill the watering can. So, I go into the kitchen. And… Aunt March and the Gramps are up against the icebox with their arms around each other. Smooching. On the lips!"

I sit back to savor the reaction. Miss Hannah claps her hands together and yells, "Woo!" Meg and Amy shriek about how gross it is for old people to make out, and Beth looks scared. The reaction is quite satisfactory, overall.

But Mooms is silent. There's no laughing or moral judgements against either of them, or even a scolding about how we need to mind our own business. Nothing.

"Mooms? How are you doing over there?" I say a few minutes later, feeling like something is off.

She says, "I just… need to go to bed." She swoops up the baby and goes up the stairs, that quick.

The rest of us look at each other and kind of shrug. But it is getting late, so we soon start heading up the stairs, too.

Chapter 9

It's a lazy winter Sunday. Larry and I lounge in his room, after smoking a doobie in his car. We hear the Gramps coming up the stairs, so Larry gets up from the bed and stashes the guitar he was half-heartedly strumming. He shoves it under the bed. He keeps his guitar away from the Gramps, for the most part. Then Larry rushes over to sit next to me, on the loveseat in his bedroom, making it look like we're up here being all lovey-dovey together, "faking out," as we call it.

The Gramps clears his throat, like he always does when he comes down the hallway, a warning sound so he doesn't walk in on anything, I guess.

He sticks his head in the room and says, "Just checking that the door is open up here." Fortunately, what I said about the Gramps's portrait seems to have blown over. I still can't look him in the eye, though.

Mr. Vaughn goes away as quick as he appeared. Larry waits a few minutes to make sure the Gramps is really gone. Then he retrieves his guitar, flops back down on the bed and continues his lazy strumming. No wonder we have the rude but well-known term, "drama fag" at school. And no wonder there are so many gay actors in Hollywood. Homosexuals have had to play a role all their lives. That adds up a whole lot of real-life acting lessons, if you ask me.

Ever since Larry and I started "dating," we've been under strict orders to keep Larry's bedroom door open, so now we have to go out to Larry's car to get high.

I say, "You won't believe what Meg did. If this shit keeps up, she might become a completely separate entity from her mommy. And what would life on earth look like then?"

Larry sets his guitar aside and sits up immediately. He adores gossip. He says, "What did she do now? What?"

"Okay, well, I was working on my story, you know, that one I told you about, that's based on the dream I had. The one where the girl gives birth to a litter of cats with human heads? Well, my pen ran out of ink and I couldn't find another one, so I went downstairs."

Larry does a rolling motion with his hand like, come on, get to it.

"How rude. You'd think my boyfriend would care that my first book-length story collection is almost done. Anyhow, I went in Meg's room, looking for a pen, you know, but Meg wasn't in there. So, then I opened her nightstand drawer, where she keeps stuff like that."

Larry pops his eyes open real wide at me.

"All right, already! You are so, so rude. So anyhow, I'm rooting around in the drawer, trying to find a pen, and what do I find but... Oh, never mind. You probably don't even care about it." I turn back to my math homework.

Larry comes flying across the room and sits on top of me.

I say, "Okay, okay. Get your smelly wiener away from me. Eww. Anyhow, remember Mrs. Moffat's missing pearl necklace and earrings, that the cops came to our house about? Well, they were in Meg's drawer."

"No!" he yells, flapping around the room, excited.

"Oh, yes. They sure were. Can you believe that shit?"

"Whoa! What did you do?"

"Well, what was there for me to do? I found a pen, then I put everything back the best I could. And then, in my story, I made the unmarried teenage cat mom dress her human-cat hybrid babies up with pearl necklaces. You know, to try to make them cuter, hoping people would accept them better. Do you think that's interesting or is the whole story just too weird to be publishable?"

"Shush. What are you going to do about the pearls? Aren't you even going to say anything to her?"

"No. Not unless she pisses me off. Then I'll have it to hold over her head. Gee, you can tell you don't have any siblings. You have no idea how these things work, son. Anyhow, the Moffats deserved it, pig-fucking thundercunts."

"Oh my God. You are the foulest -mouthed creature on the planet."

"Thank you," I say, honored.

He says, "Seriously, though. I should be furious. I'd have been in ten kinds of hot water if I got caught, when I was writing Annie Moffat's phone number on men's bathroom walls all over town. And now, after all that, we find out Meg actually did what the girl accused her of."

"That's true. Then again, I mean, it *was* your choice. Nobody twisted your arm."

"*You* twisted my arm. You did. That is exactly, literally, what you did."

I fall over on the loveseat, laughing. Larry plays "Evil Woman" on his guitar and sings along.

Generic foods came about in the late 1970s, in response to steep inflation. They covered a wide range of products, everything from applesauce to toilet paper to beer, and came in plain white packaging with black letters (yellow packaging, in some places). At the time, generic items were isolated in their own grocery store aisle. They carried a social stigma that isn't placed on users of today's equivalent, store brand products. Many generic goods came off the same production lines as their higher-priced brand name counterparts, but other products were inferior.

Chapter 10

Amy has a fit at breakfast because she doesn't like the generic cornflakes, though if she hadn't seen the plain white box with the black lettering, I doubt she'd even know they're not Kellogg's. She tosses her spoon down into her bowl of cereal and sits there pouting.

Miss Hannah says, "Oh, I'm sorry, sweetie. How about Miss Hannah makes you some toast with butter and jelly instead? Or would you like some hot oatmeal? Hey, I could put some cinnamon in it."

But it seems Amy wants the big shelf full of brand name cereals to choose from, like we had at our old house and nothing else will do. She says, "No! I want Golden Grahams. Or Froot Loops."

Mooms says, "Now, Amy. Miss Hannah is trying to be nice to you."

"Froot. Loops!" she hollers. Good Lard, she seems more like two than twelve sometimes. And then other times, she seems twenty-five. If she keeps it up, she could become her own grandma, haha.

Mooms says, "You know that we need to be careful with our money. We don't have extra to waste on expensive cereal that's not even good for you. Eat your breakfast and be glad you have something to eat. I bet those poor men over there fighting for us in the Viet Cong wish they could sit here in a nice, safe house with their family and eat that cereal."

Amy puts her head down on the table, hiding her face.

I guess she doesn't like it when everyone moves on from her complaints and gets back to eating and talking among themselves, because then she lifts her head up and clunks it back down hard, making everything on the table jump, including Moom's coffee, some of which sloshes out onto the table. Mooms glares at me. Not at Amy, at me. Just because I laughed.

Beth says, "It's okay, Amy. Don't pay any attention to those nasty kids.

Miss Hannah says, "That's right, sweetie."

"What nasty kids?" I say.

Finally, Meg explains. She tells me, "Amy went grocery shopping with Mooms and some kids Amy knows saw all the generics in the cart, and now they've been making fun of her at school."

I say, "Ah, okay. Now I get it. Amy, don't you dare be ashamed of our family being thrifty. It's stupid to pay more than you have to for the same stuff, and anybody who thinks that's something to make fun of is an ignoramus."

Meg says, "It really is pretty mortifying to be seen in the generics aisle, though. Poor kid."

Mooms says, "Excuse me, but inflation is out of control and we were barely hanging on in the first place. Anyone who thinks they're too good for plain label groceries is welcome to go buy the big brand names and pay for them with their own money. In the meantime, we all need to just be grateful there's food on the table."

"Amen," Miss Hannah says.

I only said the generics are the same stuff as the store brands because it made for a better pep talk. Really, the generic canned green beans have stems and the corn is tough.

I put my bowl in the sink and go bundle up, so I can go out and shovel the driveway.

It's hard to do since the driveway is gravel, not concrete. I've been out here for a while, carefully skimming snow off the top, at least. A woman with puffy, orange-painted lips gets out of her old Dodge and comes up the drive, sliding around on the ice under the snow. She says, "Hi there. I'm Kay Hummel, the new Avon representative for this territory. Can I show you our beautiful new products?"

It seems to me like a stupid time for door-to-door selling, right after a winter storm. The schools are closed, the snowplows are working overtime, trying to get the streets cleared. Half of Black Jack's electric is still knocked out. Then again, everyone is stuck at home today, so maybe it is a good time for door-to-door selling, after all. What do I know. I say, "I don't want any but you can knock on the door and see if the rest of them do, if you want."

I should have known. With the five little (or big, or medium-sized) women inside, the Avon lady immediately disappears into the house. Nevermind that we can barely afford to keep food on the damn table. Kay Hummel said the magic word, "Avon," and whoosh, they snatched her right in.

I can't figure out how to scoop up the snow and ice without scooping up half the damn gravel along with it. Aunt March would have a cow if we were left with a mud driveway, with the gravel flung all over the yard. I give up and put the snow shovel back in the garage.

When I get inside, the dining room table is covered with makeup and jewelry and everybody is seated, as if they are sitting down to a feast of Avon products. Which, in a way, they are.

The ladies of the house greedily rip open tiny sample packages. They spray perfume, apply lipstick and try on jewelry. The Avon lady just lets them have at it, on their own, like she's forgotten what she's there for. She is holding baby Robbie and seems as fascinated with him as everyone else is with all the frou-frou stuff.

Miss Hannah rushes off to gather up handheld mirrors so everybody can see how the makeup looks on them. Then she rushes off again to start the coffee and cocoa. Poor Miss Hannah looks flustered from the interruptions. I bet she just can't wait to get back to her seat at the girly table.

I sit on the side of the living room couch where I can watch the fun without being close enough for anybody to try putting any globdamn glop on me.

But then, there's something about the Avon lady's facial expression, fixated on Robbie. It's too intense. And there's something about how her thick lips and blue eyes look too much like Robbie's. Warning bells sound, a silent siren in my mind.

Pruitt-Igoe was a massive low-income housing complex built in St. Louis, beginning in 1954. It was heralded as a bold new solution to the terrible ghetto conditions that existed in the area at the time. The high rise, high density, public housing project was considered an innovation in urban renewal.

At first, the complex of 33 eleven-story high rises was segregated. The Pruitt side was for Black residents, and the Igoe side was for Whites. But public housing segregation ended in St. Louis soon after, in 1955.

Just four years after its beginnings, the buildings were largely abandoned, ransacked and stripped, and what remained was overrun with violence, crime and gangs. Pruitt-Igoe was a colossal failure. The last of the buildings wasn't demolished until 1976.

Chapter 11

It's Friday night and I've just come over to Larry's because I'm fed up with Meg's mouth. We're in Larry's room, or, as Meg calls it in front of

Mooms, "the honeymoon suite." The jealous rag would just love it if Mooms wouldn't let me come over here anymore.

Now Larry's getting on my nerves because Meg is driving me crazy and he is supposed to take my side and hate the bitch with me. But he just sits there playing around with his guitar. So, I tell him how Meg keeps saying that our cat Party is his and my love child, since Party is black. I hope he'll get mad about the racism but he just laughs. I say, "Meg has no idea how much I do for her."

He says, "If you're talking about making me write that poor Annie Moffat's phone number on all those bathroom walls, I don't remember you ever actually telling Meg about it. So, I don't know how she could be grateful. Not that it's anything to be grateful for anyway."

"It's in poor taste to identify oneself to the recipients of one's charity. Meg knows I'm on her side without knowing any specifics, anyway. She should have the same attitude for me."

He does that funny thing where he raises one eyebrow at me. He keeps talking. Bored with hearing him whine about the bathroom walls again, I say, "What time is it anyway?"

He pulls his cool antique pocket watch out of his Levi's. "8:45," he says. Then, he says, "What's the number of that time and temperature hotline you're always calling? I want to see if my watch is right. I tell him as picks up the receiver of his phone, "321-

2522." Larry loves that watch. He cleans its case with silver polish every week. It was his father's.

My family's coming over at nine. Mooms said she caught up with Mr. Vaughn when he was checking his mail, to thank him for all the baby stuff. She said Mr. Vaughn pulled some magazine out of his mailbox that had Sonny and Cher on the cover, and the two of them started talking about it. Mooms used to get a kick out of that show, when we had a TV. Their conversation led to an invitation for my family to come over and watch the Sonny and Cher show.

Larry starts playing that Sonny and Cher song on his guitar, "I Got You, Babe."

"Oh, you've got to play that for Mooms. She'll love it," I say, forgetting, as I do way too often, that Meg and Mooms are teamed up against me, so I really shouldn't bother being nice to them. "Let's go downstairs now."

Everybody comes. Even Miss Hannah and the baby and Beth, clutching the side of Mooms's skirt. Beth probably only came because she's just a little more scared to stay home alone than she is to go somewhere new.

Meg's been over here a couple of times, but only to tell me to come home for supper. It turns out to be a terrific way to pass an hour, watching a show we've been missing out on and drinking soda (wine for the adults). The maid set up hors d'oeuvres on the coffee table, miniature cocktail sandwiches and a nut-coated cheese ball with fancy crackers. I sure notice all these little luxuries, now that they're not part of my daily life anymore. I even feel a little weepy when the ice in our glasses is in that long banana-like shape that comes from an automatic ice dispenser rather than the rounded rectangles from the ice cube trays.

Mooms has a second glass of wine and gets giggly over Mr. Vaughn's dorky jokes. At ten, when the show's over, Larry plays "I Got You, Babe" and we all sing along. Then we all clap for Larry. Mr. Vaughn doesn't clap but he doesn't look mad, either. Beth silently moons at Larry like she's in love with him. Then Mooms says it's time to go.

My little rag-tag family walks home in the dark, snowy night, back to our cold house and bare-bones life.

Chapter 12

Meg and her new best friend, Sally Gardiner, come up to Larry's bedroom for the second time this week. Mr. Vaughn or the maid must have let them in. Larry smoked part of a joint before I got here and we were getting ready to take a ride so I could get a buzz, too. Now, with Mooms Junior here, I'll have to wait.

"Hi!" Meg says, all smiles, like we're just the best of pals. Nevermind all the crappy things she's said about Larry and me. She's decided it's in her best interest to be seen as someone closely associated with the wealthy Vaughn family, now that she wants to impress Sally Gardiner. I know how Meg's mind works, when it comes to that kind of stuff.

I can just picture the mothers of Meg's former "friends" in west county now, the country club set. They'd be expensively coiffed and manicured and rail thin from their diet pills and tennis, blabbing on over cocktails, in their slightly British fake accents. Upon hearing the March name these days, they'd tilt their surgically snipped noses up and sniff, "NOTD." (Not Our Type, Dear). That kind of thing makes me think they're crap but it makes Meg think Meg is crap. She simply has to have the approval of people like that. I bet Sally Gardiner's mother is just like that.

And the dismissal would be because we're poor now, not because our father is in jail. There was another convicted father in our old neighborhood who didn't lose his money. The Ladies Who Lunch just waved that off with, "Oh, it's all just business." I know these things from overhearing Mooms's phone conversations, before the phone got shut off at our old house.

Larry's like us, though. He's been both rich and poor. Larry's no silver-spoon shithead. He seems to get self-conscious, with these two in his bedroom. He starts straightening up the mess, picking his clothes up off the furniture and the floor. He says, "The maid's lazy," jokingly blaming his sloppiness on the maid rather than himself.

It's clearly a joke to me but it hits Meg wrong, probably because her run-in with Annie Moffat is still raw. She snaps, "The maid has to pick your dirty underwear up off the floor, really?"

Larry tries to dodge her. He's stoned so one can't expect much. He says, "I don't know. I guess not."

Meg says, "And you call her "the maid?" Doesn't she have a name?"

"Uh, I guess so."

"What is it, then?"

"Um, Tanelle? Maria? I don't remember. She's kind of new."

"She's a human being, you know."

"Oh. Okay."

Sally's looking at Meg funny. Her forehead's crinkled, like she's either deep in thought or not liking this side of Meg.

I try to change the subject. "How's the job search going, Meg?"

"Oh, I don't know. It sounded like a fun idea but I might pass."

A fun idea? She might pass? Oh, right. Meg wouldn't want Sally to know that she has to have a part-time job. I wish Meg would go home.

She says, "Anyway, sis, I wanted to ask you a favor, before you get home."

I'm suspicious. "Yeah?"

"Well, you know I turn eighteen next week, right?"

"Okay?"

"Okay, well, Sally and I want to go party with some college guys she knows, over in Illinois."

A lot of seniors go across the bridge to Illinois, where the drinking age is eighteen for 3.2 beer. It's 21 here in Missouri, for any kind of alcohol.

Meg says, "Sally and I told Mooms that Sally's cousin in Illinois has to have an operation and needs someone to stay over and help her with her kids over the weekend. I said I wanted to go help Sally with it."

I say, "Okay?" I'm wondering what it has to do with me.

"Well, you know Mooms. She said I can't go unless you go, too." It figures that Meg reaching the adult age of eighteen means exactly nothing to Mooms, whose motto is "Don't like it? Get out."

Wait. Now Meg is outright lying to Mooms Senior and trying to enlist me to help? Well now. This is wonderful. I say, "Sure. What do you need?"

She says, "Well, I need you to come to Illinois for the weekend."

"Okay," I say. "Sure." I'll have to get out of going to Aunt March's.

"Thanks, honey," Meg says, and hugs me. Meg never calls me "honey." Sally Gardiner calls people "honey."

After Meg and Sally leave, Larry and I finally take our drive. I light up a joint. He says, "Can I come?"

"You better come. Otherwise, who knows where those two will dump me off at, when they go off to the clubs with their college guys. Only, you know, Mooms and your Gramps are getting all friendly lately, so it's likely they'll compare stories. You'll have to come up with a story for the Gramps that doesn't involve you and I going away for the weekend together. Oh, did I tell you that Mooms left some brochures from Planned Parenthood on my dresser?"

He says, "Yeah. I'll work on that."

"Oh, you will, will you?"

"No, not that. I mean I'll work on coming up with a story for the weekend."

"I know, just kidding. Anyhow, Meg is such a climber, pretending to be in good with your family now. It's so desperate. I almost feel sorry for her. She's still a rat-bastard, though. Always was, always will be. I can't believe she had the nerve to yell at you in your own house."

"I know. I don't know why she thinks she has to seem richer than she is anyhow. It's not like you guys live in Pruitt-Igoe or anything."

I put the joint out. I've been hitting it too heavy and I'm not getting much writing done.

He says, "When your sister got on my case about the Gramps's maid, I almost blurted out something about you guys having a maid, too. I didn't, because of you. But if you don't mind me asking, what is the deal with Miss Hannah? You and Meg have to chip in on the bills but there's a live-in maid? Just if you feel like talking about it."

"No, it's okay. I guess it does look strange from the outside. See, Miss Hannah was our live-in at our old house, for a pretty long time, like, a few years. When everything fell apart, Mooms tried to let her go. But Miss Hannah said she didn't have anywhere else to go. She said nobody wanted to hire a seventy-year-old with heart problems. She cried and even got down on her knees and begged. It was horrible to watch. Mooms told her that she couldn't afford to pay her anymore. But Miss Hannah insisted on coming with us anyway. So here we are."

"Wow," is all Larry says.

Then out of nowhere, he blurts out, "I look in your windows, you know."

I sit up straight. "What? You weirdo. You fucker. What the hell?"

He says, "Well. That's not very nice."

That's so stupid that I crack up laughing. Larry laughs, too.

I say, "Was that supposed to be a joke or what?"

He says, "I talk too much when I'm buzzed. But okay, you and I have our secrets so I'll finish my little confession. If you promise not to call me any more names."

"Okay, fuck-face."

"Oh my God. Anyway, I'm not being a weirdo. You all just leave the curtains open a lot. And I have to tell you, I don't understand what you're always bitching about, not having this and not having that. It looks like a Norman Rockwell painting over there. Do you know who that is?"

"Another peeping tom?"

"Shush and don't flatter yourself. I don't *deliberately* look in your windows. I just open my bedroom window when I want to smoke. And I see such a nice, big cozy family over there. People together, eating dinner, laughing, the cat running around, and now the baby. See, I don't have all that. I never did. Really, I'm the one who's poor and you're the one who's rich. You just don't know it, is all.

My eyes tear up. "Wow. I don't even know what to say."

Larry wipes his eyes with the back of his hand.

It's getting too sappy around here for me. I say, "You can look in my windows any time. You're my favorite pervert."

Larry yanks my ear and twists it until I yell, and then we're back on an even keel.

Chapter 13

A few days later, I go home for supper after hanging out at Larry's, and our house is strangely quiet. Beth announces that supper's ready, so softly that I have to repeat it so everybody can hear. I don't know what all goes into making up the different moods in a home, but I feel the mood here right now and it's tense.

I notice the blinds are open and go over to shut them, because it's already dark out. Then I change my mind and leave them open for Larry, since he likes watching the March family soap opera so much. Norman Rockwell, ha! I guess Larry missed the "Daddy's Not in Vietnam, He's in Prison" episode. And the "Avon Lady Who Might be the Baby's Mother" episode. And let's not even think about the "Black Tent of Death" episode.

We sit down at the table, while Miss Hannah and Beth pass out bowls of seasoned red beans over rice, with fruit salad on the side. I didn't know this before but one way you can tell if your family is rich is if the foods in your meals are separate: the meat on one part of the plate, the potatoes on another and the vegetables on a third part. Poor people eat a lot of glop, all mixed together. Or we do, at least.

Amy's eyes are red. Her usual spark is missing. Whatever's up, it has something to do with her.

After we're all settled in, Mooms says, "Girls. Just for your information, I got a call from the principal at the elementary school today. I had to leave my job early, to go have a word with him and pick Amy up, after she earned herself a paddling."

"What did you do now, kerplop head?" I say to Amy, trying to lighten the mood. Trying to take some of the heat from Mooms off the kid, by doling out lesser heat to the kid myself, or something.

"Amy, why don't you tell everyone what you did?" Mooms says, her jaw set in that tight way it gets when she's super mad.

Amy says, "Nothing. I didn't do anything! I just, it was just, we had to stay in the classroom at recess because of the weather. It was sleeting outside. So, then some girls decided we should play "seven minutes in heaven."

I say, "You mean that game where a boy and a girl make out in the dark for seven minutes?"

"Yeah, but I only went in there because I didn't want those girls to call me a baby or anything. I didn't do anything in the closet. I just went in there when they said it was my turn, so I wouldn't get picked on."

Meg and I exchange knowing looks. I bet anything Amy did make out with a boy in the coat closet. And I bet it just happened to be that one blond boy Amy talks about all the time too, the patrol boy. In fact, I'd be surprised if Amy wasn't the one who started the whole game in first place.

Meg just says, "Beth, pass me the salt and pepper, would you, honey?" After Meg gets the tall white Tupperware shakers and over-seasons her glop du jour, she goes back to eating, minding her own business for a change instead of sticking her nose in. It's like she's forgotten she is Mooms Junior.

So, Meg has added these things to her life: stealing from her enemies. Drinking beer. Calling people "honey." And lying to Mooms, so she can sneak out to bars with college guys. She's subtracted being super nosey and being Mooms's Chief Enforcement Officer. I'm really starting to see hope for the girl.

Anyhow, we girls need to keep the weight off Mooms's shoulders, as much as possible. We need to handle ourselves, among ourselves. I say, "So, in other words, you were being bullied and you handled the situation to the best of your ability, and the principal spanked you for it?"

Amy nods, humbly. Amy acting humble breaks my heart. It's very rare.

I continue my Perry Mason bit. "And where was the adult in charge, while this game was going on?"

Mooms's jaw is still tight, but her eyebrows rise up halfway to her hairline. She says, "Right. Who did allow that kind of game to go on in the classroom?"

Amy says, "There wasn't an adult. When we can't go outside for recess, the lunch ladies just check in on the classrooms, sometimes." Beth reaches over and puts her hand on top of Amy's, in silent sympathy.

"Well. That's not right, is it," I say, and turn back to my glop, like it doesn't make much difference to me, either way.

Mooms slams her spoon down. "Why that... I didn't know that. And the way he had the audacity to speak to me. Not to mention laying his hand on my child, without my permission. We'll see about this. I'm going back up there on my lunch break tomorrow."

I say, "Oh, Mooms. You've already missed work time. Why don't we have Meg drop you off at work tomorrow, then Meg and I will drive over to the elementary school on our lunch break instead? We'll just say we heard that the classrooms are unsupervised when the weather keeps the students in from recess, and that we thought he might like to know. As for the rest, well, even if the school was partly to blame, she can't really be unspanked anyway, right?" Meg nods along with my words. I'm not sure if I'm making a lot of sense or not. I'm just trying to end the upset for Mooms.

Mooms sighs deeply, like she's puffed up with pressurized hot air that she just can't wait to release. One of these times, I wouldn't be surprised if she goes flying around the room, like a balloon that's come undone. She says, "Thanks, girls. I don't know what I'd do without you." That breaks the spell of tension and makes me feel pretty great.

Meg and I talk about it later. We aren't going up to the elementary school. Why take a chance on stirring it all up again? We agree to just tell Mooms that the principal was very nice. We'll say he wasn't aware that the classrooms were being left unsupervised, and that he thanked us for letting him know.

I pull Amy aside, when I get a chance. I say, "You know, we girls have to be careful not to upset Mooms, right? After all she's been through, she can't take much more. And I don't even want to think about what will happen to our family if she falls apart, especially for you two little girls. So, I covered for you this time. But you watch yourself, hear?"

She doesn't speak or even make eye contact but she nods. I think she got enough of a lesson today to keep her in her place for a while.

Chapter 14

Meg and I sing and dance around like spazzes to KSLQ radio while we get ready for our weekend in Edwardsville. KSLQ is the guilty pleasure of the girls in this house, playing more soft and pop rock kind of songs, like Peter Frampton, Abba and the Bee Gees. We keep that information quiet outside of the house, though. KSHE-95, the hard rock station, is what's considered cool.

Meg is all dolled up for her big night out, wearing the dress Aunt March gave me for Christmas, which somehow manages to look sexy and stylish on Meg. She was disappointed that the doctor said she still has to be on crutches though. I'm starting to look forward to getting out of town for a while, for a change of scenery. But mainly, it's cool to feel like real sisters with Meg, partners in crime and all that. That could never happen when Meg was so close to Mooms.

Then little Miss Tag-Along starts her tantrums again. Amy thinks she should get to go everywhere Meg and I go, as if a twelve-year-old belongs any place and every place that a nearly sixteen-year-old and eighteen-year-old go.

Amy yells, "I want to go! Why can't I go? Either I'm going, or else I'm telling Mooms on you guys!" She throws herself across the old suitcase that's opened on Meg's bed. Meg yells at her to get up because she might bust the suitcase's frame. Instead of getting off the suitcase, Amy starts bouncing up and down on it.

Meg tries to pull her off. She says, "I can't believe you'd even ask to come along, after how you acted at Sally's party."

I add, "Not to mention that I saved you from the whipping of a lifetime, after your little closet game at school. You ungrateful thing. You aren't invited to Illinois, and that's that. Damn, we're only going babysitting anyway."

Instead of showing even the slightest bit of remorse, Amy continues to display her evil ten percent. She bounces up and down on Meg's suitcase even harder, with a smart aleck look on her face. She says, in a sing-songy voice, timed with her suitcase bouncing, "Nope. I heard you two talking about it. You're not going babysitting. You're going partying. And I'm going to tell Mooms!"

But Mooms isn't here. She's at work. And Miss Hannah isn't home right now, either. The suitcase splits in two at the hinges.

I say, "That's it." I snatch Amy up and throw her over my lap, then spank her, hard. Two smacks, five smacks, eight smacks, until she's crying, good and loud.

I only stop when I see Beth standing in the doorway, holding the baby and looking terrified.

I say to Amy, "Now get in your room and I better not see your face again before I leave."

Amy hisses, looking like something out of *The Exorcist*. She says, "Just wait. You'll be sorry, bitch."

Bitch? Oh, my fucking stars. I start after her again, but… there's traumatized Beth and the baby, and we've got to get going. But mostly, I know I need to stop because now I'm mad enough to knock little Miss Amy into next week. That girl!

Amy flounces off to her and Beth's bedroom, but of course she doesn't go quietly. She sobs, loud and dramatic, all the way. Beth scurries along after her. At least Beth is carrying a real baby with her now.

The fun, sisters-against-the-world mood Meg and I shared has gone sour now. But somebody had to put that child in her place. Amy would never dare try the outrageous behavior she's gotten by with lately, if Daddy was here. Fortunately, Sally arrives. Meg tosses her stuff into a trash bag and we make our getaway, before Mooms gets home and Amy gets a chance to snitch.

I love riding in Sally's new blue Camaro. But between that and Aunt March's Lincoln, I really, really notice how old and shabby our old family station wagon is. In our old house, it was the extra car, for Miss Hannah to use or for if Mooms or Daddy's cars were in the shop. Meg and Amy always duck down whenever we ride in it, so nobody they know will see them in a poor people's car.

Sally hands Meg a box of Sobranies. I've seen the two of them showing off with them in the smoking area outside of school. The expensive European cigarettes stand out because they come in different colors, with gold foil around the filtered part. I'm pretty sure the showing off is the point. I don't know how much they cost but I know it's more than the usual Marlboros or Salems. It's stupid. Meg selects a pink one, then Sally hands the box back to me. I think, oh why not, grab a yellow one, and wait for Sally's lighter to make its way back to me. It's not a Bic, it's a dainty, slim thing with a little peacock enameled on it.

Meg tells Sally about the latest Amy incident. Sally shakes her bleached blonde head, from her seat behind the steering wheel, while she and Meg rehash Amy's misbehavior at Sally's New Year's Eve party. I'm sure Meg spun that story just right so it would reflect on her, Meg, as well as possible. I'm glad Meg and Sally agree that Amy had the butt whipping coming, though. The old Meg would surely have tried to put a stop to me going after Amy, just to show that she was the one in charge, the junior Mooms.

Larry will come to Illinois later tonight. He's waiting until later, so that his and my weekend trips will seem less connected to each other. I don't know what story he told the Gramps, just that it doesn't involve me and Meg, obviously.

We really are staying with Sally's cousin, as was told to Mooms. Only Sally's cousin doesn't need an operation or have any kids, and he's a guy. He rents a room in a big old house in Edwardsville, along with a bunch of other students. I feel like an outlaw, sneaking across the border at night, as we cross the long bridge over the Mississippi River, from Missouri to Illinois, the water inky, far below. It's kind of exciting, even though I'm only going there to sit around some stranger's house with Larry. I don't usually get to go very far from home these days.

#

I almost forgot it's Meg's birthday today. Sally has plans for her, though. Sally and Meg and the college friends are going out for a fancy birthday dinner for Meg, before they hit the night clubs. After we put our stuff in the bedroom that we three girls will be sharing upstairs, I hand Meg a ten-dollar bill. I tell her to have her first legal drink on me. Sally promises to send me a picture of it. She's got a camera and flash cubes in her purse.

Meg and Sally are just kind of fidgeting around, all dressed up, and it dawns on me that they probably think they have to wait until Larry gets here to leave, so I'm not left alone in a strange house. But there's another girl here in the living room, who we're watching TV with and talking to. I tell Meg and Sally not to wait around on my account.

"Well, if you don't mind, honey…" Sally says, brightening up. I act overly cheery back, so I don't drag down Meg's big eighteenth birthday. I wish I was invited along to dinner, at least, even if I can't get into the bars. But I'm trying to be cool about it. I can't afford a fancy restaurant dinner anyway. Even if I could, I don't want to be the new Miss Tag-Along on things I wasn't invited to.

Now I'm wondering if it was a mistake to have Amy fill in for me at Aunt March's tomorrow, when Amy's become such a Problem Child. Then again, I would love to see what Aunt March does to her, if she runs that smart mouth over there. No, come to think of it, I wouldn't. I keep going through the ugly scene we had earlier, in my mind. Regardless of who was right or wrong, I feel pretty lousy about it now.

I make small talk with the other girl here. I wonder if she wishes Meg and Sally had invited her to go out, too. She's from somewhere way out in the country here in Illinois and she wants to be a math teacher. I say, "Wow, that's interesting," just to be polite. But I can't think of a past or a future that would be more boring than hers.

Larry shows up and shares his weed with me and the girl. The girl offers us some generic cola from a big bottle, and serves it to us over ice. Now I'm worried, because Mooms always says not to drink the water in Illinois and I don't know if that includes ice. On the one hand, ice *is* water, obviously. But on the other hand, maybe freezing the water kills the bacteria or germs or whatever the problem is. I bring it up, and Larry and Math girl howl with laughter, like it is the most hilarious thing they've ever heard.

They keep repeating, "Don't drink the water in Illinois," and laughing their stoned and stupid heads off. I sort of laugh along, so I don't look like even more of a spaz, but it does make me mad.

I don't find Mooms's advice hard to believe on this one, though. I mean, I was so surprised in junior high, when I learned that Illinois is a far more wealthy and powerful state than Missouri. It's not like that at all, around here.

When you go across the bridge from Missouri, the part of Illinois you enter is hoosier-ville. There are shacks and trailer parks and rinky-dink churches that look like they most likely advocate snake-handling. And all manner of vice is allowed that would be crimes in Missouri. Not just low age drinking but also gambling (in the form of lottery tickets), and sleazy strip clubs, too. But Math girl was born and raised here in Illinois, and Larry's from California, so they don't know any better. Anyway, it's not worth the chance of getting parasites, or whatever. I pour my soda out in the sink. That makes Math girl and loyalty-free Larry laugh so hard they're about to lose their minds.

Sally's cousin comes home and introduces himself. I thought he was supposed to go out with Sally and Meg and whoever else is with them, so I tell him they said they were going to Rusty's Restaurant and then to the Holiday Inn bar. But I don't know where they're going after that.

Steve says, "Okay." But after a while, he says, "You know what, I think I'll just hang out here with you guys." I feel flattered that a college person would pick us over a night on the town with the cool older crowd. Well, Math girl is older too, but I couldn't see her in with any cool crowd. Not with those high-water pants and brown plastic eyeglass frames.

Steve passes out cold cans of Busch beer (no Illinois ice needed hahaha, oh, teehee). He pops two frozen cheese pizzas in the oven and sets a timer that looks like a big ladybug.

We all move over to the kitchen table, after Steve asks if we want to play Yahtzee and starts setting the game up before we can answer. He plays an Aerosmith cassette on a boom box.

I thought Larry and I would hang out here alone, just like any other night except for the location, so this is a nice surprise. After we get past the Illinois water/ice debacle, that is. I start to have fun.

We finish two rounds of Yahtzee, the two pizzas, more beer and pot, and a game of Scrabble, which Math girl wins. Then get started on Clue. Larry and Steve are flirting with each other.

I decide to leave the room before I say something that might start a fight. Getting into another clash today, after the thing with Amy earlier, that would be too much for me. Plus, I'm too buzzed to even know if being furious about Larry and Steve flirting is reasonable. I suspect it's not but that's still how I feel. I say, "I have a headache. I need to go lay down for a while."

Math girl says, "I hope you feel better. Let me know if you need anything."

I say, "Thanks, honey," trying the word out, and confirming that it's definitely obnoxious.

On the way up the steps, I conclude that you shouldn't call anyone who isn't your romantic partner "honey," unless you're at least, say, fifteen years older than they are. So, under the non-obnoxious "honey" use rule, Mooms, Daddy, Mr. Vaughn, Aunt March and Miss Hannah could all call me "honey," without sounding obnoxious. That sounds right to me. At this stage in my life, I could only call little Robbie and Party "honey." Which also sounds about right to me. I plan to pass my "honey" use thoughts along to Meg, though I doubt it will do any good. Larry and Steve don't seem to have heard me say I'm going to lay down, even though my leaving will mess up the Clue game.

I go to the bedroom where me, Meg and Sally have put our stuff. Sally brought a couple of sleeping bags because there's only one twin bed in here, for us three girls. Larry is to sleep on the downstairs couch. I unroll a sleeping bag and lie down in the dark, where I can sort out my thoughts about Larry in peace.

The thing is, first of all, Larry and I present ourselves to the world as a couple, which seems to me should have been obvious to Steve. I mean, I'm wearing Larry's ring, and Math girl certainly ·

thought Larry and I were a couple. So that's a huge disrespect factor from Steve, playing footsies with Larry under the table and all that, right in front of me. I mean, Larry and I know that we're only a pretend couple but how would Steve know that?

Second, if Larry starts hanging out with Steve, I'll be alone. Aside from being my best friend, Larry is my *only* friend. The girls at school don't count. They're only acquaintances, and acquaintances with an agenda, at that. I'm sure they'd stop bothering with me the minute they thought Larry and I had broken up. When I invited Larry along, I meant for him to be sharing jokes and stuff with me, not with Steve.

I wake up much later, when Sally and Meg come stumbling in, all tipsy. They nice-bicker over who gets to sleep in the bed. Sally says Meg should get the bed because she is the birthday girl. And Meg says Sally should get the bed because it's Sally's cousin's place. I leave the room like I'm headed for the bathroom down the hall, but I go downstairs to check on Larry.

He's not sleeping on the couch. There's no sign of him, but his car is still out front. He's most likely spending the night in Steve's room.

When I get back, Sally is ensconced in the bed, as I expected, since Sally is richer and cooler than Meg, and therefore the queen who deserves the best for herself. Meg is in a sleeping bag, in her rightful place on the floor. It makes me a little bit mad.

#

On Saturday, more people are around. Larry and Steve don't flirt with each other in front of them.

Sunday, Sally, Meg and I leave in the morning but nobody has to remind Larry to wait a few hours before heading home. He's already left for the day with Steve. They've gone to downtown St. Louis to check out some art galleries or museums or something. So now Larry has Steve, Meg has Sally and I have nobody. I mope alone in the back seat on the ride home.

When we get close to our house, I brace myself. If Amy snitched to Mooms about our real reason for going to Illinois, it won't be pretty. And I won't be able to escape over to Larry's house, either. He won't be home yet and I don't feel like talking to him whenever he does get home, anyway. I mean, I realize that marching over there as the jealous fake girlfriend would be hilariously stupid. I also know it's stupid and immature to want to be Larry's only friend in the first place. But still, I do feel dumped and hurt. So, my best bet is to just keep my distance for now, so I don't make a fool out of myself. I decide to write a funny story about a ridiculous, jealous fake girlfriend, which cheers me up some.

Chapter 15

After Sally Gardiner drops Meg and me off, the first thing I notice at our house is that the front door is locked, which I take as one good omen, at least. But when I get inside, I hear arguing. I rush up to my garret, hoping nobody notices me. They don't.

I tiptoe back down to the second floor a couple of times, but all I hear is Mooms arguing with Amy in the living room. It's not loud enough for me to pick up on much. And as long as Mooms is mad at Amy instead of Meg or me, I'm not too concerned anyway. Time goes by and the house goes quiet. I find Meg in her bedroom.

I plop down on Meg's bed, like we're real sister-buddies. I say, "What was all that arguing about?"

She says, "From what I could hear, Mooms is mad because Amy went over to Aunt March's."

"What? I sent her over there, to work in my place, you know."

"Yeah, but Mooms didn't know about it."

"True, but I'm trying to keep things calm for Mooms, like you always say we should do. Anything to do with Aunt March seems likely to upset Mooms. But it seemed better to offer Aunt March a replacement than to just say I wasn't coming, you know? Aunt March said it was okay. I called her from Larry's." We don't have a telephone.

"Don't you remember that whole thing, when everything happened with Daddy, and Aunt March wanted to adopt one of us girls?"

Aunt March did get really mad when Mooms refused her offer. In fact, Aunt March nearly kicked us out of this place over it, before we'd even finished moving in. I guess I just found it hard to take seriously because it was so ridiculous. Who on earth would seriously expect someone to give away one of their kids, just because they were short on money at the time. Like sure, here ya go. Take your pick of the litter? Besides, it seemed like that was all over and done with. I say, "But I go over there every Saturday. Mooms doesn't say anything about that."

Meg says, "Um, I think Aunt March wanted one of the little girls."

"Gee, thanks." The last thing I'd want is to live with Aunt March. But I'm not sure I like not being wanted, regardless.

Meg says, "Yeah right, I'm sure that breaks your heart. But anyway, Aunt March has started it up again. Now she's trying to bribe Amy to move in with her. I guess you couldn't hear it from the attic, but the old witch promised Amy she could go to some fancy art school in Clayton if she moves in over there. Oh, she also promised Amy a nose job."

My head is spinning with too many thoughts at once. *Good, Let Amy go. Did I really just think that about my baby sister? Why didn't Aunt March ever ask to adopt me? It's great that Meg is staying here in her bedroom, rather than downstairs acting like Mooms's shadow. Did Amy snitch about me spanking her, or about why Meg and I really went to Illinois? Where the hell is Larry when I need him? Can I get by with sneaking outside to smoke a doobie?*

Things get too complicated around here for me to keep track of. The situations I make up in my stories are so much easier.

I look out the window. Larry's car is still not back.

When we go down for supper, I shut the blinds. Fuck Larry. He can go look in his new boyfriend's windows. We sit at the table in gloomy silence, in the chilly dining room, in our jackets and sweaters. Miss Hannah and Beth dish out vegetable beef stew and buttered Wonder bread. It does smell pretty damn good.

Party hops up on the table and sits there like a centerpiece. A couple of us start to grin, then snicker, when he proceeds to prowl around the tabletop, stepping tentatively, sampling stew from our bowls, one at a time. His yellow eyes are open wide, like he just can't believe we set up this delicious buffet just for him. Larry would have gotten a kick out of it, especially after the formal dinners he's used to having with the Gramps.

Only Amy doesn't even crack a smile. With the hood pulled up on her sweatsuit top and her face in the shadows, she looks hunched and grizzly, like an elderly troll from a fairy tale.

After she finishes eating, she stands up and says, "Just so you know, I hate all of you. Except for Beth, Miss Hannah, Robbie and Party. Which means I hate you, Mooms, Jo and Meg. And by the way, Jo, good luck with your book."

She starts to flounce off but Mooms interrupts her, sounding tired. She says, "Put your dishes in the sink, Amy."

Amy comes back and places her dishes into the sink, then re-flounces. But her stopping in the middle of her big bad revolt to obey an order from her mommy strikes the rest of us as comical. Laughter erupts around the dinner table.

Meg starts to get up like she's going to follow after Amy, but then she waves her hand in Amy's direction, like *oh, just forget it* and sits back down.

I wonder what Amy means by "Good luck with your book." The comment sits uneasy in my chest. But it also reminds me of the new story I'm working on, about the fake couple and their "lovers' quarrel." I finish my supper, then go up to my garret to get back to it.

One more story will be enough for my debut collection, I think, which makes this one extra special. I have a list of book publishers to try, from the *Writer's Market 1977* that Meg gave me for Christmas. I need to get this last story written, then figure out a way to type the stories up, because the publishers expect them to be typed. My stories are handwritten on notebook paper now. I'm hoping my English teacher will help me get permission to use one of the school typewriters. I reach into my bottom dresser drawer for my big stack of stories, but the drawer is empty.

My stories are gone.

#

Amy's lying on her bed, facing the wall. I say, "Amy. Where are my stories?"

She puts her pillow over her head and holds it down with her hands.

Twelve long stories, written and re-written 'til they jump off the page at you. Two years of work. My dream. I feel sick. Exhausted really, but I need an answer and I intend to get it. I say, "You better take that damn pillow off your head before I hold it down better than that and smother you. Don't even think I won't." I shove the pillow down hard on her head. I hate us both.

She throws the pillow aside. Her tear-streaked face looks ecstatic, crazed. She says, smiling, "I ripped your dumb stories into teeny-tiny pieces. And then I soaked the pieces in the bathroom sink until they were mush. They're all gone now. We don't always get what we want, do we? Aw gee, that's too bad."

I stare at her. Who is this child, anyway? I don't want to know this girl, now or ever. I say, "We're not sisters anymore." It's all I have the energy for. I feel like my world has now collapsed completely. I'm not Larry's number one person anymore and I don't even have my stories.

I turn to leave the bedroom. Mooms stands in the doorway. She steps aside, saying, "Oh, my goodness. Oh dear." Amy is sobbing now. I just go up to my garret and sleep, because it's the easiest way to not exist.

I don't wake up until early morning. Larry's car is in his driveway next door now, covered with frost.

Chapter 16

It takes a couple of weeks after the trip to Illinois before I'm ready to stop dodging Larry. By then, Larry and Steve are on their way to becoming a real couple.

Larry and I agree that our lives are nicer when we're a pretend couple, so we stay that way. Also, sometimes I feel like Larry is my family, as much as, or even more than, my real family is. So, I adjust. It's either that or lose him completely. But whenever Steve is around, I'm not around. I just like my world better without Steve in it.

One beautiful, blue-skied, Steve-free Sunday, Larry and I go ice skating. It will likely be our last chance this winter.

Once, before I stopped being Amy's sister, Larry and I were talking about ice skating on the pond, and Amy overheard us. Naturally, she tried to invite herself along. At the time, I said okay. We have ice skates from our Old Life that we could probably make do with, even if Amy had to wear Meg's skates with a couple extra pairs of socks on.

Amy somehow thinks the invitation still stands. Mooms forgave and consoled Amy for destroying my stories just because Amy cried, but I didn't.

I ignore Amy's whining. I don't think a normal person of any age would have the nerve to expect to still be invited along, all things considered. I ignore Amy in general now. I gather up my ice skates, get warmly bundled up and go back to Larry's. He's waiting at the end of his driveway.

The pond is a short walk away. It's great to be out here in nature, with Larry, in this frozen wonderland. I like it even better than the Ice Capades shows we used to go see when they came to the St. Louis Arena. I did like seeing the talent, the costumes, the whole bit. But I'd still rather skate myself than watch other people skate, no matter how good they are at it.

Larry says, "I'm not so sure about this ice. Let's just stick to the edges of the pond, okay?"

I'm disappointed, but he doesn't usually talk without knowing what he's what he's talking about, so I go along with it. He speeds off along the pond's edge and I start after him, when hear, "Hey, you guys, wait for me!"

It's Amy. Ugh. I skate away along the edge of the pond, as far and as fast as I can, hoping to salvage some of the day's joy, at least.

A short time later, I hear a loud cracking sound. Amy screams.

She's out near the middle of the pond. She's fallen down on her knees. No, she's gone through the ice. She's halfway underwater, and flailing.

My mind is still trying to catch up with what my eyes see when Larry appears at Amy's side. He yells to me, "I need a long piece of wood, right away. Find a tree limb or a fence plank!"

I snap to, then. I wobble on my skates as fast as I can to somebody's old wooden fence nearby and yank hard, until a plank comes off.

When I get back with it, Larry's on his stomach, managing to hold Amy up enough that her face is out of the icy water most of the time. "Here!" I shout, pushing the wood to him.

He lays it across the hole in the ice, and we're able to help Amy climb out that way.

Once we're back on dry land, I have Larry turn around while I pull Amy's wet clothes off her real quick. I wrap her up in my dry coat, hat, scarf and gloves. We rush home, with the poor thing sobbing all the way. She must have been terrified, and the water was so bitterly cold.

#

Mooms gets Amy completely dried off and wrapped up in blankets on the sofa. A mug of hot cocoa has gone cold on the coffee table nearby. Amy's fast asleep, her blonde hair fanned out over the pillow. She slept through dinner and now everyone but Amy, Mooms and I have gone upstairs. Our precious little girl is safe at home, as she deserves to be. She looks a far cry from the monstrous villain I had so stupidly come to see her as, before we nearly lost her. I am so ashamed of myself I can barely stand it.

Mooms sits on a cushion on the floor. She smooths Amy's hair and softly sings James Taylor's "Up on the Roof" of all songs to pick, in her beautiful Mooms voice.

When the song ends, I desperately feel like I need my mommy, too. That's a feeling I haven't had for a long time, which is probably good, considering that I'm fifteen. I say, "It's all my fault. I was furious about her ruining my stories, so I ignored her. I knew the ice wasn't to be trusted, out in the middle of the pond. I hate myself for not even turning to see where she was. Sometimes, how I get when I'm angry, it scares me to death."

Mooms says, "I understand, Jo. I'm angry nearly every day of my life."

I'm stunned. "You? I didn't know that. I mean, I know you get mad when we've done something wrong or when you have another good reason to be mad. But that's all."

"Well, I've had more years to practice controlling it than you have. You really do need to get a grip on it because as we see here, acting out of anger, or *not* acting because you're angry, can ruin your life, or somebody else's, in a split second."

"Right. You're so right." I weirdly think about how I wish the fireplace worked. It would be so cozy, with the cold winter outside and all of us safe and warm in here. After a while, I said, So, how do you control your anger?"

"Well, I'm not saying this is the right way or the only way. But have you ever heard of what they call "mother's little helpers?"

My mouth drops open. "You mean, like, downers?"

"Jo. I am talking about prescription Valium, medication from a physician. Not dope from some shady character in a dark alley."

"Sure. Sorry. But, I mean, if you don't mind me asking, how long have you been taking those? And why didn't we know about it?"

"All right, I guess you're old enough to know. I've been taking them off and on for the past, oh let's see. How long ago did I marry your father?"

That cracks me up. It's funny in a messed-up way, though. I mean, I guess it's not really that funny at all.

Mooms says, "And of course, with children, you want to set a good example and all like that. And children should be allowed to be children, as much as possible. They don't need to know too much grown-up business."

I feel like I age a few years in these few minutes, talking to Mooms like she's a fellow human being, rather than just my mother. I want to ask why she lied about Daddy but I can't get up the nerve yet. I mean, I understand her wanting us kids to think our father was in Vietnam rather than in prison, but I don't get why she said he was dead. So, I start with an easier question. I say, "Mooms, can I ask you something?"

"Okay." She shrugs.

"Um, why did you decide to keep the baby?"

"Oh, that. Well, you know, sometimes when you're not sure what to do, the wisest choice can be to just not do anything. It was such a strange situation. I didn't want to take any action that I wouldn't be able to take back. You know, once you call the authorities, they come in and take over and that's it."

I kind of get what she's saying but she did take an action she couldn't take back. She filed a false birth certificate. And she could be arrested and taken from us because of it. I start to say more but then I realize how tired I am. At the same time, she puts her finger to her lips, like *hush*.

She takes the strand of my hair that was hanging down in my face and tucks it behind my ear. She says, "I know you're very sorry that Amy fell through the ice. I also know you're very brave and have a huge heart. I think you'll do just fine. Well, I'm going to turn in now." She hops up from her cushion on the floor and goes up the steps.

I feel like I maybe got something better than answers to all the questions I want to ask her, because now I think maybe she has a higher opinion of me than I thought she did. I go up to my garret to get my blankets and pillow, then come back and settle down to sleep on the floor, so Amy won't wake up in the night and find herself alone.

Chapter 17

My birthday's tomorrow, but all Larry can talk about is the stupid "one month anniversary" gift he's bought for Steve, as if knowing someone for only a month is a big deal. The gift is a pocket watch. Steve admired Larry's pocket watch, so Larry got him one that sort of looks like it, except it's not an antique like Larry's. It's from the *Things Remembered* shop at the mall, and it has "SL" engraved on the back, which stands for "Steve + Laurence." But there's no "+" sign or anything obviously romantic. That way, Larry blabs on, if anyone ever notices the initials, Steve can just say the store made a mistake, since Steve's last name doesn't start with an "L." Or, Larry blathers, Steve could say the "SL" stands for "St. Louis." I start to tell him I've only seen "St. Louis" abbreviated with "STL," not "SL," but I'm not interested enough to bother.

Larry continues bleating about the pocket watch, asking me what I think of it? Do I like it? Do I think Steve will like it? Is it enough to show the depth of Larry's feelings? Or is it too much, this early in their relationship? Steve won't think that Larry is trying to buy his love, will he? Should Larry wrap it or is that a bit much? Should he just give it to Steve or should he wait to see if Steve got him a one-month anniversary gift first, so he won't come across as too eager? And here I thought two guys together wouldn't be so… whatever. New couples are nauseating. I make up an excuse to go home.

But at home, there's more new couple nausea. It must be close to springtime. The mammals are pairing off like crazy. Meg's been dating Edward Moffat for about three weeks now. He is the older half-brother of the three little boys she used to babysit, the older brother of that Annie Moffat bitch. I can't even believe this shit.

Edward happened to come into Baskin-Robbins, where Meg works now. Then he kept coming back, whenever she was working. They had plenty of time to get acquainted, or re-acquainted, since there aren't many ice cream customers when there's still snow on the ground.

I don't like Edward and I don't like Meg when she's with Edward. She gets all simpery and overly agreeable with him when he's here. And even when he's not here and she's just talking about him. And him, well, he's every bit as much of a spoiled shithead as his sister. For example, he pulls into the driveway and honks, and Meg goes running out to his car.

Mooms saw that, and made Edward come into the house, where she gave him a talking-to about how her daughter was to be treated. Mooms told him he needs to come to the door when he arrives to pick Meg up. He said, "Yes, ma'am," all slippery, like Eddie Haskell on *Leave it to Beaver*. But when Mooms isn't home, he still honks in the driveway.

Whenever Edward drops Meg off, I remind her not to be a bad doggie and chase his car down the street as he drives away or anything. Sometimes I sing "How Much is that Doggie in the Window?" because Meg seems so desperate for him to decide that he wants to keep her. I haven't forgotten all the nasty remarks she made about Larry and me, before she realized it would help her social climbing agenda to be nice to Larry. She's got paybacks coming.

Meg's made Edward some sugar cookies, cut out with a heart-shaped cookie cutter. They're sitting on cooling racks and topped with pink and red sugar. She doesn't mention anything about my birthday tomorrow, either. I guess she's forgotten that I spent a whole weekend in Illinois covering for her on her birthday.

I don't understand why people always seem to put their boyfriend or girlfriend first, in general. It's like if you're not someone's boyfriend or girlfriend, you'll always be a distant second to that person, no matter what you do for them. But the boyfriends and girlfriends are usually the ones who come and go. Close friends and family are much more likely to stick around, if you ask me.

Underneath Meg's sweet and responsible act, she's always been a one-way type. She'll be super nice when she wants something, then drop the nice act as soon as she gets whatever she wanted. Her happiness is irritating anyway because it's stupid. Dating a giant turd like Edward Moffat is nothing to be happy about. I feel like giving her a little jab, a punishment for her dumbness. I say, "Sure, just what every guy wants, heart-shaped cookies. Why don't you give him a dozen red roses and a nice bottle of perfume while you're at it? Maybe some sexy lingerie."

She just rolls her eyes, a disappointing response.

I say, "You know, the first clue that Edward is a dick should have been that he goes by "Edward." Not Ed or Eddie or even Ward, but "Edward." What kind of guy doesn't have a nickname?" I realize this is kind of true as it pops out of my mouth.

She rolls her eyes again. She steps out of the kitchen and I snatch a couple of the cookies, then rearrange the rest of them so it's not too obvious. But after I eat them, I say, "Hmm. A little bland there, little woman. Add some more vanilla next time. Maybe some cinnamon."

Meg finally starts squawking. There now, that's more like it. I say, "Go make me a sandwich, little woman." That makes her squawk some more and then I get bored with her dumbness and go upstairs.

I'm rewriting my story collection. I alternate between trying to recreate the stories that were lost and working on new ones. There's hope for my book, after all.

When I get upstairs, I see two people through the glass, in the side yard of Larry's house. I move closer to my garret window in disbelief, and stand there, frozen at the corruption in front of me.

The two people are Mooms and the Larry's Gramps. And they are kissing.

Kissing.

The puzzle pieces click into place, in my mind. The look on Mooms's face when I joked about catching Mr. Vaughn and Aunt March kissing. Mooms's giddiness at Mr. Vaughn's jokes when we watched TV over there. The extreme number of baby gifts from Mr. Vaughn. Maybe even Mooms telling us Daddy was dead. Had something been going on between Mooms and Mr. Vaughn all that time?

So, here's the phase where the cracked house breaks completely apart and tumbles down the hill and into the creek. I roll a joint and wait for the horror show next door to end, so I can open the window and light up.

The tradition of blowing out birthday candles is widespread throughout the world. Among the ancient Greeks, it was thought to pay tribute to the pagan moon goddess, Artemis. The cake was round, to represent the moon. And smoke from blowing out the candles was meant to carry the honoree's wishes to the gods. In other cultures, the smoke from blowing out candles was intended to ward off evil spirits.

Chapter 18

At least my birthday isn't completely forgotten, though neither Meg or Larry seem to notice it. They are both out with their new boyfriends. Miss Hannah and Beth fixed tacos for dinner, one of my favorites. And they've baked a chocolate cake for dessert.

"Make a wish!" Miss Hannah says.

I say, "My wish is to get my driver's license." I blow out the candles.

Amy says, "I don't think you're supposed to say your wish out loud."

Mooms, Beth and Miss Hannah assure me that it is permissible to say your birthday wish out loud. Mooms says, "I don't like it when people don't, because I always want to know what their wish is."

Hell's bells. I already know enough about Mooms's wishes for a lifetime. But I only say a wish out loud that I don't mind other people knowing about. My other wishes are more private.

I get an expensive Cross pen from Mooms. It's gold and has "Jo March" engraved on She says a writer needs a good pen. I would feel honored, except that I don't think much of Mooms anymore.

I say, "Oh my gosh. Thanks so much. That's so special." I feel like I must sound the way Mooms does when she's being phony for social purposes.

Amy also gives me a pen, filled with liquid on one end, with silver glitter floating around in it. Miss Hannah gives me a homemade, pizza-sized chocolate chip cookie. From Beth, I get a keychain in the shape of the letter "J", which she tells me is for when I start driving.

Beth plays "Happy Birthday" on her guitar and everyone sings along. Then Amy urges her to play more songs, and we have a little sing-along.

Mr. Vaughn comes over later with a large, beautifully wrapped present for me. When I open it, I'm so shocked that I feel dizzy. It's a brand-new Brother electric typewriter.

I say, "Oh my gosh. Thanks so much. That's so special." It's my new phony voice. I do completely and extremely love the typewriter. It makes me feel like an elegant, grown-up professional author who is To Be Taken Seriously. But then, getting an expensive gift, or any gift, from my married mother's secret boyfriend, well I feel like my beautiful gift has come with an invisible coating of slime.

I can't bring the two strong opposing feelings I have about the typewriter together in a way that makes sense in my mind. I excuse myself soon after that and put the typewriter away in my armoire, out of sight for now.

I can't wait to get my driver's license, even though I'll only get to borrow Mooms's car now and then, like Meg does. I've already studied for my permit, with Meg's old booklet. I'm also thinking about getting a real part-time job.

Aunt March is crabby and I never know when she's going to snap at me. I don't want to go over there anymore. But quitting might cause trouble. Aunt March probably won't like it. If it makes her mad enough, hell, she could even kick us all out of here. I'll have to think about it some more.

#

Kay comes around every two weeks, when her Avon orders come in and the latest brochure comes out. Around here, somebody always orders something. I try to talk them out of it, hoping Kay will have to go away if there's no more reason for her to come around. But there's never a two-week campaign where at least one or two of them don't have a damn order coming.

Kay brings me a big wrapped box. She says, "This is for your sweet sixteen. Sorry it's late," as if she is a personal friend of the family. The box is full of Avon products. Lots of Avon products. I get some perfume, nail polish, hand cream, powder, lipstick, eyeshadow and bubble bath and a necklace. I say, "Oh my gosh. Thanks so much. That's so special." Kay is definitely trying to weasel her way with us.

Kay plays baby games with Robbie, like "How big is Robbie? Sooo big," and pulls his arms out wide while he laughs.

Then she starts on "Where's Robbie?" while she covers his eyes. Then she uncovers his eyes and says, "Peek-a-boo!"

My sisters paw through my box of Avon, greedy to see what they can get from me after Kay leaves.

I've told Meg my suspicions about Kay Hummel. Meg thinks we ought to just keep a close eye on her for now. Just make sure Kay doesn't try to sneak off with little Robbie. Telling Mooms is not a good idea, according to Meg. She adds that there's nothing Kay can do anyhow, aside from an outright kidnapping, because Mooms has the official birth certificate naming her and Daddy as Robbie's parents. I'm not sure this is good advice but I'm not sure it isn't, either. I go along with it for now.

I don't tell Meg about Mooms and Mr. Vaughn kissing. I don't want any of my sisters to feel the icky, horrified way that discovery made me feel. Not even Meg, who never said a word about my birthday, even when Kay announced that she had brought me a late birthday present.

After Kay leaves, I take the box of Avon junk into Amy and Beth's room and tell them to split it all up between them. I say, "Don't give any to Meg," which makes Amy laugh and makes Beth look worried.

#

By the beginning of April, I have my driver's license, thanks to Larry. He took me to get my permit, then back for the license, after a few torturous driving lessons that nearly ended our friendship. For some reason, Larry turns into the traffic cop from hell when I'm driving. I mean, I appreciate his help, but damn.

Larry also knows about Mooms's and the Gramps's affair, though they still think they're being sly. He was the one who brought it up, during one of the driving lessons. Just what I need to think about when I'm trying to master globdamn parallel parking. I told him it was disgusting and I didn't even want to think about it. He really is the best friend I ever had, though. After I passed my driving test, he took me to Pizza Hut to celebrate. Their salad bar is the new in-thing and Larry was just dying to try it. Personally, I don't know why anyone would bother with salad when you can have one of those amazing super thick pan pizzas, though.

One night, late, Meg comes up to my garret and shakes me awake. "Jo, Jo," she says. "Get up. It's Beth."

I jump out of bed, not comprehending. Meg snaps the light on. She says, "Hurry," and rushes back downstairs.

When I get to the little girls' bedroom, Beth is sitting up in bed, sweaty and glassy-eyed. She whispers about people watching her through the electric socket and lights. She repeats every sentence she says, in a soft echo of itself. She says, "They're watching me, *they're watching me.*"

I say, "Where's Mooms?"

Amy says, "Next door," at the same time Meg says, "Probably with Larry's Gramps."

I guess everybody knows, then.

I say, "Okay, Amy. Let's have you go find whatever you can to cover up the ceiling light and the socket. Paper, tape and scissors. And take the lamp out of here while you're at it, okay?"

Amy gets busy. I gather Beth up in my arms. I say, "It's okay, Bethie. We're fixing everything. Don't worry."

I start to ask Meg to go get Mooms, but she's better at calming Beth than I am, and I'm better at… the jobs nobody else wants to touch with a ten-foot pole, I guess.

I say, "Meg, can you stay here with Beth, while I go get Mooms?"

She nods.

Miss Hannah comes in, holding little Robbie, who was woken up by the uproar. Not finding anything urgent to do, Miss Hannah sits on the edge of the bed with him. Just having us all here might have eased Beth's fears some. Her breathing isn't so fast now.

I say, "Oh, wait. I have an idea." I go to Moom's bedroom and root around in her stuff, looking for her Valium. That would surely help Beth right now. I can't find it anywhere though, so I take a deep breath and head next door.

After I ring the doorbell a few times, Larry finally answers. He looks confused. Which is no surprise, since it's three in the morning.

I say, "Can you tell Mooms to come home, right away? Beth is having some kind of… medical emergency, and we don't know what to do."

Larry groans.

"Yeah, I know," I say. "Thanks." I'm glad I'm not the one who has to knock on that bedroom door and let those two in on the fact that we *all* know about their corruption. I hurry home.

When I get back to Beth and Amy's room, there's only the light from the hallway, since Amy's removed or covered up both bedroom lights.

"Mooms is coming," I say. Meg is kind of rocking Beth. Beth's eyes are closed. She cries, quietly.

Mooms comes rushing in. "What? What's wrong?" she says.

After Mooms looks Beth over and checks her forehead for fever, I motion for her to follow me out to the hallway, out of Beth's hearing. I explain the situation to her, then go fetch a glass of water while she gets her pills.

We all gather around while Mooms explains to Beth that the pill is a Valium from the doctor and that it will help her sleep. Amy and Meg both look at me, like *Mooms has Valium?*

I just shrug.

Chapter 19

We cater to Beth for a few days, and we take care to keep things calm and pleasant. Meg and I help Miss Hannah with the cooking and cleaning. We treat Beth like we treated Mooms, right after Daddy got taken away.

Beth recovers from the incident, which comes to be known as "Beth's nightmare." She returns to her usual self. But when you stop and think about it, Beth's usual self isn't really what you'd call "doing well," in the first place. If you ask me, it's more like we've all just gotten used to her. Taking Beth to the doctor is brought up a couple of times but the idea fades away as we get back to our usual daily routines.

We've just sat down to supper, grilled government cheese sandwiches and Campbell's tomato soup, when Mooms makes an announcement. She says, "Girls. There's something you should know." We all kind of freeze in place because there's just no telling what she'll say.

She continues, "It's wrong to try to keep people for yourself. We should all be free to associate with whoever we please. We don't own other people and they don't own us. This came to me in a dream."

"Okay," I say, and dip my wonderful sandwich into hot tomato soup. The crunchy toasted bread, the gooey cheese, and the hot soup, it's all just heavenly together. One thing that's amazed me since our fall from grace is how delicious cheap, simple food can be. I mean, not always, but a lot of the time. It's also cozier, somehow, to snuggle in at night in a smaller, chillier house, one where you hear the rain on the roof quite clearly. It's like the closer you are to not having, the more you're aware of what you do have. If that even makes sense.

Speaking of being grateful for the smaller things when you're close to not even having that, I wonder if it would be too obnoxious to ask for a couple more grilled cheese sandwiches and another bowl of soup. It probably would, since it would make more work for Miss Hannah or Beth. I'm thinking about what I could offer in exchange, when Mooms continues. I don't feel like listening to any more of Mooms's nutty announcement now. I guess I just don't really like her anymore, now that I know the extent of her corruption.

She says, "Girls. Mr. Vaughn and I are a couple. And that's all right!" She nods emphatically, like she's backing herself up, seconding her own motion, voting for herself. She says this like she doesn't know that we already know it, and like we don't know that Daddy did not die on any globdamn battlefield in Vietnam, either.

Meg has the nerve to raise her eyebrows at me, giving me the signal she said she'd use on me at the New Year's Eve party, to let me know I'm not behaving appropriately. I'm the one who's not behaving appropriately here, really? I guess Meg doesn't like the look of disgust that must be on my face right now. I raise my eyebrows back at her, then sneakily do my hand in a motion like jacking off a wiener. I wonder if Meg thinks I'm doing that appropriately. She should know.

Little Miss Smarty Pants Amy pipes up. She says, "Does that mean I can go live with Aunt March then, if nobody owns anyone and we should all be free to associate with whoever we want?"

Mooms puts her soup spoon down. She clears her throat. After a long moment, she says, "Yes, Amy, it does. You may go stay with Aunt March, if that is your wish. Keep us in mind again, if it doesn't work out."

I'm horrified. You don't just let a sixth grader go live with somebody else any old time they feel like it. I catch Amy's eye, and silently shake my head, *no*.

Amy says, "Oh goody! Goody goody gumdrops! Thank you, Mooms. Oh, thank you! When can I go, Mooms?" Amy gives me a smug look, like she's emphasizing that it's between her and Mooms only.

Mooms, whose face has that glazed, faraway look it gets when she's being especially insane, says, "You may go whenever you wish, dear."

I'm wondering now if Amy really dislikes us that much. I mean, everyone here gets on my nerves sometimes, to varying degrees. But there's not one of them I'd want to get completely away from. Well, except for Amy herself, and even that was only for a little while.

#

On Saturday, Aunt March's driver shows up to take Amy and her belongings to go live with Aunt March. I chicken out on telling Aunt March I want to quit working for her. Instead, I tell Amy to tell Aunt March that I don't think I'll be needed anymore, since she'll have Amy there now. I mean, may as well, as long as Amy insists on going there anyway.

After Amy leaves, Beth curls up on Amy's bed. Meg and I lounge on Beth's bed, with our heads at opposite ends. We just hang out there together, feeling pretty awful.

I try to cheer them up. "Oh, don't worry. Youse don't know Aunt March like I do. She's even more of a bitch than you guys can imagine. Nobody can live with her. Even her own husband committed pie suicide. And I'm pretty sure it was just to get away from Aunt March." That makes Meg cackle. I think I should probably feel bad for saying that. I probably will, later. But right now, we kind of hate Aunt March. We sink into our sad silence again.

I try again. I say, "You know, I think I've got this figured out. Amy really, really hates her nose and Aunt March promised her a nose job. I'll bet you anything, that's what this is all about. I'll bet you anything Amy's back in a couple of weeks, with a big bandage on her silly little nose." I say it like I know what I'm talking about.

Mooms wasn't even here. She went over to Mr. Vaughn's house.

#

Mr. Vaughn and Larry bring over Imo's pizza for supper, which, if you ask me, is the best pizza in the entire globdamn universe. But this time, it comes with the same invisible slime coating the typewriter did. I choke it down, feeling like I'm accepting bribes to be disloyal to Daddy.

Is the pizza surprise a celebration of Mooms getting rid of Amy? Does she hope to get rid of the rest of us now too, just as she apparently wants to get rid of Daddy?

Larry gives me a kiss on the lips in front of everyone, to keep up our facade that we're a couple. Just when I didn't think it was possible for things to get any grosser. In Science class, we had to scrape a plastic spoon-like thing on the inside of our mouths and look at it under a microscope. It was so, so icky. People need to keep their globdamn mouth germs to themselves.

I think of Daddy, locked up in prison. I know what he did. It was a big news story, in both of the big papers around here. I read all about it in the *St. Louis Globe-Democrat* and then I read it again the *St. Louis Post-Dispatch*, hoping the *Globe-Democrat* had somehow got it wrong. But they didn't.

And now, I feel like Mooms is just as corrupt as Daddy. In a way, she's worse. We all counted on Mooms to hold the family together until Daddy got out, and then we'd get back to our old life the best we could, all together again. The time here in Aunt March's rent house was just supposed to be one deep, dark valley, among many peaks.

But what Mooms is doing now, it would tear our family apart even if Daddy was never locked up in the first place.

You think of the enemies of your family as being outside, people you lock your doors to keep out. It really does your head in when the enemy of your family is a member of your family, especially the member who is the center of it all. Come to think of it, Amy was right to leave. I don't know how much more of this corrupt environment I can stand.

Chapter 20

I go to the prison in May. I was going to take the bus but then Larry offered to drive me. It's a two-hour drive, so here we are, skipping school, on the road to the prison, the Rolling Stones blasting, smoking a joint. Oh yeah, we're pretty globdamn cool.

On the way, Larry says they might not let me in. He's already said that a couple of times in the past week. He says, "My Pops was locked up once and I remember how mad my mom was when they wouldn't let her see him."

"Ooh. I didn't know that. What was he in for? I mean, if you don't mind me asking?"

"Just weed, I think. And it was just jail, not prison. I'm just saying, don't be too upset if they turn you away. I think they're gonna turn you away."

"Okay. If I can't see him today, at least I'll be able to find out what their globdamn rules even are."

When we get there, the woman at the desk looks like she's about to fall asleep in her chair. She asks for my ID and I tell her I just turned sixteen and haven't had a chance to get my driver's license yet. I tell her I just want to see my father. She sighs, then says, "A short visit, that's all." She waves Larry and I into an empty visitor room with tables and vending machines. It smells like cigarette smoke and piss.

Larry says, "Uh, I don't think she was supposed to do that."

"Do what?"

"Just let us in here like this."

"Oh. Well, I'm not gonna argue with her about it. Hey, want to play "Trouble?" There are a few games stacked up on one of the tables. Larry grabs the game and we pass some time with it. Then we ask the half-asleep lady for change for the vending machines. After reading their rules and such, I leave some money with her, for Daddy to have later on.

When the guard brings Daddy in, Larry excuses himself. He goes out to the car, so I can have some time alone with Daddy.

Daddy looks smaller, and older. His hair is thinner and more gray than I remember. He gives Larry a long, hard look as Larry walks away, which I'm glad Larry doesn't see. Then he looks at me the same way.

I say, "Oh, I know that guy from school. I paid him to bring me here. I whisper, "He's gay," like that's a funny secret I'm letting Daddy in on.

It seems to satisfy Daddy that the Black boy won't try to impregnate his daughter, at least enough to spare me the old "I'm not prejudice but" talk. He gives me a hug, squashing me so hard I can hardly breathe. He says, "What happened to your hair?"

I could ask him the same. But I say, "My hair? Oh, right, I forgot about that. I sold it, so I could buy a bus ticket here. But then I got a ride for less, so I didn't need the bus ticket. I put the extra money on your books."

Daddy winces a little and I think maybe I shouldn't have told him that I sold my hair for him.

But then he says, "My little Jo. You're a peach. Looking out for your old man."

We get chips and sodas from the vending machines. We talk about old times, my life at home and his life here, and the family. I try to keep it light and I get the feeling he's doing the same. I tell him some happy little news bits about the girls and some funny ones about Party and Miss Hannah.

I say, "Do you have any idea when you can come home?"

He says, "I might have something in the works. Aunt March got me a lawyer who's been known to do great things."

And then, our time is up. We only have time for one more quick hug, as the guard waits to take Daddy back.

Larry and I don't talk much on the way home. The strangeness of seeing Daddy after all these months, and in prison stripes no less, keeps playing through my mind. I'm glad I came, just to let Daddy know we still care about him, I guess. And to clarify the situation to myself.

What I clarified was, first of all, that Daddy is not dead. I really didn't think he was, but that's only because what Mooms said about *how* he died was obviously a lie. I mean, there was still a chance that the part about him actually dying was true.

I also learned, from the things he said, that he still considers himself solidly married to Mooms.

Which makes her look totally terrible, until you consider that maybe she just doesn't want to tell him it's over while he's still locked up. Maybe she's sparing him that bad news when he's already probably totally miserable, out of kindness. Or is she just plain old cheating, with no real reason to make it seem any better than what it is?

I'm so glad when Larry passes me a lit joint. That's enough thinking in circles for now, better to just take a couple of tokes and relax.

Inhaling the joint reminds me that I bought Daddy a pack of Marlboros from the vending machine and he chain-smoked during our visit. He never used to smoke.

#

Larry and I get a Saturday detention for skipping school. Mooms and the Gramps don't seem to care about it too much. They both just tell us not to do it again. I wonder what Mooms would say if she knew where I went.

The girls at school comment on my extreme haircut. I didn't think about what to say, or what not to say, beforehand. Then, not wanting to get into a discussion about what I needed the money so bad for, I blurt out that I donated my hair for cancer patients who need wigs. Then I feel bad when that gets around and I get praise all week long for the amazing, selfless deed that I didn't do.

Chapter 21

Kay comes over after supper. She lets everyone play with the Avon stuff unattended while she plays with Robbie again. I decide to tell Mooms about my worries because I don't know what Kay is up to. If she just wants to see little Robbie a couple of times a month, that's one thing but who knows what more she might have in mind? Mooms should be warned.

I keep an eye on Kay while she's here, making sure she doesn't try to sneak out with my baby brother. After she leaves, I catch Mooms alone. I say, "I need to talk to you about Kay."

She says, "You mean Robbie's biological mother?"

I'm floored.

Mooms says, "You can close your mouth now, before you swallow a fly." Then she laughs.

It makes me mad. This has weighed on my mind a lot, and I don't think it's funny. But I just say, "You already know."

"Jo. Come on, now. It's not hard to figure out. I haven't spoken to her about it yet but, you know, trying to have ownership over other human beings is not right, it's abnormal. Remember?"

"Yes, I remember. It came to you in a dream." I try not to roll my eyes.

"That's it!" Mooms claps her hands together. She says, "The next time Kay comes, I'm just going to talk to her and then I'm going to let her start sharing little Robbie, if she wants to. A little bit at a time, so we can make sure she's more responsible now. Then little Robbie will get to know his other mother too, and we'll get more of a break now and then." She smiles hugely, thrilled with her idea. I am not sure about this. I wonder if she just wants to dump little Robbie off, now that she has her affair to keep her entertained instead.

Mooms says, "Well, I'm off to go see my boyfriend next door. Isn't that cute, you and I dating a grandson and grandfather?"

She whooshes out the door before I can answer. But no, it's not cute. It's not cute at all.

#

I think about Mooms's new philosophy of not "owning" other people. Of course, she probably only came up with it to try to justify cheating with Larry's Gramps to herself, after she got caught anyway. It does make me think about Larry and Steve, though.

I wonder what it would be like if I could just drop my grudge against Steve. I picture the three of us hanging out together. But even the thought of it makes me feel kind of nauseated. Nah, I'm not doing it. I guess I do want to own my people, or something like that.

Five minutes later, Larry's at the door. Sometimes I think he can read my mind. He says he has a Great Idea for me, which makes me nervous. He looks too eager. We go for a walk around the pond, the same one I almost let Amy drown in.

We walk along, sharing a joint. I say, "Okay, what is it?"

His eyes light up like he has a giant present for me. He says, "Steve knows a cute lesbian. She said she's up for going on a double date, you two and us two."

"Eww!" I shove him, then hold my breath while he scrambles to regain his balance, inches away from tumbling into the pond. Which would be hilarious, except that he'd probably never speak to me again.

"What do you mean, "Eww? You haven't even seen her yet. You don't know anything about her." He stands up tall, trying to regain his dignity after I made him helicopter all over the place on the edge of the water. It cracks me up.

I say, "I don't want to go out with a girl."

He does that one eyebrow raised thing at me, which makes me laugh harder. He says, "You like guys. Are you kidding?"

"I didn't say that. I don't like anybody. I mean, not in that way."

He says, "Stop being stubborn."

"I'm not being stubborn. Let me spell it out for you, bonehead. I am not attracted to guys. And I am not attracted to girls. I am not attracted to anybody. Get it?"

He snaps, "Okay. If you say so." He sulks for the rest of our walk around the pond. I guess he still thinks I'm being stubborn.

It pisses me off, being pushed to announce my most private business in the first place, then having it blown off like it wasn't the biggest revelation I've ever made to anybody.

When we're back at his driveway, he mutters, "I was just trying to help you out."

I just keep walking, to my house and up to my garret. An attic room, alone at the top of an old house is a good place for someone like me. They always keep the crazy lady in the attic.

Now I've finished recreating the stories Amy ruined. They're all typed up, on my electric typewriter. The collection is finished. Finally! Now I just have to work up the nerve to send it out.

But right now, I start a story about a hidden group of aliens that end up on Earth, including one alien who's so weird that even the other aliens don't want him around.

Chapter 22

There's nothing better than summer vacation. School's been out for a week now and I still feel like twirling round and round with joy whenever I think about it. I still set my alarm clock every night too, just so I can wake up when it's time to get up and get ready for school and remember that I don't have to.

I'm not a hundred percent carefree, though. Meg got me on with her at Baskin-Robbins. But it's only twenty hours per week.

There's a fancy graduation dinner for Meg, at Larry and Mr. Vaughn's. The table is set with vases of flowers, china and crystal, the whole works. Meg wears a flowery red summer dress and she just glows. Red is definitely her color. Meg is now officially an adult, out of high school. It makes me feel a little like crying, for some reason.

Unfortunately, Edward Moffat is here too, seated next to Meg. Now that is a good reason to cry. They look like little red riding hood and the big bad wolf.

Meg has a tiny diamond on her finger now that she dips into a jar of jewelry cleaner twice daily and puts away in its little blue velvet box each night. She stares at it all the time too. The diamond is so small you can barely even see it with the naked eye but she acts like it is the Hope diamond.

So, I guess Meg forgot about the time Edward made out with that other girl behind her back. She forgets about the time they got in an argument and he smacked her in the mouth, too. Or rather, she thinks it doesn't count since they were both drinking and she shouldn't have yelled at him first.

Every week or so, there's some new nastiness having to do with Edward Moffat. Edward sets off all kinds of warning bells but Meg insists on skipping down the road to hell.

Sally Gardiner is here, too. She is actually pretty nice, aside from the feeling I get that she thinks she is the queen or something. Tonight, she even had the nerve to wear a sparkly band on her head that kind of looks like a crown. Meg called it Sally's "tiara." The Queen of Black Jack, ha! Sally has her hair permed into a white girl afro now. I wonder what Larry will think about it. He says things about race that I never even imagined.

Also, Sally hangs out with Annie Moffat, that bathroom bitch. Unbelievably, Meg also likes Annie Moffat now, just because she is Edward's sister. And, of course, Steve had to come to the dinner, too, since it's at Larry's. I can't wait to go home.

Mooms is all giggly, as usual when she's had a couple of drinks, though she doesn't sit next to Mr. Vaughn tonight. I'm pretty sure it's because Aunt

March is here with Amy, and Aunt March probably wants Mr. Vaughn for herself.

Aunt March and Mr. Vaughn went to school together, back in the olden days. It just highlights how ancient he really is. Way too old for Mooms, if you ask me.

And, of course, Aunt March is Daddy's aunt, and Daddy is married to Mooms. So, there's that to consider, too.

Mr. Vaughn always tells me to call him Vince but I call him Mr. Vaughn. I could think of many other things to call him, though.

Amy and Aunt March sit side by side and mostly only talk to each other. Amy's nose looks like a plum, still purple and swollen from her nose job. It looks like she has two faded black eyes, too. She's got makeup on, but it's not completely covering it. I didn't think plastic surgeons would operate on thirteen-year-olds for vanity purposes, but what do I know. We've all been warned by Mooms not to mention Amy's plum, I mean nose. Amy has always been overly sensitive about her nose, so I already figured this.

The people at this table who I don't like are: Steve, Edward Moffat, Mr. Vaughn, Aunt March and also Mooms, due to her extreme corruption. The ones I do like: Meg (sometimes), Amy (sometimes), Beth, Robbie, Miss Hannah and Larry. Neutrals: Sally Gardiner.

Miss Hannah interrupts my categorizing activity when she hands Robbie across me, over to Beth.

She says, "Hold your brother a minute, dear. I need to use the powder room."

I'm wondering why I was passed over for the task of holding Robbie. Aunt March stops whatever she's saying to Amy. Her face goes all owlish, staring down its prey, which is Mooms. She says, "That baby is Beth's brother?"

Amy looks down at her plate, her face turning red, which makes the surgery discoloration even more purple. I'm glad Amy still has the loyalty to not have told Aunt March about the baby. From the looks of her though, Amy expects to have hell to pay for the omission.

Mooms says, "Yes, he's ours, mine and Robert's." Then she turns back to her beef

Wellington. "My, this is delicious. I really need this recipe." Mooms doesn't seem very cowed by Aunt March now. In fact, Mooms hasn't paid much attention to Aunt March at all. Aunt March continues her bird-of-prey stare at Mooms, who just continues eating and talking to others near her at the table.

The dinner progresses to coffee and not one but two flaming desserts, cherries Jubilee and bananas Foster. Mooms seems like the old self she was before everything fell apart, stylish and bubbly, not the burdened old woman she became afterwards. But the whole thing between Mooms and Mr. Vaughn still gives me the icks.

Chapter 23

Meg and I are working this shift together. "Yeah, let me try the tutti frutti," the scraggly teenager, Jeremy, says. I've seen the kid around enough to know that he's homeless. I get one of the little disposable tester spoons and hand him an overloaded spoonful of the multi-colored ice cream.

"Hmm. Pretty good. Hey, can I try that black walnut, too?" he says. I give him another overloaded spoonful of ice cream. I wonder if something is wrong with me because I'm enjoying this. For some reason, it reminds me of when my sisters and I were little and used to feed bread to the ducks, in west county. They were so cute, so imperious and greedy. If you weren't fast enough, the biggest one would waddle up and snatch the bread right out of your hand.

During his seventh or eighth overloaded spoonful, Meg comes out from the back and the kid slinks off. Meg says, "Jo, you know the rule. Two sample spoons per customer, per visit."

Meg is my boss whenever the two of us work together, but she's okay for the most part. She's floating on a cloud about stupid Edward Moffat and doesn't seem interested enough in anything else to bother being too bossy anymore.

I like working at Baskin-Robbins a lot better than working for Aunt March. Here, even the most obnoxious customer only sticks around for a short time. And if you get stuck working with somebody you don't like, you're both too busy with the customers to have much to do with each other anyway.

We get a free ice cream cone every shift we work, but Beth gets so excited over ice cream that we both bring every other free ice cream cone home for her. The ice cream goes in a lidded container, with the sugar cone separate, for easy transport.

After Meg and I close up the shop, we're walking home together and I see Jeremy at the side of the building, sitting with his back against the wall, a dirty backpack next to him. I say, "Good night, Jeremy. See you later." Meg shakes her head at me, like *don't encourage him*. It makes me mad. I hand Jeremy the ice cream I had gotten for Beth. He looks so skinny and young as we walk away, just sitting there alone in the night. Jeremy is gay. His shithead parents kicked him out of the house over it. I make a mental note to talk the situation over with Larry.

#

Larry and I buy secondhand camping equipment out of the classified ads. We get Jeremy set up in the woods near the pond, with a tent and sleeping bag and some other stuff. Then we help him get a part-time job, cleaning a local family-owned tavern late each night.

Soon afterward, another homeless kid joins Jeremy in the tent. It's mostly Larry chipping in the money of course, since I don't have much to spare. But we both check in on "the boys" and do what we can for them. Steve helps out too, though I stay away when he does.

Chapter 24

In July, Meg and I are walking home after closing up Baskin-Robbins, and she tells me that she and Edward are getting ready to elope.

I say, "Um, that seems kind of drastic, doesn't it? Why not just have a wedding? I mean, if you absolutely insist on marrying him."

"Edward's parents told him they won't help pay for it or even come to it. They don't like me."

The jerk's parents should be eternally grateful any woman would accept their crappy creep of a son. I say, "What the hell? You're polite, pretty, undemanding, and you put up with the asshole. Why in the world wouldn't they like you?"

Meg shrugs. "Who knows. First, Edward told me they said we were too young and that he needed to finish his degree first, even though Edward says college was a joke and he's never going back. Then he and I got in a fight over something else and he said his parents think our family is trash. Later, he said he only told me that because he was mad but I think that's the truth of it."

"Why? Just because our family's not wealthy anymore, so they think they're too good for us, right?"

"Maybe. Who really knows. But Edward said it's because of that whole thing with Daddy, you know, that he's in prison for. That, and because of when Mrs. Moffat's jewelry went missing. Edward said after his parents made the police report, Annie started getting a bunch of perverted phone calls. Because of the timing and everything, you know, they think I was behind it."

Oh, right. The pearls. I'd forgotten about that. "Oh, screw them. Listen, you've got to know by now that there's something wrong with those people. And what about us? Why does it all revolve around them? You would cut your own family out of your wedding just because his parents are jerks? Oh, wait. I get it. You're pregnant!"

Meg laughs but it's not a jolly laugh. She says, "No, I'm not pregnant. I just don't want to give Edward's parents the chance to snub me publicly, by having a wedding that the groom's parents refuse to attend. It would be so humiliating. This way, it just seems like Edward and I got carried away with the romance of it all and couldn't wait. It just kind of smooths it all over, as much as possible. See? I'm sure that over time, they'll see that I'm a good wife."

"Mooms is going to have a fit."

Meg just shrugs again. It seems like she's completely switched over now, from being

Mooms's shadow to being Edward Moffat's shadow.

People like Meg, who drag you into their business but then refuse to help themselves, they can drive you nuts. I mean, like what am I supposed to say? Oh, how lovely? No, it's really, really not lovely. Meg wants a puppet-friend who only says what she wants to hear. I'm not doing it. I say, "Edward Moffat is a conceited, spoiled jack-off. He's mean, too. No girl with half a brain would want him."

She says, "Thanks. I should have figured you wouldn't just be a friend for once."

Meg's stubborn stupidity is exhausting. I just want to get away from her now. I say, "I feel like jogging. I'll see you back at the house."

The jog is nice. It's not too hot out and the night air is perfumed with wild honeysuckle. I feel calm again by the time I get home.

#

Meg doesn't just plan to elope, she plans to move away for good. Meg and Edward Moffat take off for the Four Corners region of the country. It doesn't make much sense to me, as far as life plans go. I looked it up when I went to the library, and there doesn't seem to be much there. Just some Native reservations, where they probably don't even like white people. And miles and miles of empty wilderness in all directions, with nothing but mountain lions and bears. Oh, well there *is* that round thingie where you can sit your ass down on Arizona, Colorado, Utah and New Mexico, all at the same time. Maybe sitting their asses down on very empty regions of four states at once *is* their life plan though, knowing them.

When I asked Meg what the hell they were going there for, she just said "Edward thinks it would be cool." Then she did that half-sided twist of her mouth that she's started doing. She might be trying to put on airs and thinks that goofy half-grin looks mysterious or interesting or something. Or maybe shithead Edward hit her in the mouth again and permanently damaged her smile this time.

Me and Mooms both try to talk Meg out of running off with Edward but of course she won't listen and just starts blabbing about how we're against her and not being her friend.

The next thing I know, we're all standing in the driveway: Mooms, Miss Hannah, Beth, little Robbie and me, sadly waving good-bye as Meg rides away with that bastard Edward Moffat.

Chapter 25

In September, a couple of weeks after school starts, I come down from my garret to ask when supper will be ready. Mooms has just come home from work and is tending to Miss Hannah, who's holding onto the kitchen counter, bracing herself. The color's drained from her face and she's all sweaty and shaky. There's mac and cheese on the stove, getting a burning smell. I turn the burner off and move the pot off it.

Mooms says to Miss Hannah, "It's okay, hon. I'm just going to drive you to the Emergency Room and let the doctor have a quick look at you." Mooms starts walking her out to the car, Miss Hannah's arm around Moom's shoulder. Beth rushes out the door after them, which surprises the hell out of me. Beth hardly ever goes anywhere besides to school, and she even manages to get out of that pretty often.

Mooms and Beth come back about an hour later, without Miss Hannah. Mooms said they made it to the ER and Miss Hannah was rushed away. Mooms and Beth were told to stay in the waiting room for the time being. About a half hour later, the doctor came out and told Mooms and Beth that Miss Hannah had a heart attack as soon as they got her back there. Even with immediate medical attention, they were unable to save her. Miss Hannah is dead.

#

Miss Hannah's passing leaves some coldness where there used to be comfort. I didn't realize how much it meant to see her cheerful face whenever I'd come home, asking how my day went and seeming genuinely interested in the answer. It's like we were so used to her being around that we didn't fully notice how like a doting grandma she really was to us. She didn't criticize or correct us, she just offered help and kindness. Now, it's like there's a Miss Hannah-shaped empty spot at our house, especially in the kitchen and living room.

The emptiness she left almost seems like a ghost. That sounds like a great story idea, a ghost being the striking absence of someone who used to be there. I grab a pen and jot the idea down on a piece of paper towel and stick it in my pocket for later. But then it feels wrong to use Miss Hannah as a story character. It seems like it would be cheapening her memory or something, so I toss my paper towel note away.

I help Mooms write an obituary and we have it published in the paper. We don't hear from anybody, though. Mooms said she didn't expect to but it just seemed respectful to have a public announcement of

Miss Hannah's passing. Mooms says Miss Hannah's parents and brother died years ago. She was married briefly when she was young but had been divorced for many years, and never had any children. So, she really was alone in the world, except for us. I feel bad that I never even thought to ask Miss Hannah about her life but Mooms said not to worry. She said kids aren't expected to think of things like that but that she, Mooms, had talked plenty to Miss Hannah about all that.

Beth was closest to Miss Hannah, since they did household chores together every day. Even before, in west county, Beth stuck close to Miss Hannah whenever Mooms wasn't around. Beth is very quiet now, even more quiet than usual. Even Party seems to grieve. He starts sleeping on Miss Hannah's bed, which he never did before. He keeps it up until Mooms and Beth strip the bed and empty out the room.

Mooms tried to call Amy, to tell her about Miss Hannah's passing. I was the one who tried to call Amy when Meg left. Beth has also tried to call Amy, and so did Miss Hannah, before she died. But Aunt March doesn't answer the phone anymore and neither does her maid. Aunt March has hired some kind of answering service now, where the only person you can talk to is whoever works for the service. Nobody ever calls us back. We haven't seen or heard from Amy or Aunt March all summer, not since Meg's graduation dinner.

This is a problem with not trying to own people, as Mooms calls it. It doesn't mean somebody else won't try to own that person. And then you're just left out in the cold. It's an especially ridiculous theory to go by when it's your own child, for globsakes. There's no telling what the old witch has done with Amy.

I tell Mooms, "We should take a ride over there. I mean, isn't this kind of like kidnapping?"

But Mooms doesn't seem too interested. She is busy kneading dough from a box of Chef-Boy-Ar-Dee complete pizza mix. She says, "Hold on a sec. I have to pay attention here." Mooms isn't used to cooking. She says she doesn't want it to all fall on Beth, now that Miss Hannah is no longer with us. But Beth always stands right there anyway.

I've brought up going to Aunt March's to check on Amy a few other times too, since nobody even answers our calls, but Mooms doesn't seem like she's in any hurry about it.

#

Things keep changing around here, mostly in the opposite direction of getting our family back together. We had six people here: us four girls, Mooms and Miss Hannah. Now there are only three and a half: me, Mooms and Beth. Robbie's the half, since he's here about half the time now.

Mooms' offers to let Kay watch Robbie started out small, just asking her to keep an eye on him while Mooms went to pick up a gallon of milk or something, with Beth and I here anyway. Then she asked Kay to take him to his baby doctor appointment by herself, and it went on from there.

Kay seems to be walking on clouds, she's so thrilled to work out the weekly schedule with Mooms now, sharing time with Robbie. Mooms's no-people-ownership policy, loony as it sounds, does have its benefits sometimes, especially now that there's often nobody here to take care of Robbie, now that Miss Hannah's gone. Mooms has work and Beth and I have school. I don't know what we'd do now, if Kay didn't help out. Besides selling Avon, Kay tends bar at Meyer's Tavern, which is mostly nights and weekends, so it works out great.

Kay comes by to drop off Robbie and to drop off Mooms's and Beth's Avon orders. Mooms hands the baby to me. She pours generic cola into glasses of ice and takes them to the dining room, ready for their usual twice a month Avon ritual.

I play with blocks with Robbie on the living room rug. Or rather, I stack the blocks up and Robbie gleefully knocks them down, again and again. He's grown a pair of top choppers to go with his two bottom choppers. So cute!

I halfway listen to the talk at the table, trying to figure out what the hell a "lotion shampoo" is, or a "powder spray." Two forms of glop, mixed together, seems to be the latest girly fad.

Mooms says, "Oh Beth, I almost forgot. You know that work friend of mine I told you about, the woman who runs the hospital laundry room?"

Beth says, "The lady who reminds you of Miss Hannah?"

"Yes. Well, she said they have an opening for a part-time laundry worker and that you're a shoo-in, if you bring her an application. I brought you one. It's folded up, in my purse over there. Interested?"

Beth says yes, which I can hardly believe. But then, Mooms has been working on this for a while, talking to Beth about how nice the laundry room supervisor is, and about how there's hardly anybody in the hospital laundry room most of the time. I bet Mooms knew an opening would be coming up there. Also, I can't remember the last time I saw Beth with a doll. That's some damn fine progress, if you ask me.

Chapter 26

The week before Halloween, Larry and I are bored and high one afternoon, and we decide to do some decorating. We go buy some scary junk at K-Mart and do up both of our houses, mostly outside but a little bit on the interiors, too. Then we go over to the woods and stick a couple of plastic skeletons on Jeremy's tent, thinking ourselves hilarious, since we're high as kites and put the skeletons in sexual positions. We also have fake cobwebs, big plastic spiders and bats. It seems cheesy once my buzz wears off, but it was fun at the time.

If only I'd known. A couple nights later, I get home from Baskin-Robbins about seven, because they're on winter hours now. Our house is dark, but that's not unusual these days, when we all leave early in the morning and might not get home until after dark, now that the days are getting shorter again.

I go inside, flip the lights on and put Beth's ice cream treat in the freezer. Then I rummage around, trying to find something to fix for supper. Party meows. He wants his dinner, too.

Party runs to a big black thing that's hanging out from under the dining room table. This is weird as hell. My heart pounding, I grab the paring knife in one hand and grab the wasp spray, from under the sink, with the other hand. I stand there with my weapons, trying to decide between charging at whatever's under the table or running out the door.

I opt for running out the door but when I'm halfway outside, I hear "Spiders. Bats and ghosts. *Bats and ghosts." Beth.* I run back inside. Beth has apparently dragged Mooms's black tent of death in from the garage and crawled into it. It's under the table, collapsed, not tied up to anything now.

I fumble with the pile of tent, trying to find my way in. "Beth? Beth! What are you doing?"

I finally get Beth separated from the collapsed tent enough to see that she's in some kind of stupor, conscious and awake, but barely. Then I see it, the prescription pill bottle. Mooms's Valium. The lid is gone and there are only a couple of pills left in the container.

I run to the phone, grateful that Mr. Vaughn got it for us, but furious that Mooms is most likely over there with him, again, when Beth needs her. I call for an ambulance, then rush back to Beth's side to wait for its arrival. I keep kinda shaking her, telling her to get up. Maybe Mooms should consider that she is the reason her kid has so many problems. One thing I know for sure, if Mooms was at home instead of screwing around with the creepy old man next door when she's married, Beth wouldn't be in a tent under the table with a mostly empty bottle of pills beside her.

#

After the Emergency Room, Beth is admitted into the psychiatric ward. Her psychiatrist says he expects her to be there for a while, though he won't say what he means by "a while." He just says they need time to run tests and observe her and she needs time to rest, away from the worries of the larger world.

Mooms starts to argue but the doctor says that Beth is obviously not able to navigate that larger world very well right now. So, she needs to stay here for the time being, where she's protected and monitored twenty-four hours a day. I catch Mooms's eye and nod She seems to accept it then. It feels like some kind of milestone moment, when your mother follows your lead on something serious.

Also, I was blaming Mooms but underneath that, I really just wish Larry and I had never bought those stupid Halloween decorations. It seems obvious that's what set Beth off. The next day, I take all the decorations down at our house, inside and out, and throw them in the trash, though Halloween's still three days away. The day after that, I notice they're gone from Larry's yard, too.

Mooms stays home for a few nights, after she gets home from work, instead of going next door to see Mr. Vaughn. It's like we're both trying to do the things now that we wish we'd have done before Beth overdosed herself. Mooms talks about how she should have stayed home more and how she shouldn't have pushed Beth to take that job at the hospital, that it was just too much for her, especially so soon after losing Miss Hannah.

I tell her no, no, it wasn't her fault, there was nothing she could have done. After seeing how much Mooms blames herself, I feel lousy for blaming her in the first place, even if I only blamed her in my own mind.

We have many more problems than we would have had if Daddy hadn't been taken away, if you ask me so it's really more fair to blame him, if we're blaming anyone. I seriously doubt he'd have let Amy move in with Aunt March and I'd lay money on it that he'd have put a stop Edward Moffat right away. I don't know about Beth, but she's a sensitive girl and her family breaking up surely figures in to her problems. Of course, none of that can be proven but I know it's the truth.

I've done a lot of thinking about finding a way to leave too, after Amy and Meg both did. I mean, two sisters taking off and the other in the psych ward kind of reinforces that it's not just me. But this situation here pretty much kills off my hopes of leaving. When Beth comes home, I can't leave her here alone with just Mooms.

I hate to say it but just as Daddy, Meg and Amy seem to me 90% good but 10% evil, I'd rate Mooms 90% good but 10% crazy, ever since things fell apart anyway. Ten percent isn't that much, except that you never know where it will show up. One mistake with Beth now, that could be one too many.

Mooms and I go together to another conference with Beth's psychiatrist. He says they haven't uncovered anything in her environment that would seem an obvious explanation for an episode like Beth had.

Mooms says, "Well, there have been a lot of changes in the past couple of years."

The doctor says, "Yes, I'm aware of that. And of course, some patients are just more fragile than others. So, while what she's been through wouldn't typically be at a high enough level for such an extreme reaction, that certainly doesn't mean it couldn't be. Or that it wasn't at least a contributing factor."

Mooms says, "What is her diagnosis?" Mooms has picked up some knowledge from working as a hospital receptionist.

"There isn't enough evidence thus far, to label her with any specific mental illness. At this point, she's at "wait and see" status. The recommended course of action will be to keep a close eye on her and keep her environment tranquil, after she's discharged."

I already figured that. Mooms says, "What about school? She frequently comes home upset and begs to be allowed to stay home."

The doctor starts writing. "All right. We'll put her on absentee schooling, with a teacher stopping by once per week to pick up her completed assignments and drop off new ones. She'll also be prescribed medication but it will have to be closely controlled. I believe you work during the day, Mrs. March?"

Mooms nods and the doctor says, "I can also write a hardship excuse for your other daughter to have her assignments at home as well. Is she responsible enough to supervise Beth?"

Mooms assures him that I am. That part makes me feel pretty good, at least.

The doctor also gives Mooms a number to call to get Beth enrolled in a teen therapy group. He says, "Beth should be ready to go home soon. I'll call you."

Getting out of school is fabulous. I don't know what I was thinking anyway, about leaving home. I don't even know where I'd go.

Chapter 27

Beth comes home from the hospital the day before Thanksgiving. Beth and I will both be doing our assignments at home, at least until after the Christmas break. Mooms asked me to get a leave of absence from my job too, which my boss granted.

Since Beth just got home, Thanksgiving dinner will be kept quiet, just me, Mooms and Beth.

Beth is settled in on the couch, watching *Leave it to Beaver.* I hear Ward call June Cleaver "the belle of East St. Louis" on the show and I think I must have heard wrong. Then I stifle my laughter, to keep Beth's environment extra calm. But oh, my glob, East St. Louis is across the river in Illinois, and it is a total bombed out slum. It's nowhere you'd ever go, if you like remaining alive.

Mr. Vaughn bought us our television. It's just a portable black and white one though, the basic cheapo model. Our new phone is the same, the wall mount type with the round dial, not the cool bar-shaped one with push buttons. Mooms will accept help from Mr. Vaughn but only the most basic help possible. It's annoying as hell.

Mooms has just brushed Beth's hair and clipped it on the sides with new barrettes. Strangely, considering that Beth is obviously not doing so great, she's the prettiest I've ever seen her. She's like a life size, delicate porcelain doll, all snuggled up in her blanket with Party. I tell her so and she smiles.

I take the boneless, skinless turkey breast out of the freezer and put it in the icebox to thaw. Tomorrow, we'll also have gravy, stuffing and mashed potatoes, all from boxed mixes, along with storebought rolls and a storebought pumpkin pie.

Mooms and I agreed that the hustle and bustle that goes into fixing a holiday meal from scratch wouldn't be good for Beth to be around, this soon. But we also don't mind getting out of it anyway. To be honest, Mooms and I are actually a bit proud of ourselves for nixing our original idea of just getting Swanson's turkey TV dinners.

The next afternoon, we've just sat down to our simple and lonely Thanksgiving supper when Aunt March's baby blue Lincoln pulls up in the driveway. I don't know about Beth, but Aunt March is too much for my nerves on a regular day. But Aunt March is not in the car. Amy gets out, followed by Aunt March's chauffeur, who loads himself up with boxes and bags.

"I came back as soon as I heard what all's been going on around here!" Amy bustles in importantly, as if the March household couldn't possibly continue on for one moment longer without her oversight.

The chauffeur puts down his burdens to help Amy out of her coat, then follows her directions on carrying her possessions upstairs. Amy comes back downstairs and takes a seat at the dinner table while the chauffeur goes back outside for another load. "Go ahead and continue eating," she says, granting us permission.

Beth gets up and starts fixing a plate for Amy. Mooms and I look at each other, the question between us being if we should let Beth start resuming her usual role already or stop her. I guess we don't know exactly what the doctor meant by "a tranquil environment." Mooms shrugs, and we don't say anything.

Amy airily dismisses the driver now. I imagine he'd like to turn little Aunt March Junior over his knee. Amy's picked up a lot of Aunt March's tone and mannerisms. It's not any cuter on a thirteen-year-old than it is on old Aunt March, that's for sure.

But I just say, "Welcome back, girl. We missed you."

Amy says, "I simply couldn't go another day over there, knowing what Beth is going through. Especially after I heard that Meg was gone, and Miss Hannah died. Why didn't anybody call me? Why didn't anyone tell me anything?"

The haughty act falls away and Amy just looks hurt. The snipped nose makes her face look a little larger, and a bit pan-like or something. I have to make myself concentrate on her words rather than her face.

For now, I just say, "Oh no, I'm sorry. Who caught you up on the news?"

"Aunt March," she says, like it should be obvious.

I say, "Hmm. Well, first of all, you were definitely missed. Very, very missed. Let's sit down and have a talk about the rest of it later, okay?" After checking that Beth's not looking, I look at Amy and nod towards Beth, like *not in front of her.*

Amy catches on. No one could accuse the girl of being slow. She says, "Aunt March is going to the country club for Thanksgiving dinner. They have waiters in tuxedos and big ice sculptures. There's even fountain that has melted chocolate instead of water."

"Wow, cool. I'd love to see that," I say, wondering why Amy really came home. Well, really, I should wonder why it lasted as long as it did.

Mooms's face has that tight look about it, underneath the smile. She says, "Oh, is it the St. Louis Country Club? Because Vince and I were just talking about taking you there. Maybe in a couple of weeks, after things settle in here."

"What a coincidence. What are the chances of that?" I say innocently, trying not to crack up laughing. I really doubt that Mooms and Mr. Vaughn had any plans to take us to any country club. In fact, I've never heard anything about Mr.

Vaughn even belonging to any country club. Mooms's face is flushed, like she's all worked up about it. Sometimes Mooms is hilarious. Like, sure, take my kid away but don't you *dare* take her out for a fancier meal than I did.

We've progressed through the turkey supper and we're on to the pumpkin pie when Kay's old car pulls up in the driveway. Kay gets out, carrying a big fluffy blue snowsuit, which I assume contains Robbie, somewhere inside of it.

She makes her way to the door. Amy looks around like she just realized Robbie was missing. She says, "Why does the Avon lady have Robbie?"

Mooms says, "Oh, Kay watches him sometimes now."

Beth puts a piece of pie on a plate for Kay, who bursts in like a blizzard, as soon as I open the door.

Kay says, "I can't keep Robbie next week, after all. I've been kicked out. I'll have to move and it will be really hard to find another place, on my budget. In fact, I'll probably be living in my car." As if tornado Amy wasn't enough, now we have hurricane Kay, too.

Mooms takes Robbie. We all make a fuss over the return of the most adorable baby in the universe and, oh yeah, Kay's impending homelessness too, I guess.

The pie is gone and we're having coffee and cocoa in the living room before I notice that Beth seems strange. She's kind of staring off, blankly. I motion towards Beth to Mooms, hoping Mooms gets my drift. I'm sure doing a lot of silent signaling today. Mooms seems to understand though, and she walks Beth upstairs for a rest.

When Mooms comes back down, Kay's still ranting about how her roommate didn't have any right to kick her, Kay, out when she hadn't even done anything wrong. Apparently, the roommate just wanted to get rid of Kay because the roommate's boyfriend seemed too interested in Kay, which wasn't Kay's fault, especially when Kay wasn't even remotely interested in the roommate's boyfriend in the first place.

Mooms says, "Yes, it causes all sorts of problems for innocent bystanders when people don't play fair in the love department. Doesn't it, Kay?" Hell's bells, that had a bite to it. Mooms didn't speak the words as much as spit them out.

Amy perks up, looking interested. Amy is too aware of grown-up issues for a thirteen-year-old. Meg said once she thought that was because Meg and Mooms watched all those soap operas, at our old house. *As the World Turns* and *Days of Our Lives*. Meg said it was a mistake to let Amy watch them, too. They should have made her go play.

Kay's eyes get big. She reaches over and lays her hand on Moom's arm, the arm that's holding the baby. She practically whispers to Mooms, "I'm so sorry, Margaret."

Oh, I get it now. Kay wants to stay here and Mooms is getting snippy because she feels like she has to say yes, although she doesn't want to.

Mooms already has too many people of her own to take care of. It's like when we had to keep Miss Hannah, all over again. I mean, when you figure up what one person eats in a month, that's a chunk of cash right there, especially when you're on the edge to start with. If you ask me, Mooms and Kay's little friendship, or whatever you'd call it, is corrupt as hell in the first place, all things considered.

Mooms closes her eyes like she's meditating. Then, after her trademark Deep Sigh, she says to Kay, "You can stay here, if you help out around the house. Amy, please show her Miss Hannah's old room. Quietly, though. Beth needs her rest."

I don't get the reason for showing Kay the bedroom. Who cares what Kay thinks of it? What's she gonna do, say, thanks anyway, but I like the layout and décor of my old car better than this free room. And even if she did say that, wouldn't Mooms be happier anyway?

Time goes by and Amy and Kay don't come back down. What's taking so long? There's not much to see. It's just a plain, small room, with a twin bed and a chest of drawers.

I go up there and find Kay in Meg's old room, putting Amy's things away, while Amy sits on Meg's bed and orders Kay about.

Amy says, "No Kay, move the socks to the left side of the top drawer. I said the *panties* go on the right. The *bras* go on the left."

Apparently, Miss Amy has decided to take Meg's room, now that Meg's gone, instead of going back to the shared room with Beth. She should have asked Mooms first.

But one offense at a time is all I can handle right now. I say, "Oh no, you don't, Miss Priss."

Kay says, "I'm sorry, ma'am."

I hold back laughing. "I don't mean you, Kay. Amy, let me explain something to you, and keep in mind I'm telling you this, not asking you."

Amy flounces once on the bed, folds her arms and sticks her tiny new nose in the air. She looks kind of adorable, a baby girl villain.

I say, "Don't even start the attitude with me, missy thing. You are a child, understand? You take orders, you don't give them, least of all to *any* full-grown adult."

Amy purses her lips at me, so I grab her by the chin and make her say "Yes, I understand."

I tell Kay she doesn't ever have to wait on Amy. Then we all go back downstairs. When we get there, I tell Amy, "Now, you need to ask Mooms if it's okay, before you move into Meg's old bedroom."

Mooms thinks for a while, rocking the baby in her rocking chair. Then she says, "No, Amy. I want you in the bedroom with Beth. I need you to keep an eye on her for me. You understand?"

Rather than the expected argument, Amy seems pleased. Like she likes being trusted with a serious responsibility. She sits up straight, as if she's accepting a formal honor. "I will keep a close eye on her."

Well, there's a thought. Maybe giving Amy more responsibility will improve her attitude. I guess she's never had much chance at that, as the youngest. Then I realize I must sound just like Meg used to. Oh, my glob, what a horrifying thought. I'm turning into the new Mooms Junior.

I remember the issue from earlier and say, "Oh, by the way, Amy, we did call to tell you we had a phone, and about all the other things, too. We called more than once, when Meg eloped, when Miss Hannah passed away, and when Beth went in the hospital. We always had to leave a message with an answering service, and nobody ever called us back."

Amy gets tears in her eyes. It breaks my heart. I say, "You know, we also called more than once to tell you how much we missed you and that we all wanted you home."

Little Miss Bird Beak starts sobbing into her hands, all hunched over. I swear to myself to always remember that under that stubborn exterior, there's a soft girl who feels like she needs a tough shell.

After a short nap, Beth comes down and wants to play with the baby, so Mooms hands Robbie over. We find something boring to watch on TV. Nothing scary or upsetting or even too wildly funny, per Beth's doctor's instructions.

Kay says, "I guess I'll start cleaning up the kitchen."

Mooms suggests she start moving her stuff over instead, so she can be done with the roommate mess. Kay leaves, and to my surprise, Amy goes

into the kitchen and starts washing the supper
dishes.

Crime comes in many more colors than the most well-known, white-collar and blue-collar. The color names are mostly not official though, and can overlap with each other:

blue collar crime is a large, broad category and mostly committed by individuals of lower socioeconomic status. It's typically more obvious and direct than white collar crime and also more likely to include violence. It's what we probably most often think of, when we think of "crime." Examples include drug deals, assault, and shoplifting.

white collar crime is nonviolent crime for financial gain, most often committed by white, middle-class males. It usually involves the perpetrator's high level professional position. Examples are securities fraud and embezzling.

green collar crime is a subset of white-collar crime. It is specifically committed against the environment, for profit.

red collar crime occurs when a white collar criminal resorts to murder to silence victims or witnesses.

pink collar crime is various types of theft from employers. It isn't limited to women but refers to lower-level office positions, which include a relatively high percentage of women. These perpetrators have limited access to information and funds.

orange collar crime is a subset of blue-collar crime. It's committed by workers in the manual labor industry and connected to their work. It can include any level of seriousness.

black collar crime is crime committed by a member of the clergy.

gold collar crime involves many people in a hierarchal complex. It includes war crimes, crimes against humanity and genocide.

gray collar crime is use of technology to commit crime, without ever meeting the victim.

silver collar crime is elderly exploitation, financially motivated, usually by someone close to the elderly person and using official paperwork to do so.

<u>*plaid collar crime*</u> *(if we're counting "plaid" as a color) is crime that directly affects farm workers, such as theft of products grown or farm equipment.*

Chapter 28

A couple weeks later, we've settled into a new routine. Kay steps into Miss Hannah's old role and Beth helps, just like she used to help Miss Hannah. Beth still seems weak though, and kind of robotic.

Mooms says that's a side effect of Beth's new medication. Amy is a big help now too, playing mother hen to both Robbie and Beth.

My schoolwork only takes me about two hours a day. Some lady from the school district comes by once a week to pick up the finished assignments from me and Beth and drop off new ones. I wish I could keep it this way for the year and a half I have left of high school. Well, maybe only a year, if I can get enough credits to graduate early. With Kay here to keep an eye on Beth, I mostly stay in my garret and write.

We've just sat down to a late lunch one day in mid-December: Kay, Beth and I. Amy's at school, Mooms is at work and Robbie's taking his nap. We're having tuna salad on toast, Campbell's chicken and stars soup, carrot sticks and apple slices. A taxi pulls up in the driveway. It seems every damn unexpected thing that goes on around here happens when we're trying to eat.

We all stop eating and stare out the window, wondering what the hell is going on. Taxis never come here. Some old man gets out and hobbles toward the door.

It takes me a minute to realize the old man is Daddy. He's aged some more since I saw him at the prison.

After Beth and I finish swarming him with hugs and kisses, I encourage Daddy to sit down and eat, motioning to the seat at the head of the table. Kay and Beth bustle around in the kitchen to find something to feed him. I say, all chipper, "See, we even left your seat empty for you."

He sits down. It soon becomes apparent that he doesn't fit in with us like he used to. It's like under all the hoopla, he's really a kind of shabby visitor who I don't know very well. If he was younger, I could see Larry and I taking him to our growing tent village in the woods and scrambling to find the basics to keep him going for a day or two. I say, "What a great surprise this is!"

He says, "Your Aunt March, she got her magical lawyer on it and, why, next thing you know, here I am."

A while later, he says, "I'll tell you what. Freedom is a beautiful thing. I felt like Phil the gorilla. It was before your time but he was famous at the zoo. Why, he'd turn the hose on you, flip people off, sometimes he even threw doo-doo. After being locked up in a zoo myself, I can't say as I blame him."

I laugh along. I start to recognize Daddy in there somewhere. He'd told the famous gorilla story many times.

Kay comes to the table with silverware, and a small plate of apple slices and carrot sticks. Daddy's mouth drops open. His eyes look like they're about to pop out of his head. He says, "What are you doing here?" His sharp tone startles me.

Robbie starts crying and I rush up the stairs to get him. I take him upstairs to Kay's room and change him, then play with him on the floor with some baby toys she has up here.

Lunch is over when I finally come back downstairs with Robbie. Daddy and Kay are in the kitchen, arguing, though their voices are low. Beth is on the couch, curled up in a blanket, intently watching the television and kind of nodding like she agrees with what's going on there. But the television is not turned on.

When I get closer, I see that she's not shaking exactly, more like trembling. Whatever you'd call this, it's clear that she's not doing well.

I go into the kitchen, still carrying Robbie, getting mad now. Daddy and Kay both look up. Daddy says, all bright and cheery, "Hey, what's up, kiddo? Who have you got there?"

I think *hell's bells, buster, just wait til you find out!* I say, "Listen, you two have upset Beth and the

doctor said she has to be kept calm. I think you…
should leave. At least until Mooms gets home."

They head straight for the door. Daddy doesn't
ask what Beth is under a doctor's care for.

Kay says, "I'll take Robbie with me."

I almost hand him over but then I don't. I say,
"You can ask Mooms when she gets home."

They leave, and I feel like I've aged a decade. I
just gave my father an order, and he obeyed me.
Wow. I get a glass of water and Beth's pills, the
ones we're supposed to give her if she starts getting
agitated. I say, "Here you go, Bethie. Now, let's see
what's on TV." We settle in to watch *Bewitched*.
Trying to lighten the mood, I chat about the show.
"Isn't that cool how Samantha can just wiggle her
nose and get whatever she wants? Maybe we should
practice that."

Beth smiles.

I say, "Can you just imagine little Tabitha from
Bewitched, with Robbie? That would be so cute.
Hey, we should try to find another baby for him to
play with."

During a commercial, Beth says, "I heard them.
Kay said Robbie is hers and Daddy's." She starts
that trembling thing again, though she's wrapped up
in a blanket. Just when I thought I'd gotten her
calmed down, globdammit.

I try to make it like it's no big deal. "Oh, I don't
know about that. But I'll tell you what I try to do,
Beth, and that's to ask myself 'Is this my problem?'

whenever something upsets me. And nine times out
of ten, it's not. I mean, the ones who are involved in
something, that's for them to worry about. And if
they've wrong, that'll be for them to answer for. But
you and I? Nope. Fortunately, we're not involved.
Therefore, we don't need to get ourselves involved.
Am I right?"

She nods, like she's taking in what I'm saying. I
say, "How about some pink milk?" That always
seems to cheer her up. I come back with two glasses
of milk with Nestle's Strawberry Quik powder
mixed in, and two of those big loopy straws.

When Mooms comes in from work, I take her
aside and fill her in on the day's developments.
Then I realize there's no supper, with Kay out and
Beth all drugged up.

Mooms says, "I'll tell you what. I'd almost agree
to a second wife, just to get out of the cooking and
cleaning." I laugh with her, without meaning to. I
mean, how gross and corrupt is it even possible to
be? I think of a new story title, "Laughter in the
Loony Bin." Oops, no. "Loony bin" isn't a word to
joke about anymore, not after my only nice sister
was in the psych ward.

Mooms picks up the half full ashtray from the
dining room table. Her jaw is clenched. She says,
"You were smoking?"

I say, "Oh, no. That's Daddy's."

"Daddy doesn't smoke."

I said, "Well, I guess he does now."

Mooms looks at me, suspicious. Then she says, "Where's Amy?"

With everything else going on here today, I didn't even notice that Amy didn't come home after school.

Just then, Amy comes slinking through the door, trying to sneak up the stairs without being noticed. Like I don't know that trick. But right now, I'm just relieved that she's okay, I swoop her up, swing her around, and say, "Where the moth balls were you? You about worried us to death, girl."

She cracks up laughing. She reeks of pot. I put two and two together, because I've been thinking my stash seemed a little light lately. I don't know how she could find it though, under the loose floorboard in the corner of my garret. Amy's a little bitch but she's not stupid, unfortunately.

Mooms says, "And where were you, Miss?"

"Eh, out with some kids. We just hung around the Quick Shop and stuff." She pulls a Marathon candy bar out of her coat pocket as proof. The Quick Shop, ugh. The liquor store is right next to it, in the same building. Some girls at school were talking about the old red-nosed alkie who owns the liquor store. He likes to sit in a chair outside his shop and bother people, when he doesn't have any customers. The girls at school were saying he sells booze to underage girls, if they show him their tits. I'm going to have to keep closer tabs on Amy before she gets completely out of hand.

Well, at least she's fitting back in with the local kids. She came home from Aunt March's all snobby and threw a fit when she had to go to Kirby junior high. But there was no chance in hell Mooms could afford to keep her in the fancy art school Aunt March had enrolled her in. Mooms wouldn't even be able to afford the gas money to get her there and back.

Amy moped around for a while after her return from Aunt March's, saying the kids around here were "north county trash." But at least she stayed around the house then, which kept her out of the reach of old alkie perverts.

Amy got the worst traits of Meg and I. Meg's snobbishness and my, I don't know, upfront-ness or whatever you'd call it. We probably both inherited it from Aunt March ha. Anyway, there are nice new subdivisions all over the place around here, and some grand old homes too, including Larry's Gramps' house, right next door. I hate to tell Miss Fancy-Pants but we are the trash in north county.

Mooms wanders off to start fixing dinner, so I follow Amy up the stairs and into her bedroom. I say, "Give me that candy bar."

She starts to argue but I say, "You better shup up, you little thief, or I'll tell Mooms you're high."

She looks at me, incredulous. "But it's *your* weed!"

"Aha. You admit it." I snatch the candy bar, then open the hope chest at the foot of her bed. What thirteen-year-old girl has a hope chest? What girl of any age who isn't in the eighteenth century, has a hope chest? I go shopping in it. I take the ceramic mushroom-shaped condiment container that Mooms got with her green stamps, then decided she didn't want. I also take Amy's four potholders. That's a good punishment. Amy is proud of the potholders, since she made them herself, from some kit that had a little metal loom and a bunch of little loopy things to weave through it.

I say, "If you take my stuff, I take your stuff. See how that works?"

Amy doesn't say anything. She knows she deserves it.

I say, "And don't ever go to the Quick Shop by yourself. That old alkie in the liquor store is a pervert."

She rolls her eyes. "Like duh, who doesn't know that?"

Just then, Amy with her new nose reminds me of fussy toddler Amy, before that time when Meg and I put a diaper on her head and were acting out that show with her, *The Flying Nun*. I accidentally dropped Amy, on top of Moom's antique coal hod, which sat on the fireplace hearth. That big old metal bucket used to hold Mooms's big dried flower arrangement, with the cattails and everything. I wonder if Amy remembers it, if she knows it was my fault the bridge of her nose was smashed flat in the first place.

I set her stuff down on the dresser: the candy bar, the mushroom container and the pot holders. I say,

"Eh, I'll let it slide. This time only, though. Hey, me and Beth are gonna make big soft pretzels tonight. Want to help?"

She looks suspicious for a minute, then she says, "Wow, sure. Thanks."

Amy is the type of kid who needs a firm hand though, as Mooms always says. I say, "You better watch yourself, though. Don't think I won't kerplop you, bitch."

Chapter 29

Now Daddy, his mistress Kay, and their love child Robbie live with us in our house, or rather, in Aunt March's house. They don't have anywhere else to go and neither do we, so here we are. As if that's not corrupt enough, now we're all gathered here together at Mr. Vaughn's house for Christmas dinner, for some reason. It's all just super gross and corrupt. Ultra corrupt.

Amy, Beth and I sit on the floor, crowded into the butler's pantry off the kitchen. Robbie toddles around while we talk about this and that. Anything I can think of to keep them away from the weirdness in the living room, which if you ask me, is about two steps away from becoming a globdamn glory hole situation.

The girls' chatter dies down so I ask Amy why she left Aunt March's, when she obviously lived in such big-time luxury there.

She says, "Oh God. She made me stay right with her every minute that I wasn't in school, lecturing me and bossing me around and dragging me to old people places, like the symphony. I couldn't stand another minute of it, not even for a trillion dollars."

"Yeah, I figured something like that."

She says, "Oh, Tony's restaurant, though! That's Aunt March's favorite. I don't think we ever went there, but Mooms and Daddy might have. Anyhow, it's super expensive and Aunt March would make me sit there with her for hours. That's another thing, she just loves to drag dinner out for ages. It's so boring. But get this: There's stairs at Tony's and the waiters have to walk up them backwards, so the snooty customers don't have to see their backsides."

We laugh about that. I say, "So, I guess it's more polite to display their front sides, then?"

The maid sticks her head in. She says, "Can you girls take the baby into the other room now? We're about to start carrying hot dishes and I don't want him to get hurt."

I scoop Robbie up, bracing to head to Sodom and Gomorrah, I mean, the living room. Amy says, "I think I hear her now. Ugh. Wish me luck." This will be the first time Amy's seen Aunt March since the big argument that ended in some combination of Amy storming out and/or Aunt March throwing her out.

Aunt March stands in the middle of the living room, a giant, alarmed bird of prey. The rest of us, except for Beth and Robbie, have been helping ourselves to Mr. Vaughn's liquor cart since noon.

Daddy and Kay snuggle together on a loveseat, arms and legs entwined, which draws a puffed up, neck-out response from Aunt March. Going by the expression on her face, her mind seems to be struggling to comprehend what's in front of her eyes.

Amy slips by Aunt March, dragging Beth along with her. They hide behind the other loveseat, which is occupied by Mooms and Mr. Vaughn. The matching loveseats face each other. Mooms and Daddy and their respective paramours seem to be having some kind of competition to determine which new couple is the most hot-to-trot. Kay rubs the back of Daddy's neck. Mr. Vaughn rests his hand on Mooms's thigh. Daddy kisses Kay's ear. Mooms tucks her hair behind her ears and gushes again about the diamond earrings Mr. Vaughn gave her for Christmas.

While they think everyone's distracted, Larry and Steve steal a quick kiss under the mistletoe that hangs in the doorway between the living room and dining room.

The maid announces that dinner is ready. After we're all seated, Mr. Vaughn says grace at the head of the table. I steel myself for lightning to strike.

The dinner is almost worth it, though. There's both beef roast and turkey. Mashed potatoes, sweet potato casserole, green bean casserole, various cold salads, and rolls.

Aunt March gulps down two glasses of red wine and holds her glass out for more.

For a while, all you can hear is the clatter of silver forks on china.

A half hour later, everyone seems full. We're sitting around the table, waiting for the maid to serve the dessert and coffee. Kay, obviously still tipsy, puts her hand over Daddy's hand where it's resting on the table. Not about to be upstaged, Mooms caresses Mr. Vaughn's cheek.

Suddenly, Aunt March scoops up a heaping serving spoon full of mashed potatoes and flings it across the table at Mooms. It slaps her upside her head, then plops wetly onto the table.

We all just sit there for a minute. It's like we're trying to figure out if that really just happened. Then Mooms's jaw tightens and I know it's not over. She sticks her hand into the baking dish of green bean casserole and volleys a heaping handful right back at Aunt March. Except she doesn't throw hard enough and it kind of splatters everyone at the table.

The next thing you know, food's flying everywhere: the sweet potatoes with marshmallows, the apple sauce, slices of beef. Mooms get ups and stomps right over and empties the china gravy boat, over Kay's head. Amy gleefully begins pelting us all with Waldorf salad.

The maid comes in carrying a big tray on her shoulder, loaded with slices of French apple cake and dishes of chocolate mousse. She skids to a stop when she sees the maelstrom. An errant turkey drumstick bounces off her ample bosom.

She yells, "Fuck all a youse crazies." She lets go of the big tray. It clunks loudly on the hardwood floor, dishes flying every which way. She stomps out.

The whole ordeal probably only lasted a few minutes but globdamn, I'll remember it to my dying day. It ends with some people screaming with laughter and other people just screaming.

Aunt March stalks off in her arch and stately way, unaware that a buttered dinner roll is caught in her elaborate hairdo, no doubt glued in there from the excess of Aqua Net hair spray. She mutters, "disgraceful, disgraceful," like she wasn't the one who started the whole thing.

As if on cue, everyone else scuttles away, too. They seem to just silently disappear.

Then Mooms and I notice at the same time that Beth and Robbie are missing.

We run all over the house and all over the yards. We find them next door, back at our house, huddled together under the dining room table. Mooms gets Beth's medicine and I change the baby, then we put them both to bed.

Mooms makes me go back to Mr. Vaughn's with her to clean up, saying over and over, "Some of that stuff will stain."

It looks like a miniature tornado made a direct hit inside the dining room. There's chunky, gloppy and liquid mess all over the table and floor. Gravy drips from on the chandelier, red wine is splashed up the curtains.

It's not funny now. Aunt March's word "disgraceful" is right. Our family, trashing our host's home, the evening cut short, and possibly permanently hurt feelings, all around. The gifts remain under the tree, unopened, including the ones for the kids.

#

Aunt March kicks off the Big Re-Shuffle. She comes over to our house the day after Christmas, when lunch and its clean-up are done and we've just finished unwrapping all the presents that had been left untouched at Mr. Vaughn's house yesterday. We're lounging around in the living room with the TV on: Mooms, Daddy, Kay, me, Beth, Amy and little Robbie.

Beth embroiders a flower on the pocket of her Levi's. Mooms set it up for her, to give Beth something calming to focus on. Amy's sketching a picture of Party. I just came back from smoking some weed in the garage so I'm all nice and zoned out, just watching the colored lights twinkle magically on the pitiful Christmas tree. Nobody talks. We're probably all thinking about the question mark hanging in the air, wondering what comes next.

There's a sharp rap-rap-rap on the front door. Before anyone can answer, Aunt March unlocks it with her key and barges in. She points a long, red-painted talon at Mooms, who's only made it halfway to the door by then. Aunt March says, "I want you out. You have three days." It cracks me up because just then, that commercial about that Zykan company that hauls away trash comes on. "If nobody can, Zykan!"

If Aunt March thought of it, she'd probably have just called the Zykan brothers and had Mooms delivered to the dump. Nobody else gets the joke, though. They all stare at me.

Amy starts arguing about how that's not fair. I try to decide if Amy is brave or just ill-mannered. I know they're not mutually exclusive, so I try to picture the issue on a Venn diagram in my mind. Is the pointy-ended oval between the two circles fat or skinny, that overlap where Amy is both brave and ill-mannered?

Aunt March's beady raptor eyes bore into Amy now, the talon rotating accordingly. Aunt March says, "You too." It sounds owly, like "Who. Whooo."

Amy leaps up, tossing her sketch pad onto the coffee table. She shrieks, "Your dog is a homo!"

There's a collective gasp in the room. Aunt March's beak falls open, then clamps shut.

I drop my face into my hands. I'm just dying. It's so funny I can't breathe.

Then I recover. And what the hell is everyone staring at me for? Amy's the one who said it, and her parents are the ones who didn't correct her. If I spoke like that to an elderly relative when I was her age, even an old witchy one who'd just evicted my mother, I'd have gotten such a whooping that I wouldn't be able to sit down to this day. I can't even help it if I laughed, especially since I'm stoned.

Laughter is involuntary. I'm the least guilty one of everyone involved. I glare back at each of them back, in turn, except for Beth and Robbie. Kay gets an extra glare portion, since she's the homewrecker who started it all. That seems to break up their highly corrupt group staring project.

Beth runs upstairs. Daddy follows, like a dutiful and worried father, but it's obviously an excuse for him to escape.

Aunt March calls after him, "Robert, you may continue to live here." Oh my glob. Amy's right. It's not fair at all.

Mistress Kay sits there holding little Robbie. Am I imagining it, or is she smiling and nodding her head, barely perceptibly, totally digging the thought of positioning herself on the winning side of this shake-up? Oh yeah. She is.

When your stoned mind slows the action down, you see what others miss. Or at least it seems that way to me.

Mooms doesn't say anything. She just steps around Aunt March and goes out the still-open front door. Through the window, I see her cutting across the front yards in the snow, headed for Mr. Vaughn's house.

Aunt March swoops out, as suddenly as she appeared. I wonder what happened to the dinner roll that was on her head.

I go upstairs to pack my things. Any hope I had of my family patching it up after Daddy came home is 100% gone now. I guess both parents being involved in affairs, not to mention an affair baby, should have been my first clue that the house had broken wide apart and tumbled down the hill.

Part Two

One Year Later
January 10, 1979

People from St. Louis area are sometimes surprised when they go to other parts of the country and discover that no one knows what a "pork steak" is.

According to Wikipedia, in 1956, Winfred Steinbruegge of Florissant, Missouri asked Tom Brandt of Tomboy Grocery Store to cut a pork butt into steaks that could be grilled. The new "pork steak" quickly became popular with local residents.

Chapter 30

I'm staying with Daddy and Kay now, in the house that used to be for Mooms and my sisters and me. Every globdamn time somebody shows up without notice around here, it's still when we're trying to eat. Not that I'm crazy about this ground beef and rice mixed with Campbell's vegetable soup anyway. It's one of Kay's specialties, which she will actually tell you with a straight face.

I'm thinking about moving next door to Mooms and Mr. Vaughn's house for a while, where things like a steak dinner at Yacovelli's once in a while would not be out of the question. Heck, I'd gladly settle for pork steaks barbecued in the back yard, but it's still too cold out for that.

Or maybe I'd just rather focus on small complaints than on the big disaster standing in front of me, I don't know. But you can be sure Meg's fallen to pieces, since her face and hair aren't fixed. Meg walked in looking like a street urchin straight out of *Oliver Twist*. She's hugging a big plastic trash bag that I assume is filled with her clothes and stuff.

We're all silent and still: Meg, Daddy, Kay, me and even little Robbie. It's a strange moment, frozen in time.

I feel for Meg. I do. Going by the way she looks now, she's been through some mess. It's a sad contrast with the thrilled, overly confident attitude she left with. I remember that day. She was beautifully put together, from her Candies wedge sandals to her carefully cultivated Coppertone tan and hair newly cut short by a beautician rather than one of our usual home haircuts. She was so proud to be at Edward's side (you know, back when she wouldn't listen to me, back before she proved me right). Most important though, I am infinitely relieved just to know that Meg is alive.

But that's the thing, she just left me, left all of us, to wonder. Nobody's heard from Meg since she left, a year and a half ago. Mooms sobbed her heart out more than once over it, too. I even thought I was going to have to call an ambulance over it once. That time, Mooms cried so hard it seemed like she was either having a nervous breakdown or a heart attack, or both at the same time. I'll never understand how Meg could go from practically being Mooms's shadow to having no concern about her at all.

The rest of us were worried sick, too. Every one of us tried to find Meg, even the non-relatives like Kay, Mr. Vaughn and Larry. We repeatedly called the hospitals, and even the jails, from here to the Four Corners region.

It doesn't even make sense. Meg wasn't on super great terms with us when she left, but that was only because we did care about her and didn't like that she was marrying a total bastard, never mind that we weren't even welcome at their wedding. But there was no big fight or anything like that, nothing would make us think she wanted to leave us behind for good.

So, all I can figure is that Me-Me-Me-Meg doesn't give a shit about us. She's probably only here because she wants something.

She gives us an awkward smile and I see that she's missing a tooth.

My feelings about Meg, the positive and the negative, collide with each other violently, giving me an instant nervous stomach, which is pure misery, since I also happen to be starving to death right now.

Meg sets the trash bag down, revealing a gigantic belly. Meg is pregnant. Pregnant! Hell's bells. She looks like she's about fifteen months along, too.

Daddy's eyes narrow. He crosses his arms across his chest. Meg's gaze meets his, then she looks down at the floor. What the hell is he looking all disapproving for, he's the one who set that example. At least Meg is married. Well, Daddy was too, so I guess I should specify that Meg is married to the father of her almost-kid. I guess she is, anyway.

Kay is the first to speak. She says, "Sit down right here, hon. Let me fix you a plate." Kay is probably overjoyed to no longer be the only one around here who goes about plopping out babies indiscriminately. I feel like reminding Kay of *that* now, like maybe by singing "Oh, Christmas Tree." Haha. Meg showing up has reminded me that most everyone else around here is highly corrupt, too. It's so disappointing.

Meg slumps into the chair that Kay pulls out for her. Kay goes into the kitchen. Little Robbie starts to fuss. He says, "Mama! Ma-ma!" I get up and tend to him, glad to have a distraction, while I try to figure out how to react to Meg. A hug? A slap upside the globdamn head? I don't know. I mean, this is way beyond yelling, "I'll kerplop you, bitch." This is serious.

Kay sets a bowl of glop and a slice of buttered bread in front of Meg. I fight back the urge to quote from Oliver Twist, "Please sir. May I have some more?"

Yep, Meg's arrival reminds me that I'm not sure I like any of these creatures. Well, except for little Robbie, of course. Little Robbie is an angel. And Beth. Beth is an angel, too. I just misunderstood her before, that's all.

Meg thanks Kay, though I don't know if it's for the glop or just for being nice to her. After we all get settled in and the meal resumes, Meg looks around and says, "Where is everybody?"

I open my mouth to start explaining the new screwed up changes to the slightly older screwed up changes, but it's all so screwed up that I start laughing and can't stop. That's a problem I have. I think ignorant things are funny. Especially when I'm stoned.

Everyone glares at me. After all they've done, all globdamn three of them, they have the nerve to glare at me. They have a way of doing that.

I'm already on the edge right now so their dirty looks totally fire me up more and more, until I reach my breaking point. I run upstairs and get a joint from my new and improved hiding place inside the electric box. I come back down smoking it, then sit down at the table to enjoy more tokes off it, right in their faces. I snatch Daddy's ashtray. I glare back at them, just daring any of these hypocritical, corrupt people to open their snouts.

They don't open their snouts. They just sit there for a minute and then they all start eating the cheap-ass glop again. Then it dawns on me that I'm an idiot. A mortified idiot, now. For one thing, if anyone had said anything to me, what would I have done about it anyway? Answer: Nothing.

But mostly, I get this weird feeling that I've just become an adult. Yes, at this moment, smoking a joint at my father's dinner table, and realizing how immature it is that I thought that was so brave and tough, I feel strongly that right now is the moment I become an adult. And I did it so stupidly. You only become an adult once, so it's another permanent failure.

I think of those questions people ask in a group sometimes, like at the cocktail parties my parents used to throw. Somebody might say, "So, where were all of you when President Kennedy was assassinated?" Or "Where were youse when the men walked on the moon?" More recently, it might be "Where were you when Elvis died?" In years to come, I'll think "Where was I, when I realized I'd become an adult?" and I'll think of this moment and how damn ridiculous I am.

In a flash of stoned self-loathing, I jam the lit end of the joint into my palm.

There's a gasp around the table. Then another silence. And this silence hits me harder than if they'd all shouted dirty words at me.

Kay finally breaks the spell. She says, "Whoopsie!" like my psycho self-attack is some kind of normal accident, like spilling a drink or stubbing a toe or something. She jumps up and rushes to the kitchen, then comes back with a bag of frozen peas to put on the black, pink and red circle in the middle of my palm. For a second, it smells like steak on the grill.

Meg sits there, shaking her head. *The nerve of her!*

Robbie bounces gleefully in his high chair, laughing at me rocking back and forth with the bag of frozen peas and moaning, "Oh fuck, oh fuck." I guess people do look pretty funny when they're in extreme pain, when you think about it. I mean, just going by the facial expressions and stuff, if you didn't understand what was going on.

Daddy puts his face in his hands, which is pretty globdamn dramatic for someone who… Oh, I don't have the energy to think of everything he's done.

I say, "I think I'm just gonna go upstairs and rest for a while."

Kay says, "Okay, hon. I'll come check on you in a bit." Kay is an uncomfortable swirl in my mind, one of several. Kay seems so nice and normal, more so than any of us Marchs, really. But then, she helped break up our home and she abandoned a baby. I don't know how to put those two sides of Kay together. I don't like mind swirls.

In bed, up in my garret, I settle in and try to float along with what's left of my buzz, and not think too much. I graduated a semester early so I've been done with high school for three weeks now, ever since Christmas break. I don't have much of a plan for what to do next. I just feel stuck because I'm pissed off at Daddy and Kay, and equally pissed off at Mooms and Mr. Vaughn. I know I'm right to be pissed off, too. Sleazy double-crossers, all of them. Yet, they're my family. What am I supposed to do with that?

I feel most at home in the tents in the woods, with the other outcasts. It's hard camping out there in freezing weather, though. And I don't always like whoever else is there, either. For the past year, I've been like a nomad, me and my backpack, going between here and the tents and sometimes Mr. Vaughn's house too. And nobody seems to care if I'm there or not anyway, at any of my three homes.

Chapter 31

The next day, Meg comes with me to work my shift at Baskin-Robbins. I don't know why they don't just shut this damn place down in the wintertime but hey, it's easy money. I also don't know why I let Meg come with me, well, except that she didn't really ask. She just sort of joined me and I wasn't expecting it. She looks better today.

We get the re-stocking and cleaning done in a half hour, between the two of us, even with my left hand all bandaged up and Meg being 64 months pregnant. The only talk is just Meg making comments, like "Wow, I forgot how cold the walk-in freezer is," and "I don't miss scraping down the sides of all these cartons." There's a coat and gloves hanging outside the walk-in freezer but it's still no fun to have to rummage around in there, looking for whatever type of ice cream we're out of.

We find a new thing of vanilla and then we get the sides of the cartons scraped down out in the display case, so the ice cream looks fresh. And of course, nobody likes cleaning the restroom. I mean, it's one thing to clean your own bathroom at home but cleaning a public one is nasty.

We get done, then we sit at the employee table in the back room, with a sugar cone apiece. I pick the jamoca almond fudge ice cream and Meg has pralines n' cream. I haven't gone out of my way to talk to Meg since she's been back, aside from barely answering her on the small talk she keeps starting up.

She says, "So much has happened since the last time we were here together, huh?"

"Yep."

"So, are you still with Larry?"

"Eh, I don't know."

"Yeah, you're probably better off alone. I know I am."

"Hmm," I say, wishing a customer would come in or something. My strong mixed feelings about Meg are obviously too much for me to carry so I've deliberately dropped that load. I figure my one flip out last night was enough. She's spent many months showing me where we stand with each other and now I just need to respond accordingly. I plan to treat her like an acquaintance.

She says, "Kay and Daddy filled me in. They said they're a couple now, Mooms moved in with Mr. Vaughn next door, and Miss Hannah died. Wow, that's a lot."

"Are you going to stay with Mooms then? It's a lot cushier over there." I'm going to stay at whichever house she's not staying at. I expect Meg to pick the more prestigious address, naturally. "I'm sure you're welcome over there. Mooms and Daddy and their new fucks all said we girls are welcome at both homes."

"Their new fucks? Really?"

"Maybe you better just tend to your own behavior, Meg." Fortunately, someone comes in right then. I figure it's the big red-haired guy who always picks out a different ice cream flavor, then has me put two scoops in a coffee cup and melt it in the microwave oven.

But no, it's that globdamn pig, Edward Moffat. And there's an older woman in a navy blue dress with him. His mother, maybe?

Remembering my decision to keep a safe distance from Meg, I don't even speak to them, but just go in the back and tell Meg he's here.

Meg goes out to talk to Edward. I stay in the back room and turn on the radio to drown out whatever they're talking about. I get my notebook from my backpack and try to work on my latest story. But I can't concentrate, so I dig out my cards and play a couple rounds of solitaire. I lose both rounds.

Meg comes back. She's crying. "That bastard," she says.

I'm so glad I only work a half-shift today.

Meg says, "Edward and some woman from an adoption agency just tried to push me to sign the baby away. Before this, Edward was going around saying the baby isn't even his. I'll tell you one thing, I'm keeping this baby, and that's that."

I try not to find this interesting. But it is. I mean, I'd assume Meg would give the baby up, if she couldn't keep Edward around. I'd guess Meg's biggest concern then would be how to finish out her pregnancy and give the baby up with as few people as possible knowing about it. That would be followed closely by losing the baby weight, so she could get back out there and try again for the lifestyle and status she craves.

I say, "So, you're thinking that you and Edward won't go through with the divorce in the end, then?"

She laughs, bitterly. "Divorce? Oh no, we're not married. Edward changed his mind about eloping before we were even out of Missouri. He decided we should wait a while, which turned into not getting married at all. And now I'm so glad we didn't. He's just… bad. Evil. I don't want him anywhere near me or the baby, ever."

Whoa.

I say, "You should definitely stay next door, then. Heck, Mr. Vaughn might even get you a nanny."

She says, "I thought I'd stay at Daddy's. For a while anyway."

"Oh. Well, yeah. I guess there are a lot fewer people coming and going at Daddy's. That keeps it all quiet, until you figure out a cover story for the out of wedlock part. I mean, for social purposes, right?"

Meg surprises me again. She does that bitter little laugh again. She says, "That's the least of my worries. I just thought Kay and I could, maybe, hang out and take care of our babies together. At least for a while. It would be great to be around another mom and baby. You know, someone who knows how it is."

This doesn't sound like Meg at all. I've heard pregnancy hormones can make women crazy, though. That must be it. A huge as that belly is, she probably has enough pregnancy hormones to qualify for the *Guinness Book of World Records*.

I continue to engage with her in spite of myself, just flat-out nosey now. "Oh. Well, I hope you're at least going after Edward for a big fat child support check."

"Oh gosh, no. Then he'd have custody rights. Him and his new wife. I mean, he obviously doesn't want anything to do with this baby right now. But what if he ever changed his mind? Or, more likely, what if he decided to use the baby to get even with me somehow, for keeping it when he doesn't want me to? I do not want Edward Moffat in my life or my baby's life in any way, shape or form. He's dangerous, Jo. And I mean that sincerely, not just because we broke up. In fact, I'm glad he ran off with someone else."

"Is his new wife from a well-to-do family then?"

"Noooo. She's a stripper."

"Whoa. I bet his snooty parents shit an elephant!"

Meg and I crack up, two sisters together against the world. Just like I always wanted.

Then I come back down to planet Earth.

Meg says, "Edward's parents are beyond horrified. They cut off his allowance when he took off with me. But for this, they cut him out of the will."

I know how to help Meg. I mean, it's what I'd do for anybody in her situation. I pull my chair over to the high cabinet, stand on it and get the White Pages down.

Meg says, "What are you doing?"

I look up what I want and write down the address and phone number of a man I know about from the tents.

I say, "You can call this man if you want. He'll put his name on the birth certificate for you. From what I understand from Mooms when she did Robbie's birth certificate, the parents whose names are on the birth certificate are the parents, period. So if this other man signs it as the father, Edward Moffat will never be able to claim the baby.

This man will try to help out if you need anything else, too. I've only been to his place myself once myself, but he seems to be the real deal."

Meg says, "What real deal? What in the world are you talking about?" She's looking closely at my eyes, like she's trying to see if I'm stoned. But she takes the paper with the information on it and puts it in her purse.

I say, "His name's Roger Royce, but he's known as Father Roger, or just Father."

"He's a priest?"

"No, a millionaire. He's, like, Daddy's age. See, he was raised without a father himself and he and his mother had a rough way to go. So, this is kind of his retirement mission. He says if any child doesn't have a father, he'll be that child's father. I know a couple of girls who have gone to him for help."

She still looks confused, so I explain more. "Everybody was suspicious when he first started it, wondering if he was some kind of weirdo, but you never hear a bad word about him. He's got a couple dozen "kids" so far. Every Sunday, they're all invited to his farm over in the Missouri Bottoms, with or without their mothers. He has babysitters there, and he puts on a big supper for everybody. He made a playground in the yard and there's an indoor play area, too. He's amazing."

Meg kind of nods so I go on. "I wouldn't be surprised if, in a few years, half the damn people you meet around here will have the last name 'Royce.' Oh, and if you ever get married, he'll bow out if you want him to."

Meg says, "Wow. I never heard of such a thing. Thanks. I'll definitely think about it. Hey, if I go see him, will you come with me?"

I only intended to give Meg the information, not get more mixed up with her. I say, "Why don't you ask Kay? Since she's a mother herself and everything."

Meg nods. She's gazing off at nothing, like she's deep in thought.

When the evening shift girl comes in, I tell Meg, "I'll see you back at the house later. I've got some stuff to do."

She's saying something but I just turn around and shout, "Go see Mooms," then I pick up my pace.

#

After ditching Meg at Baskin-Robbins, I go over to the tents. The black tent of death is holding up well, for being set up in the woods for a whole year. I've fixed it up, a little at a time. I added on to it to make it longer, for one thing, so I can stretch my legs all the way out when I lay down and also have a little storage space. And now it rests on a wooden platform, which I even made a secret cubbyhole in, for hiding valuables.

I think I drove the poor man at the hardware store crazy with all my questions, that man with dwarfism. I could swear he goes to the back room when I come in now. But my tent is solid. Mooms never seemed to notice it was gone.

As I get near the tents, I hear "Blue Mist" by Mama's Pride playing on somebody's boom box or radio, a clue that Larry or Steve are here. Steve's really into the local bands and now Larry's always talking about some group they went to see. Larry blabbed on for day about the Bob Kuban band, that time he and Steve took an evening river cruise on the Admiral.

I was trapped at Mr. Vaughn's dinner table when Larry kept going on about it. I got tired of it, so I said, "Oh, yeah. isn't that the goofy guy who makes everybody do the hokey-pokey?" That shut him up for at least two minutes. He sulked, as I made faces and put my right arm in and shook it all about. I guess it never occurred to him that everyone might not feel like hearing about all the great big whoopie fun he has when he's out with stupid Steve.

I hear voices too, and all the sounds are coming from the largest of the half dozen tents that are scattered around here now. I count four pup tents, including mine, and two larger ones. The camp has grown enough that it's starting to get a lot of hassle by the cops. There was a complaint about it in the paper recently, too.

I stand outside the big, occupied tent and call, "Alice? Is Alice here?" That comes from *Go Ask Alice*, a book about a runaway girl. "Alice" somehow became our code word, letting the people inside a tent know that you're an insider, not a cop or other problem person. The original code word was "hoosier" but we changed it after somebody didn't know it was a code word and it started a fight.

The tent flaps open and I'm waved in. It's cozy in here, with the camp light and a candle lit for warmth. It's surprising how much heat a single candle will give off, in a closed-in space. The candle must be scented; the air is lemony, but in a chemical, furniture polish way. Jeremy holds his hand up for a high five. A hug would be too complicated in this crowded space.

I say, "Just visiting or have you moved back in?" Last I heard, Jeremy had a live-in job taking care of some old man over in Whispering Lake Apartments.

"Eh, I'm back. The old geezer shit the bed."

"You quit over that? I mean, don't you think cleaning up some dookie is kind of expected with a job like that? And, it *was* three hots and a cot, plus cash." Sometimes the kids here need a talking-to. Even if it is too late to change anything, this time.

Larry says, "It's an expression. 'Shit the bed' means he died."

I just say, "Oh." I was kind of ignoring Larry. It's the same thing I just went through with Meg, trying to stay distant from someone in a small area. At least Steve's not here.

Larry's like me, as far as the tents do. We stop by to check on everybody and also drop in just for the company sometimes. But we also both camp out here when we don't like how things are going at home. Mooms and Mr. Vaughn have both backed off on monitoring our whereabouts. I guess they're more interested in other things now. Each other, for example.

I settle in next to Jeremy. We all sit in a circle, around the UNO game that's going on at the center.

It's me, Larry, Jeremy and two girls who I don't know. The more guy-ish looking girl has her arm around the other girl. A lot of the runaways, and throwaways, are gay. I introduce myself to the girls and they nod back instead of speaking. They look tired.

Steve has dumped Larry again. Apparently, my coming in interrupted Larry's retelling of the break-up. He resumes it and his eyes water up. He says Steve found somebody else, a fellow student at SIUE. Steve said he was tired of being alone so much, with Larry living an hour away, not to mention still being in high school. Steve gave the same reasons the other time he broke up with Larry.

Jeremy, rubbing Larry's back, says, "That sucks, man. Sorry he did you like that." It's no secret that Jeremy has a crush on Larry. Larry laughed it off when we first met Jeremy, saying Jeremy was too young for him. But Jeremy doesn't seem like a little lost waif anymore. He usually manages to hold down a job and keep a roof over his head. In a way, he seems more grown-up than Larry now. Larry and Jeremy. I could see it.

Up until my recent early graduation, Larry and I had sort of kept up our "romance" at school, in that I still wore his ring. School was just easier that way. But even though we used to be best friends, and now even both live at the Gramps's house sometimes, we've been pretty distant from each other, ever since The Incident.

When Steve and Larry broke up before, I foolishly got my hopes up. I embarrassed myself so badly. I was even worse than the girl in my story, the one who forgot she was in a fake relationship, not a real one. I begged and cried and then my feelings got so overloaded that I slammed my face into the corner of Larry's dresser and got a black eye.

I still cringe when I think about it. Everybody says weed makes you too laid back, but it makes my self-control too laid back. I can't blame my crazy self-attacks completely on weed, but they *have* only happened when I was stoned.

I brought up my face slam with Larry a couple of times after that, just so I could make a big deal about how high I was, as an excuse for acting like a psycho from spaz city.

Now, I've finally got it through my head that Larry and I will never be partners. I would love to find my special person, soulmate, whatever you'd call him. But to me, that does not include sex, because the whole idea of sex makes me want to throw up. But me and my dream partner would still be each other's number one person in life, just like any other couple.

But no matter how much I wanted that person to be Larry at one time, Larry wants a partnership that includes sex, and he wants it with a male only, which Larry does not consider me to be. And that will not be changing.

Anyhow, as the saying goes, I might be crazy but I'm not stupid. If I attack myself over someone, I know that means I can't handle that person and I need to back away from them. So, I consider both Larry and Meg acquaintances now.

I'm hungry, so I decide to go home. By home, I mean to Mr. Vaughn's house, since Meg is staying at Daddy's. At Daddy's house we have supper but at Mr. Vaughn's, we have dinner. At Mr. Vaughn's, we have everything.

I stayed at Daddy's house a lot more than at Mr. Vaughn's because I felt sorry for Daddy, after both of my sisters picked Mooms. Beth and Amy stay at Mr. Vaughn's all the time. They don't move around. If I didn't stay with Daddy at least part-time, then none of us girls would have picked him, which just seems cruel. But now, Daddy has Meg.

Chapter 32

Amy went back to her fancy art school at the beginning of the school year. She said the kids at the public junior high school here are low class and rough, and that she was afraid of them. Beth goes to the private music school that's next door to Amy's art school. Now that makes sense. The typical loud, rowdy public school is too much for Beth. She's too fragile. Amy though, she's about as fragile as a hippopotamus. But Mooms let her have her own way, as usual.

Mooms doesn't have to work anymore, so she drives the little girls to their posh private schools in Clayton in the morning and picks them up in the afternoon. Mr. Vaughn lets Mooms have anything she wants. And Mooms has her old Mooms bloom back, with her regular hair and nail appointments resumed, and her exercise classes, and just an all-around return to the easier life that she was used to.

Right now, Mr. Vaughn and Mooms are having a cocktail at the table after dinner, while the newest new maid does the dishes. Mooms got rid of the last new maid. That maid was after the maid who walked out during the Christmas food fight.

Mooms claimed that the last new maid was lazy and possibly stealing her things, too. But I heard Mooms and Mr. Vaughn arguing about him supposedly looking at the replacement maid's behind, while she was bent down cleaning the baseboards. I guess that maid needed lessons from the waiters at Tony's Restaurant, ha ha.

Anyway, I think Mooms really just wanted to eliminate any possible competition. It's all really too sickening to think about. Beth is helping the newest new maid clean up from dinner now. Everybody keeps telling Beth she doesn't have to help so much around the house anymore but I guess it's just become her habit.

Amy comes in and starts begging to have an art party. Mooms appears to be half-listening, if even that. She's busy turning her new sapphire ring this way and that under the light from the chandelier, apparently fascinated by the shifting colors of its facets.

Mr. Vaughn is listening, though. He says, "What do you mean by an 'art party?' What does one do at such a party?"

When he learns that Amy just wants to have somewhere between six to twelve kids over to draw and have lunch on a Saturday afternoon, he tells her to go ahead. He tells her to ask the newest new maid if she wants to come over and help out, on overtime pay.

#

I didn't have anything else going on, so I accepted an invitation to Amy's art party. She's set me up with pencils and an easel. The other guests bring their own supplies. One showy car after another pulls into the driveway and drops off a kid, until all eight guests from Amy's school are here, setting up their easels on the back patio, six girls and two boys, plus me and Amy.

The serial maids of Mr. Vaughn all seem like they're used to working for rich people, so I'm not surprised at how nice everything is. Classical music plays softly in the background, while we wait for the art model to arrive. The maid brings around a tray of red fruit punch with flower garnishes, then she makes a couple more rounds, with different hot tidbits on the tray.

The art model comes out in a robe and gets up on the picnic table, which has been covered with white sheets in preparation for him. The kids settle into their seats. They pick up their pencils.

Okay, I admit that Amy confessed her plan to me and that's really why I came. I'd never have expected it in a million years, but sometimes I get the idea now that Amy might be on her way to becoming the sister-friend that I'd always wanted Meg to be.

The model takes off his robe. And now he's naked. Completely naked. He strikes a pose, lying on his side with his nuts and ding-dong a-dangling.

A stunned silence electrifies the air. Oh man, this is gonna be great.

Some of the kids start to point and laugh. One girl stomps off in a huff. She says, "I'm calling my mother!" which brings on a fresh roar of laughter.

I hide my face in my hands because I'm just dying. I mean, these are seventh graders, so this is just so inappropriate it's hysterical.

Amy's sitting there with her new wine-colored beret on. It's been carefully arranged at a jaunty angle atop her blonde curls, as has the long paisley scarf tossed around her neck and over one shoulder in a bon vivant fashion. She's quite seriously drawing. She is showing off to her little friends about how grown up and sophisticated she is. Of course, she won't admit it but that may have been the whole point of this in the first place. It's adorable.

I look at the naked man, suddenly really noticing him. Whoa! Lying on the table naked is no other than Edward Moffat.

Oh, my fucking stars. I run inside to get my camera, tripping on the stairs in my haste. I make it back just in time to snap a couple of well-focused, well-centered photos, right before Mr. Vaughn rushes out and throws a blanket over Edward.

Mr. Vaughn says, "You do realize, don't you, that exposing yourself to children is a felony?"

"What the hell? I was sent here by the employment agency. What are you talking about, old man? Fuck off."

Mooms hears him speaking to Mr. Vaughn like that. She dashes over to the side of the house, comes back with the garden hose, and starts spraying Edward down. Edward makes a startled sound like "wonk!" It just slays me. Then he runs for his car, cursing and holding the blanket around his waist, stumbling on it as he runs. Mooms trains the hose on him and continues watering him until he's inside his car.

My ribs ache from laughing and I can't catch my breath.

A couple of girls shriek about what a nasty and weird pervert Edward is. The two boys are cracking jokes and cracking up. Miss Priss Amy continues to draw. She's drawing the empty picnic table now, cool as a cucumber in Paris. No doubt, she thinks herself an extremely sophisticated seventh grader.

The new maid, an older woman selected by Mooms this time, seems unfazed, like she's so used to seeing dinguses, children and hosings all together that it pretty much bores her, if she notices it at all. She simply rings a little crystal bell to politely get the kids' attention, and calls them to come have lunch.

While we fill our plates, buffet style, with fancy sandwiches and chips in the kitchen, Mooms and the maid slap together a large still life that runs the length of the dining room table, with somewhat random items they snatch up from around the house: houseplants in their pots, a collection of owl figurines, a decorative bird cage and some whole fruits from the kitchen.

Mooms breezes into the kitchen. She says, "Change of plans, dears. When you're through with your lunch, feel free to take a seat at the dining room table and draw what you see from your vantage point. And don't forget, there will be prizes."

And that's the end of it. Mr. Vaughn doesn't say anything else about it. Amy doesn't get in trouble, no parents call, nothing. Oh, my glob. I'd have been murderized for pulling a stunt like that.

I accidentally overhear Mooms and Mr. Vaughn talking about it later. They're on the living room couch and I'm in the hallway. He says Amy is obviously having a hard time adjusting so they should just be patient and try to ignore any acting out. I hear laughing then, and I catch on that Mooms recognized Edward Moffat, before she turned the hose on him.

After I get my film developed at the tiny drive-up Kodak booth, I go ahead and have the best naked photo of Edward blown up, into notebook paper sized posters. When I get those back in the mail, I drive Mooms's car all over town, late one night after everybody goes to bed, taping all 300 posters up on telephone poles, in telephone booths, on the windows of businesses and everything. I'm smoking a doobie, with K-SHE 95 rock radio blasting as I go. It's like a party for one, on wheels.

Chapter 33

As time goes on and everybody else has got school or work to go to, I start to feel lost. All I've got, besides my writing, is my part-time job at Baskin-Robbins. And hell, they even hire fourteen-year -olds there. It's embarrassing. And it's become painfully obvious that my so-called parents don't even notice. Back before everything fell apart, my parents would talk about our college funds and stuff like that but now neither of them has said a word to me about college.

It dawns on me that if I'm ever going to get anywhere, I'll have to figure it out myself. It hurts my feelings, especially since Mooms drives the little girls to and from their private schools every day.

So, I borrow Mooms's car between her morning drop off time and afternoon pick up time for the girls. I take a drive over to Florissant Valley Community College.

The lady behind the desk says it's too late to enroll in the spring semester since it's already started, which I already know. But, she says, it's a good time to get everything all filled out for the summer session. She gives me a catalog and some paperwork to take home.

I'm pretty proud of taking this step to Invest in My Future, as the catalog cover says. I reward myself by lighting a joint on the way home.

And then there are lights and sirens behind me.

#

I call Mooms, but for some reason Daddy, Meg, Kay and little Robbie are the ones who come to pick me up from the police station. The female police officer at the station looks like a beagle and I'm not just saying that because I'm mad about her putting in her two cents, either. Even though, as far as I know, the desk cop sharing her many personal opinions about your arrest situation is not a part of the legal process. She has sad brown eyes with darkened skin under them and long ponytails that hang down on the sides of her head, just like the ears on Robbie's Fischer-Price pull-along beagle on wheels toy.

Officer Beagle keeps saying things, in a stern voice like she's teaching me a lesson. She says, "You're lucky you're not eighteen yet. Dern tooting you are." And "Boy, you cut it close, missy. You just barely missed this being on your permanent record. You'da been toast!" And, later, "What a way that woulda been to start your adult life. Woo-wee!" Other people stand around nodding and agreeing.

Kay drops me, Meg and Daddy off at Mooms's car, then drives away in her car, with little Robbie waving bye-bye from his car seat.

Daddy gets behind the wheel. Meg gets right into the front seat of Moom's car, which pisses me off. Meg has always just assumed the front seat is for her. She's always gotten away with it, too. Whenever I drive Amy and Beth anywhere, I make them take turns riding shotgun. Who asked 106 month pregnant Meg to come anyway?

But I try to be friendly anyway, continuing the joking around that Kay and I were doing, making fun of Officer Beagle. I mean, I already thanked everyone for coming and apologized for the inconvenience, and Daddy and Kay said not to worry about it. And really, hell with them anyway. I babysit for them for free all the time and they ruined my childhood, so who really cares if they like coming to pick me up at the police station or not.

But Meg just has to butt in. In full Mooms Junior mode, she says, "The beagle lady is hardly the point. And I sure hope you do get the point."

Oh, my glob. After everything this bitch has put our whole family through, she thinks she's going to correct me? I don't think so. Reverting into childhood mode, as weirdly happens so often around either of my parents, I say, "Shut up, fatty."

I thought that was pretty mild, especially when Meg started it in the first place, but Meg starts to cry.

Daddy snaps, practically growls, "Are you happy now?"

The tone of his voice is so harsh it brings tears to my eyes. Yes, Meg was out of line but gosh, it wasn't *that* big of a deal. And after all, she is 150 months pregnant and everything.

It takes me a minute to realize that he's yelling at me, not Meg. Oh, this shit again. I mean, is it really too much to expect things to be globdamn fair once in a while? And when things aren't fair, which is always, why am I always on the losing end of it?

Not to mention that I was nice enough to stay at Daddy's crappy poor person's house all those months, just so he wouldn't feel abandoned by all of his daughters, even though he damn well deserved to be. And this is what I get? Mooching Meg finally shows up and he snarls at me like a pit bull.

I'm pissed. I've just had it. I say to him, "I don't know, are *you* happy now, you big fat turd?"

He kicks me out of the car. Kicks me out! He pulls the car over to the side of the road, points at me, then points at the side of the road, and says, "Out." Unbelievable.

As they drive away, I give them the old two-fisted middle fingers, just in case they're looking. I give the double flip-offs some motion, big arm circles, little arm circles, like they made us do in PE class ha. I have the shittiest family in the entire world, the shittiest in all of recorded history.

Then the car is out of sight. I feel the urge to lay down and slam my forehead onto the road, or maybe zip my own dumb face up in my coat.

But I just keep stomping along the side of the road, towards home. Eventually, I just walk. A long walk alone in the cold will clear your mind at a very deep level.

I take the two joints out of my bra, still surprised that the cops didn't search me. I flick them into the icy mud water in the roadside ditch. I'm done with weed.

Chapter 34

Meg gave birth to twins, a boy and a girl. Jesus penis guacamole! As if one baby isn't enough for a girl with no husband, no education, no job and no home of her own. All things considered, I'm not sure what there is to celebrate here, but I guess celebrating is just the done thing.

I haven't seen Meg or Daddy since I got kicked out of the car, but Mooms says to just go in there and be polite and friendly, and act like nothing happened. I'm pretty sure Mooms has already talked to Meg and Daddy about it, so I take her advice, even though Daddy and Meg both completely ignored my birthday.

When Mooms and I get to the hospital, everybody else is already there. Daddy, my sisters, Sally Gardiner, and even Kay, which makes Mooms mad, though she doesn't let on about that to anybody but me. I guess she changed her mind on that not owning other people thing. She makes me call Mr. Vaughn from the pay phone in the hospital lobby and tell him to come right away. I guess Mooms thinks his presence will even some weird score in some weird way.

The babies are, like, half the size little Robbie was when we first got him. They're both in incubators, so we can only look at them through the big plate glass window of the hospital nursery. It reminds me of the big window at Shakey's pizza parlor. I'm halfway waiting for someone to toss a baby up in the air and twirl it like they do the pizza dough at Shakey's.

Mooms interrupts my thoughts. She's carrying on about how precious the babies are. They're really not, though. I mean, I'm not going say anything if no one else brings it up first, but Meg's babies kind of look like monkeys.

When Mr. Vaughn gets here, all four of the cheating bastards act awkwardly cheerful and polite. They suck the air out of the room with their corrupt hypocrisy. I wish the homewreckers, Kay and Mr. Vaughn, would just go home. Preferably together, leaving Mooms and Daddy to correct their corruptness as much as possible, by getting back together. I doubt I'd forgive them even then, but it's the least they could do.

Roger Royce, Father Roger, comes in. He kisses Meg on the forehead and shakes hands all around, all jolly and everything. He's grown a bushy white beard since the other time I saw him. When he starts handing out cigars from a red bag, real cigars for the men and bubblegum cigars for the ladies, he looks like Santa Claus.

Father Roger signs the birth certificates. Meg says she decided to give the babies the March last name, though. She seems to agree with me that there are so many little Royces in town now, that the name might draw more attention than just sticking with March anyway. She says all she wants is for her children to be permanently out of the reach of Edward Moffat.

I wonder what she thinks of Edward posing naked at the art party and the naked posters all over town. Plus, Mooms turning the hose on him. Damn, that still kills me. It may be the funniest thing I've ever seen. I guess this isn't the time to bring it up though. I don't really feel like talking to Meg, anyway.

I'm relieved when Larry shows up. I can probably get a ride home with him before long. Everyone else looks good and settled in.

Meg has named her babies Donald and Daisy. Everyone acts like it's just precious that Meg named her children after cartoons. What the hell. Oh well, I guess it's better than Mickey and Minnie. Or Rocky and Bullwinkle.

#

On the ride home from the hospital, Larry tells me I should put an ad in the personals section of the newspaper.

I say, "Me? What the hell for?"

"To meet a special someone, silly."

Huh. I never thought of that before. I say, "Hmm. But I thought personals ads were only for creepy old alkies and other undesirables. Oh, wait. Is that what you're saying, that I'm an undesirable?" I bug my eyes out, just acting goofy.

He laughs. "Oh stop. Yeah, the personals ads don't have a real good reputation, that's true. But it's really just all about whoever happens to answer your ad. The personals can be very good for trying to find someone off the beaten path. Let's face it, there are far, far, far more mainstream heterosexual people around than any other type of person, like twenty or thirty to one, at least. The rest of us, we have to try harder. And there's nothing to lose, it's completely anonymous. Well, except for people you actually meet up with, obviously. That wouldn't be completely anonymous. You could give them a fake name though, if you wanted." He lights a joint, takes a toke, then holds it out to me.

I say, "No thanks."

"No thanks? Are you sick or something?"

"Nah, I quit. I don't smoke weed anymore."

He says, "Very funny."

"I mean it. I don't."

He takes another couple tokes, then puts it out in the ashtray. "Okay, if you say so. More for me. Anyhow, the personals. I thought of you because what you're looking for seems pretty rare. You'll probably want to expand your search. If you aren't just pulling my leg in the first place, about your straight, no-sex partnership thing."

"I wish I was pulling your leg. I might have to go to Mars to find my special someone."

We're home now, meaning at Mr. Vaughn's, Mooms's and Larry's house. Larry says, "Come up to my room and hang out for a while."

I think it over for a minute. I really am over hoping Larry will ever be my partner in life. Plus, I don't get high anymore, so my self-control is much better. Not to mention he's, like, the best friend I've ever had. I seriously miss him. Yeah, I can be friends with him now, without flipping out again. I say, "Okay. Let me stop by my bedroom and get your ring. I've been meaning to give it back to you." I'm don't go to school anymore, so there's no reason to wear it.

I go up to his room, with his ring. I'm thinking over what he said about the personals ads. I hand the ring back to him. I say, "Did you say that you use the personals ads yourself?"

"I did for a while. I met a couple of cool people and a couple of real weirdos."

"Hmm. Which did you like best? The weirdos, right?"

"Uh, yeah. Obviously." I've missed our way of joking around.

"Haha. So, you quit using the ads, then? How come?" Being here makes me want to smoke some weed, it makes the old habit want to kick in. I've been using a pamphlet I sent away for, on how to kick the habit. Changing your environment was at the top of the list.

I hadn't realized how much I got used to leaning on weed to cope, even with little things.

Like, the other day, I took Beth to the doctor for Mooms. Beth gets sick a lot. Anyway, the traffic light stayed stuck on red for a long time and I actually burst into tears over it. Poor Beth looked scared because I am not the type of person who cries, like, hardly ever.

I pull the pack of Fruit Stripe gum out of my pocket and chew on a piece, as the pamphlet says you should do when you get a craving. I offer a piece to Larry, who snatches it right up.

He says, "I got the munchies."

"What the hell. It's gum. You chew it. You don't eat it."

"Shush. Oh, about the personals ads. I go over to Faces now, in East St. Louis. It's a new gay bar. Have you heard of it?"

"I remember hearing a few things, at school. Someone said they hardly card anybody or something like that. But East St. Louis? Oh, my glob. I hope you don't get a flat tire over there or anything."

"That wouldn't be as dangerous for a black dude as it would be for you, Joseph, but I get what you're saying. Anyway, here, I've been wanting to give this to you. It's the lonely-hearts ads. This one's out of date but it's got the number to call and the pricing. And you can look at the other ads too. You never know."

"Wow. Maybe I will. Thanks for thinking of me." I try to take the newspaper page but Larry yanks it away. He says, "It'll cost you another piece of gum."

"Did you swallow the piece I already gave you? Open your mouth." There's no gum in his mouth anymore. But he keeps yanking the newspaper page away until I give him two more sticks of gum. The more he withholds the page, the more I feel like I want it.

I forgot to ask him about Jeremy. But I guess it's obvious, really. For whatever reason or no reason at all, Larry just isn't into Jeremy.

Chapter 35

I had copies made of my short story collection and mailed them to four small presses that seemed like likely prospects.

And I've just finished writing out my "lonely hearts" ad for, like, the twentieth time. Now I just have to work up the nerve to drive down to the newspaper office and place the ad. I'm so nervous, my hands are shaking. And here I haven't even left the house yet. This latest version says:

"Young WF seeks male soulmate who does not want sex, for LTR. Absolutely no sex, ever. Under age 23 preferred."

I have second thoughts again now. I'm wondering if "soulmate" sounds too corny and if saying the "no sex" thing twice comes across as kind of crazy.

Mooms starts talking to me and I about jump out of my skin. I can't get used to this intercom system. Larry must have turned it off in his bedroom because I don't remember ever hearing it there. Mooms asks me to go pick Beth up at school and take her to the doctor. The poor kid's sick again. I'm kind of annoyed and kind of relieved to put my personal ad aside for now. It's nerve-wracking, that's for sure.

When I get Beth to the doctor, they make me stay in the waiting room, which makes me mad because Beth gets scared easily. She won't like being in the exam room by herself. But I don't feel sure enough of myself to argue, in a medical setting. Heck, I don't even know if you can argue. It always seems more like they tell you what to do and that's that.

I'm reading an old *Readers' Digest* when the doctor comes back out, alone. He says he wants to keep Beth for some tests. He wants to admit her to the hospital. He won't tell me what kind of tests, either. I don't like the sound of this at all.

Mooms will be picking Amy up at school right now so I stay in the waiting room reading *Reader's Digests* for another hour, until Mooms should be home. The nurse has just blown me off, and I don't know what to do about it. When it's past the time that Mooms should be home, I go up to the desk and ask to use the phone. But the receptionist says they've already spoken to Mooms and that I should just go on home.

Weirdly, what sticks in my mind and nags at me is that we never got Beth into the teen therapy group that her psychiatrist advised us to do. I don't know why my brain thinks that's related to Beth being hospitalized for testing for what is obviously a physical problem. I guess it's just general guilt, like proof that we didn't take good care of Beth.

I make a mental note to push Mooms to get that started, as soon as Beth comes home.

#

Beth never comes home again. She was diagnosed with leukemia in the hospital and remained hospitalized until her death, three weeks later.

It still just about knocks the wind out of me all over again, every time I think about it. It's so unbelievably final, so hard. The sweetest girl in the world, dead at only sixteen.

The night Beth died, Amy woke up screaming from bad dreams. Larry and I moved Amy's bed into my room.

I've stopped listening to the radio, at home and in the car. Too many sad songs catch me off guard, especially since Beth was so into music herself. "Seasons in the Sun." "Starry, Starry Night. "Don't Fear the Reaper." "Only the Good Die Young."

Somehow, the bouncy, upbeat rhythm of that last one is the worst. Cutting out random songs isn't nearly enough, though. You never know what will hit you hard, or when. Just before dawn one morning, I woke to a lone bird singing outside my window. I cried until my stomach ached, fist pressed against my mouth so as not to wake Amy.

Another time, I was at Schnuck's, picking up some bread and eggs and a few other things from Mooms's grocery list. In the canned vegetable aisle,

I saw a girl who looked like Beth from behind, tall and thin, with long, dark hair in a low ponytail like Beth often wore. I started after her, heart pounding. For a crazed, gorgeous minute, I thought it was Beth.

Things will never be the same. From now on, life for me will be sharply divided into Before Beth Died and After Beth Died. Mooms's lesson about getting used to death, taking turns in the little black tent, it didn't make any difference.

Chapter 36

Meg's babies, along with Beth's short illness and passing, bring us all together more as a family, in our re-configured way. Help was simply needed from one house to the other, for more important things than holding on to grievances. We worked together to do whatever needed to be done, and then things just kind of gelled that way. We got over the Christmas food fight.

Mooms and I are alone in the living room after dinner and I sort of accidentally blurt out a question. I say, "Why did you tell us Daddy was dead?"

She does that teeth clenching, jaw tightening thing, like she's getting mad. I don't care, though. I mean, that's not right, telling us our father was dead when he wasn't.

She says, "Okay, fine. I lied. I decided I was not going to forgive your father for what he put us through after all, and I wanted to be with Vince. And I wanted to do that without walking around with a big "A" for adultress on my chest, as far as my children were concerned. Happy now, Jo?"

There was no apology. "Yes, *Mooms*," I say her name back in the same tone, to see how she likes it. "I'm quite sure I'm the one in the wrong here, not you. Isn't that the way it always goes, no matter what?"

She kinda wilts and I feel pretty great for a minute. But then she shrieks, "I wish your father *had* died, instead of Beth." Then she starts sobbing into a dishtowel and I feel just terrible.

But after another minute, it dawns on me that she's doing it again, that thing where she starts shrieking and playing the victim. I get pissed off all over again. She should apologize for what she did.

But she keeps mixing it up with Beth's death, which doesn't have a damn thing to do with it. I stomp next door to my garret, to let her know I'm not buying what she's selling. The maid was making her special pork chop dish over there, too and I missed out because of Mooms.

Oh, my glob, the maid's pork chops are heavenly. She makes them all garlicky, stuffed with a cornbread mixture and almost fried or something, then topped with mushroom gravy.

#

The next day, I sneak back over there to see if there are any pork chops left. I'm in luck. There's one left. I eat it cold because I'm too greedy to take the time to heat it up first.

Mooms and Kay have coordinated taking turns watching the twins so Meg can take a summer course at Miss Hickey's Secretarial School. Mooms usually watches little Robbie too, when it's her turn to babysit. Amy and I fill in as needed.

Mooms has strapped the babies into their baby seats and we're each feeding one of them from tiny jars of baby food, while Robbie pushes his Tonka truck around the living room. Everyone but me has started calling him "Uncle Robbie," because, well, that's what he is. Now he calls himself that, "Ukka Wobbie" and it's cute. The whole thing is still corrupt, though, Daddy's kid only being a couple years older than his grandkids, and all of them illegitimate, JPG. (Jesus penis guacamole). The ducklings are cute now, too. That's what we've all started calling them. I mean, what else would you call them when their names are Donald and Daisy. They've pudged up and lost that simian look, which no doubt came from the Moffat genes in the first place.

Robbie lives with Daddy and Kay now. I say to Mooms, "So, are you going to try to get Robbie back in the divorce?"

She looks startled. She says, "Are you kidding? Listen, no woman in her forties who's already raised four kids wants to start all over again. Unless she's got a hole in her damn head."

That cracks me up but it also surprises me, how definite her answer is. I say, "Kay's in her forties too, isn't she?"

"Kay hasn't already raised four kids. And you know, then there's that hole in the head thing."

"Haha! But I thought you liked Kay again now."

Mooms sighs like I'm just endlessly annoying, but she does it in a jokey way this time. She says, "Well kid, 'like' covers a lot of ground. In fact, technically you could consider 'like' to be anything between love and hate, you know?"

"No. I mean, okay. I guess."

Daisy starts crying and gnawing on her little fist, letting me know that I've paused entirely too long in bringing those spoonfuls of pureed pears to her itty-bitty precious rosebud mouth. I get back to work, earning a happy squeal.

Little Robbie has decided to try to climb the curtains. Mooms runs after him and our little chat is over.

Most surprising of all is that Aunt March has joined in on this one big happy family bit. She's started coming to Daddy's house (actually, her house) on Sundays.

Come to find out, Aunt March is crazy about babies. And there are three of them at Daddy's now, so she loves to go over there. She always brings toys and baby clothes, and a dessert for us all. She brings her little dog Mop too, who enjoys wild chases through the house with Party. (Party hangs out at both homes and has been known to get himself two dinners, by mewling as if he's starving, at both places). Party especially likes to attack the colorful bows on Mop's head. I don't know who's giving Mop his baths and new weekly bows and all the rest, now that it's not me or Amy. I don't bring it up because Aunt March might ask me to start doing it again.

After Aunt March is through with her weekly visit at Daddy's, they all come over to Mr. Vaughn's, where Mooms and Kay have prepared a big Sunday dinner. Meg and I think Aunt March goes to Daddy's first so she can play with the babies with less competition.

Mooms and Daddy and their new partners, all interacting with each other beyond what's strictly necessary, seemed highly corrupt to me at first. It still does, to some extent, and probably always will.

But we do all share family in common, and Mooms and Kay were already used to working together for us all, anyway. And I guess we've also just caught on that, even with our various grudges and disapprovals, it's still a lot nicer to have friendly family next door than it is to retreat and glower.

Mooms seems to almost like Aunt March now. For example, Mooms shows sympathy for her. Mooms has said more than once that it was a crying shame Aunt March never got to have any children of her own, when she's so good with the little ones. Mooms even called Aunt March's house to check on her once, when Aunt March didn't show up for dinner one Sunday. Aunt March seemed tickled pink to be called and rushed right over. Apparently, she got rid of her answering service after she no longer had "ownership" of Amy. Meg thinks Aunt March stayed home that Sunday just to see if she'd be missed.

It's been three months since we lost Beth and we're moving on, since there doesn't seem to be any choice. For a while you'd hear a lot of "Oh, Beth would have wanted you to" take this class, go on that date or just enjoy a quick family trip to pick up McDonald's. We assured each other that us getting on with our plans was Beth's greatest wish. It was like we wanted reassurance that it was all right to progress in our lives, when Beth could not.

Chapter 37

I borrow Mooms's car and drive to the
newspaper office to check my lonely-hearts box. I
find three envelopes in it, which I snatch up, then
hurry out of there before anyone recognizes me.
Though I could always just tell them I was checking
my still-married parents' lonely-hearts messages for
them. Ha! Or as Meg and I used to say, "Ha-mit!"
Which rhymes with vomit and means something is
funny and gross at the same time.

I pull in at Steak 'n Shake and wait for the girl to
skate up to the car and take my order then skate
away again, before I open one of the envelopes. I
recognize the waitress, or skate-ress or whatever the
hell she is, from school. I wouldn't have expected
her in this job. She always seemed super shy. I have
to talk my nerves down before I read these letters.
Times like this are when I really, really miss weed.

But I assure myself that there is nothing to be
anxious about. These are just inanimate objects,
only letters, right? And I don't even have to answer
them if I don't want to. That works, a little.

The first letter is from an eighty-six-year-old
woman who wants a live-in companion and helper.

What a globdamn let down, more proof of how abnormal and weird I am. People don't even understand what I'm asking for. The only times I've heard my type of person mentioned were very uncomplimentary. I mean, "frigid" is never a compliment, and that's only part of it.

I guess I was just born at the wrong time, in the middle of the sexual revolution, where apparently, everyone is extremely eager to pull down their pants at the first opportunity and get all gloppy down there together. Ew. It probably smells. They probably leave snail trails all over the furniture. Ewww!

Just what I don't want to think about when I'm getting ready to eat. This is one way the Victorian times would have been better, though. I mean, they even covered up their piano's legs, for modesty purposes. Yeah, keep that mess to yourself. I shred the letter and envelope into teeny-tiny pieces.

I wait for the waitress to hook the tray with my burger, fries and soda onto my car door, then skate away again. I don't give any sign that I know who she is. It would just come across weird since she probably doesn't know who I am. I couldn't see myself working here and wearing that dumb little skirt, but maybe I should try somewhere else that involves tips. I hear waitresses make a lot more than the $3.00 an hour I get at Baskin-Robbins, which is the $2.90 minimum wage, plus my dime an hour raise that I'm embarrassed to admit being a little bit proud of. I heard Sambo's is hiring. It's kind of a dump but maybe they'd let me wear pants there, since they seem to have a hard time keeping any employees at all, from what I heard. I'm not wearing a globdamn skirt or dress, even if I'd make twenty bucks an hour. Well, maybe then. Okay, enough stalling.

The second letter is from someone named Pussy Licker, who promises to ream me out, which will make me change my mind about being an ice queen. He can't give me his phone number, he writes, because his domineering bitch of a wife might answer the phone. But he says to let him know when and where to meet me, so we can get started. He includes a box number of his own. P.S. he adds, if you're a blubbo, don't bother.

What a reptile. I tear the letter up. I can't imagine that anyone in the entire would answer a message like that. Does he really expect an answer?

I was stupid to get my hopes up in the first place. Larry had the nerve to tell me I might change my mind about what I want when I'm older. I told him he might change his mind about what he wants when he's older too, then. That shut him up. I'm just an odd duck, that's all there is to it. Well, to be honest, I think I'm normal and everyone else is weird. But that doesn't help me.

I wait until I finish eating to open the third letter. It says:

Hi there,

I'm looking for the same thing you are. I've never been into sex, either. But I would still love to find a partner to share my life with. I am over the

age range you listed though. I'm 30 years old.
Please call if interested anyhow, phone number
below.

Regards,

Fred

Wow. I feel almost paralyzed for a minute, while
the words sink in. Is it possible? Could this really,
possibly, maybe, be my future soulmate, my future
husband?

I feel like hopping out of the car and jumping up
and down with joy. After my dinner tray is cleared
away, I do get out of the car, but only to put the
pieces of the other two letters in the trash can. I
slide Fred's letter back into its envelope, fold it
neatly in thirds, and place it inside my bra, next to
my heart. I'll definitely answer Fred but I need time
to work up the nerve first. Or maybe time to calm
my nerves down first.

I nearly run a red light on the way home.

Chapter 38

Amy and I are at Daddy's, watching the twins and Robbie. Meg's gone out on a date with John Brooke, who is not exactly her boyfriend yet since this is only their fourth date, but he actually seems nice. He is also poor, according to Meg, who weirdly almost brags about it. She seems to think she is doing some kind of brave and selfless volunteer work by dating a guy who's not rich. He's thirty years old, the same age as Fred, and teaches in the Ritenour school district, a few miles away.

I don't understand Meg's definition of "rich" anyway, since slimeball Edward Moffat didn't even have a job and lived off his parents. John Brooke has a college degree and a career and owns a house.

Daddy and Kay are going out on a date, too. If I'd known it was to celebrate my parents' divorce being finalized, I would have told them to shove their date where the sun don't shine.

But by the time I find out, they're practically walking out the door, and Kay is so pitifully glowing with happiness I don't have the heart to spoil it. Even if it is really to celebrate the success of the homewrecking venture that helped destroy my family.

Kay wears a strange two-piece outfit with a design of large purple, green and orange triangles and hilariously huge, billowing bottoms, which she proudly tells us are her "palazzo pants." As if her gigantic pants aren't hysterical enough, she wears a huge, curly orange wig. It's like she's trying balance out the huge bottom with an equally huge head.

It's lucky for her that she has big boobs. Men just seem to go crazy over big boobs. To men, I'm sure big boobs more than make up for tragic fashion sense. Kay, the poor mammal, is all a-twitter. She seems to think Bonanza is a fancy steakhouse. I thought they'd at least go somewhere like the Flaming Pit or Steak and Ale. But I guess they just don't have a dime to spare. I guess they're just living on Kay's bartending and Avon money, along with whatever Aunt March gives them. Daddy doesn't have a job. I don't know if he's even looking for one. He doesn't say anything about it. The whole thing reminds me of the song that plays on the country music station Kay listens to, called "Third Rate Romance." I hum it under my breath. They can take that any way they want to.

The whole thing is gross, obviously. Mooms won the homewrecking contest anyway. I mean if I had to pick a winner. Daddy started it, but Mooms sure had the last laugh in that game. When Mr. Vaughn takes Mooms out to dinner, it is not to cheap-ass Bonanza.

After the babies have been put to bed, Amy and I get into the Kool-Aid and popcorn Kay fixed for us. I get the big jug of vodka from under the sink and add a splash to each glass, then add tap water to the vodka bottle to conceal our crime, while Amy giggles.

I get into Daddy's old albums and put on the one with "Raindrops Keep Falling on my Head." My parents used to play that all the time when they'd have company over. Amy and I settle in to chat, which we hardly ever do, which I guess is strange when we've shared a bedroom for the past few months.

She says she thinks she's ready to move back to her own bedroom now. It seems like she's trying to not hurt my feelings or something. It's sweet but that kind of concern seems un-Amy-like. But I have to remember she's still a kid and has probably just grown up a little. I assure her that I understand. We decide we'll move her bed back tomorrow.

She does seem more grown up. I decide to confide in her. I say, "Oh, I forgot to tell you. I have a date tomorrow night."

She says, "Really? Who with?"

The surprise in her voice stings. Is it really that shocking that someone would want to take me out? Then again, Fred hasn't met me yet. Maybe he won't want to go out with me, after he does. I say, "His name is Fred. You don't know him."

"How did you meet him?"

Ugh. I didn't think of the line of questioning my announcement would bring about. I take a sip of Kool-Aid with vodka and grab a handful of popcorn, while I think of how to get around her question.

"Eh, nevermind. I'll tell you more if it goes well. So, what about you? What have you been up to lately?"

Amy starts talking about herself and I breathe easier. She says, "I really like the people around the neighborhood so I think I'll go back to public school again in the fall. The people at the art school, I don't know, they get on my nerves. A lot of them are spoiled and stuck-up. I'm not as good at art as I thought I was, anyway. Not compared to people who go to a school for art."

"Hmm. Well, the art school kids are from richer families, overall. But that doesn't mean much either way, I don't think. I mean, there will be people you like and people you don't, either way. As far as the artwork, hell, you've got plenty of time to improve, if that's still your thing. But, just a thought here, it might be better to just stay put. When you switch back and forth, you don't have time to get in solid with any friend group, and that makes that school a less friendly place." If anybody knows the difference between school being a friendly place or not, it's me.

She nods, and seems to be considering what I'm saying. The old Amy would be more likely to just start arguing, no matter what you tried to tell her.

Then she tells me about some fun stuff she's done with the neighborhood kids, like go down into the drainage sewer and walk through big underground tunnels all over Black Jack.

I'm about to blurt out my fears that a storm might pop up and drown them all or that an old wino pervert might be hiding out down there, and that no one would ever know what happened to her.

But by then, she's already on to talking about the old farmer who died and how they hang out in his old farmhouse, and about the old dirty post cards they found there, one with a topless girl who had a donkey's thing in her mouth. I open my mouth to start lecturing her about how dangerous both of these adventures are, but what comes out of my mouth is, "Can I come?"

Chapter 39

Mooms and Mr. Vaughn are getting married next week in Las Vegas. Mooms tells us this during dinner. The fabulous fried lobster ravioli that the maid fixed makes this news easier to take. I mean, I know dinner and marriage are on two completely different levels, but JPG, the ravioli's fantastic.

Mooms informs us that St. Louis is known for its fried ravioli, which I already know. But the lobster filling in these makes it way beyond any fried ravioli anywhere, and the dipping sauce isn't the usual tomato sauce but something pink and garlicky. This maid can cook. I hope she sticks around. Maybe Mr. Vaughn won't run her off by looking at her butt, since she's old.

Mooms says, "What's so funny?"

I didn't realize my face showed my thought about the maid's butt. I didn't think it would be a good idea to share that with Mooms so I just say, "Nothing," and keep eating until she stops looking at me.

Mooms didn't make one of her big announcements about her upcoming marriage, she just kinda slipped the news in. She says she knows we kids are busy and they don't want to disrupt our schedules, then she asks Amy what time she needs a ride to the Aloha roller rink tonight, like the wedding topic is already over with. Meg and I would have gotten twenty questions about going to the roller rink and then we'd have to go together.

I already knew Mooms and Mr. Vaughn planned to get married as soon as Mooms and Daddy's divorce was final. And I'd dreaded the thought of having to sit there smiling, while one of my parents married someone else, especially someone who was involved in breaking my parents up in the first place.

So, I'm real happy to dodge all that. And Mooms is right, we do all have the summer pretty booked up. Amy has the usual upcoming scheduled activities and birthday parties and stuff that a non-poor fourteen-year-old girl would have on her calendar. Meg has her twins, her summer course and her new guy. And I have my summer classes and part-time job. Larry has graduated from high school and is taking summer classes at the junior college too, before he goes to stay in the dorms at St. Louis University in the fall.

That's a damn expensive school and my grades were better than his, so it's another burn, on top of the original burn of nobody saying anything at all about my post-high school plans.

I mean, as far as St. Louis U, that might just be because the Gramps is old and doesn't think girls need an expensive education. He probably thinks girls will just become housewives anyway. And he does think I'm a girl.

Between bites of the heavenly lobster ravioli, I just say it. "How come nobody ever said anything about me going to college?"

Mooms does that jaw clench thing, along with the raised eyebrows thing. She says, "Well. Congratulations to you too, Miss Josephine."

"Oh, sorry. Congratulations." With effort, I make the ends of my big mouth go up so it looks like I'm smiling. She is the one who slipped her news in real quick, then changed the subject, though, like she didn't want to talk about it.

Larry and Amy congratulate the cheaters, too.

After a while, Mooms clears her throat in a way that makes everyone go quiet. Oh no. It's one of her announcements.

But what she says is, "Jo. I owe you a big apology, hon. There was so much going on and, well, you just seem so grown up and self-sufficient. I did let your post high school plans slip through the cracks. I'm sorry."

Wow. I feel like I'd been stuck in one of the gloomy overcast days there are so many of around here, and then the sun just broke through the clouds, unexpectedly. That's corny but I do suddenly feel super great. Mooms doesn't usually apologize so I just got something rare. I guess I'd just thought, again, that she didn't like me.

But really, who knows why some kids get more attention than others in a family. Maybe the parents just think some of their kids need more attention. I think it's always been pretty clear that Meg and Beth got more attention than me and Amy. But me and Amy are also stronger, if you ask me. I notice that everyone is looking at me. I say, "Oh. That's okay. I understand, Mooms."

She says, "Let's go buy that *What Color is Your Parachute* book. Let's start there, to see what direction you should take.

"I already know. I want to major in Creative Writing."

Mr. Vaughn clears his throat. After another bite of ravioli, he says, "I understand that you want to follow your dreams. But the arts are very iffy, as far as making a living. Most often, people with those degrees end up teaching or in another relatively low-paying field. I simply don't see the return on an expensive degree there."

He say, "So, I'll offer you the same deal I offered Larry. If you study for the type of degree that is most likely to pay off, say, a business degree, I will pay for it, including the dorm fees, at whatever university you can get in at. But if you really want to stick with the arts, I will pay for a public college only, and you can live at home."

"You mean, you'll pay my tuition?"

"I will."

Mooms says, "Vince, honey, she really hasn't gotten as much as the others. How about a little allowance for her too, instead of that job? And a secondhand car? A second car would help me out too, with all the driving around we need."

Mr. Vaughn doesn't answer for a while. Then he says, "All right, but I want to check out the car before you buy it. Jo, I agree you've been overlooked, and I apologize for that, too."

I'm embarrassed at all this unexpected attention. Just trying to be funny, I say, "Gee thanks, Daddio." But Mr. Vaughn smiles so big in response that I feel my face heat up.

Chapter 40

I meet Fred at Burger Chef. I arrive early, order my meal and pay for it. This way, I won't feel weird spending his money, if it turns out I don't like him. I've followed Meg's instructions on everything. I'm at Burger Chef's nifty little burger toppings bar, nervous, but just trying to focus on putting tomato and onion slices on my delicious burger. I ordered my meal to go, in case a quick getaway is called for.

Fred's a little early himself. I spot him right away since it's 7 p.m. on a Tuesday night and the place is nearly empty. He wears a plain black t-shirt, Levis and aviator sunglasses, like he said he'd be wearing. I'm not wearing the cut off jean overalls with a red t-shirt underneath that I said I'd be wearing. I don't want him to be able to recognize me. Meg's said I should be able to give him the slip if he looked creepy.

He looks like a normal person though, which is a huge relief. He has kind of a medium build, brown hair and a mustache. He looks too old for me but I already knew that we oddest of the odd ducks can't be too picky.

I say, "Hi, I'm Jo. I, uh, spilled iced tea all over the outfit I was supposed to be wearing."

We both laugh a little at that. He's smiling. I guess that means I pass his first inspection, too. Or I don't pass his first inspection and he's too polite to let it show.

"It's very nice to meet you," he says. "I'd shake your hand but you look busy at the moment, so I'll go get my food. Man, I'm starving."

I finish fixing up my burger and getting ketchup for my fries, then I sit at a random table. My thoughts are too scrambled now to remember what Meg said about the pros and cons of sitting up front near the employees, versus at a more private table in the back. My thoughts are too scrambled for anything right now. I just take the nearest seat and focus on eating my burger. Then it hits me that it might be rude to start eating without him, so I stop.

Larry couldn't understand why I was so nervous about meeting Fred, since I "don't want sex anyway." Being outside the norm himself, Larry has the best chance of understanding me of anybody, but he doesn't. Yep, I'm super weird. Well, hopefully Fred is equally weird. But not too, too weird. Oh, my glob. What have I gotten myself into?

Here he comes. He sits down across from me. He smells good. He has on a nice aftershave or cologne or whatever. I've heard that's a good sign. Bothering to wear cologne means a dude cares about making a good impression. At least he seems to have some sense and manners. So far, so good.

He says, "I love the burgers here. The flame broiling adds great flavor." He takes a bite. I nod.

He says, "So, what do you do? Are you a student?"

"Yeah. I go to Flo Valley. I also work at Baskin-Robbins but I've put in my two weeks notice. Two plus years of that place is enough for me."

He tells me he's a general contractor. I don't quite know what that is, but from the rest of his talk about his work, it sounds like he works for himself, remodeling houses and stuff like that.

He says, "And what do you do for fun, Jo? By the way, is it Joanne or Josephine or what?" He's got an easy smile, and a calm voice.

"Josephine, but I just go by "Jo." Eh, I do this and that, you know. I plan to go inside an abandoned farmhouse with my sister this week, and then we're going to walk through the sewer tunnels under the street." Oh, my glob. I sound like an idiot. Running around in the sewer tunnels like a rat, like in that Micheal Jackson movie, Ben. I had just meant to seem at least a little bit interesting.

But he says, "Really? Sounds wild. I wouldn't mind doing things like that myself."

I get more comfortable with Fred, one bite at a time and one sentence at a time. We keep talking until an employee starts pointedly mopping the floor right under our table. Fred walks me out to

Mooms's car and gives me a hug. He says he'll call me when he gets home, to be sure I make it home okay.

He does, and we talk for another hour on the phone.

Then I go down the hall and knock on Larry's bedroom door. Before I left, he said he'd be expecting to hear every detail. Now that's a friend.

After I give him the gist of it, he says, "Wow. You hit the jackpot. So, he's from the first batch of responses. And he's the only one you've met in person. You need to quit saying you're an odd duck. What you are is a lucky duck."

"I'm trying not to get my hopes up, though. I mean, so far, so good. But who knows, he might never even call again, right?" I desperately want this to work out. I feel like I'm in love already. I try to keep that to myself because I don't want to seem like a giant spaz to Larry, especially since I already was a giant spaz, right here in this room.

Larry says, "Wow. I wish I could meet somebody I hit it off with that well."

"Wait a minute now. First, you already had your turn. And second, I'm sure it will be your turn again soon. I mean, you don't seem to have any problem meeting people."

"I guess," he says. He wants to smoke a doobie and I talk him into sneaking me a glass of wine from downstairs first. I saw an open bottle in the fridge earlier. He comes back with a chilled, nearly full bottle of Chardonnay.

I say, "Thanks. Um, can I have a glass?"

He pops his eyes at me. I get it. Two flights of stairs is too much just for a damn glass. I take a swig straight from the bottle.

We hang out for a while, listening to Larry's boom box and talking, just like old times.

Then he stops talking. I look around the room, trying to figure out what caused the interruption. He says, "Hey, wait. You're not supposed to have any type of drugs or alcohol at all, ever, once you have an addiction to any of them. Some guy I met who goes to Alcoholics Anonymous told me that."

"Shut up."

"Okay."

"On second thought, you're right. Please get me a Coke."

He pops his eyes at me again, but then he takes what's left of the wine back down the two flights of stairs and comes back with a can of Coke. I say, "Um, can I have a glass, and some ice?"

He snatches the Coke away and makes me call myself a bunch of names to get it back. Man, I've missed Larry.

Larry has a stack of new cassettes he got from Peaches, which is just about the coolest store in the world. Any record or tape you want, they've most likely got it. But it's kind of far from here. I say, "I can't believe you went there without me. Don't you ever do that again, or else. Or if you do, you better at least bring me back one of their cool crates. Or a Peaches t-shirt."

He says, "Yes, sir," which cracks me up. He pops in his Three Dog Night tape. I say, "Hey, do you know what a "three dog night" is?"

"Uh, duh. It's the name of this band?"

"Well, yeah but it originally meant a night that was so cold you'd need three dogs in your igloo or tent or whatever, with you, to keep you warm."

"Interesting. We've had plenty of those over in the tents, huh? Or at least a three-person night, where you cram everyone you can find into one tent so all the body heat keeps you from freezing to death. Where did you hear that, anyway?"

"Well, I *am* an expert on all things frigid, you know. In fact, I'll have you know I've looked up "frigid" in the dictionary many times, just to see if there were any new developments. You'd never believe how many synonyms there are for it. Let's see, there's: gelid, hyperborean, brumal, algid, hiemal---"

"Stop, stop. I don't think they're talking about the same kind of "frigid" you were looking for," Larry says, stoned and cracking up.

I continue anyway. "Boreal, rimy, cryogenic, apathetic, heartless, soulless, antisocial, unfeeling…Hmm." Suddenly, it's not that funny anymore.

Larry says, sobering, "Oh, I hear you on the slurs. I get: faggot, sissy, pansy, deviant, fruit, poof, fairy, and those are the polite ones…And don't even get me started on all the slurs for Black folks."

I say, "Yep. People are disgusting."

"No, no. Only some people are disgusting. And you and I aren't going to have a thing to do with them, darling. Chin up!"

"Yeah. Chin up." We toast. Or we try to, anyway. But the end of his joint gets soggy and sputters out when it meets the condensation on my Coke can."

The night wears on, and I say more about Fred than I'd ever think it was possible to say about someone I just met. Analyzing every little thing and all that. I see Larry's face get a bored, glazed-over look and it cracks me up. I say, "Uh-huh, now you know what it's like to listen to somebody go on and on about their new honey-pie. How do you like it?"

It feels super great to get to be the one who does that kind of babbling for once, though.

Chapter 41

There's an envelope on my dresser at Mooms's house, from the Red Lion Press. Two other publishers already rejected my story collection. Each sent a rejection slip, which are on colored half-sheets of paper for some reason, along with my returned manuscript.

I read once about a writer who collected those green, blue, yellow and pink rejection slips and used them to wallpaper the wall behind her desk, as a badge of honor for effort. I've saved my two so far. I might do the same someday.

I've already picked out a few more publishers for my next round of submissions. The advice in *Writer's Market* is to send your manuscript out in small batches because you might get advice from a rejecting editor that you can use to improve your work for the next batch.

But what's sitting on my dresser now is a regular business-sized envelope, not one of the large manuscript-sized packages that the other two came sent my manuscript back in. *Could it be an offer of publication?*

I take a deep breath. I probably just messed up on sending the return postage. They won't send your whole manuscript back if you don't include enough postage to pay for it. That's most likely it. I shouldn't get my hopes up.

Like the other publishers I picked, the Red Lion is small, but respected. I figured the smaller presses would be more likely to work with a new writer. Besides, the huge New York City publishers are too terrifying to dare approach. Even if they ever did accept my book, I'd be too intimidated to even talk to them. I open the envelope:

Dear Miss March,

We very much enjoyed your story collection entitled *Missouri, Misery* and we're honored to extend an offer of publication to you. Please read the enclosed information and sign the contract, if the terms offered are acceptable to you, and return it within the next 30 days. Do not hesitate to call, if you have any questions.

Sincerely,

Ms. Janet Moss, Acquisitions Editor

I read it over a couple of times to be sure I didn't misunderstand. I didn't misunderstand. *My book is going to be published!*

I run through the house yelling like a lunatic, waving the letter around. Mooms, Mr. Vaughn,

Amy, Larry and even the maid come right away, most likely thinking there's a medical emergency or a fire or something.

Mooms takes the letter out of my hand and reads it out loud. And then I get congratulations from everyone, and hugs all around.

Mr. Vaughn and the maid get a bottle of champagne and champagne flutes and there's a round of toasts for me.

I can't wait to tell Fred.

#

When I tell Fred my collection of short stories was accepted for publication, he says he's very impressed, and that it's so wonderful he just can't believe it. He insists on taking me out for dinner the very next night.

It's another great vibe from him, that he seems to get what it means to me. I say, "I don't know. I mean, of course I'd love to. But I'll have school work to do, and I know it's a work night for you, too." I say that last part just so I don't sound like I only think about myself. Then I cringe because it might sound like I'm scolding him.

He says, "How about just a quick, casual supper at the Ground Round and then I'll bring you straight home. I can pick you up at six and have you home by 7:30. Will that work?"

"Cool. I'll have to get some extra studying in tonight though, so I guess I'll hang up now and see you then." Globdammit. Did it sound like I just said I plan to hang up on him?

He doesn't sound annoyed, though. He says he wants to take me out for a real celebration too, so this is just for right now. I tell him he doesn't have to, that the Ground Round is plenty. I don't want him to think I'm inconsiderate about his money.

We say our good-byes. I have to take a bunch of bullshit core classes for the next two years before I can even declare a major and Algebra is kicking my butt. I have no interest in it whatsoever, so it's hard to make myself keep up on it. And this summer class is condensed as hell. It's done in half the time the semester class is, with the same workload. If I get behind, I'll be toast.

In class the next day, I can't wait for evening to arrive. It's hard to focus on the stupid Algebra chapter. Also, it strikes me how much the college looks like the prison I went to see Daddy at. Ha! They must hire the same builders.

Evening finally rolls around and we get to the Ground Round. As soon as we get inside, I slip and slide and just barely keep from falling on my ass. After recovering from an awkward and mortifying half-split, I notice that the entire floor is littered with peanut shells.

Fred says, "Oh, sorry. I didn't realize you didn't know. That's the gimmick here. They give out free peanuts and you get to throw the shells on the floor."

"Wow. That's fun. I hope they don't get sued, though." I can just see Meg giving me her raised eyebrows signal that I'm not being appropriate. She's advised me to watch my alleged sarcastic and sour demeanor with Fred. I do a laugh to try to add levity, then worry that I just brayed like a weird donkey. It seems so hard to make the right impression, when you really want to.

Fred orders a beer and the steak and shrimp. He tries to get me to upgrade from my order of a burger and fries. But I'm sticking with Meg's advice to always order from the lower half of the menu, pricewise, if you really like the guy and hope to make it long term. She says guys notice, regardless of what they say, and that they think a nice girl is one who's thoughtful with their money.

He asks about my stories and I offer to give him a copy of my manuscript. I'm super happy when he says he's honored and looks like he means it.

He tells me about some guy he'd hired to help him remodel a family's kitchen. He caught the guy kissing the lady of the house today. The lady and Fred's helper are both married. Fred just finished firing the guy after they finished up their days' work, just before he came to pick me up.

I say, "What on earth is wrong with people?"

"Oh, I know. It's crazy what people will risk just for a cheap thrill. I feel kind of crappy about it all but I just can't have that sort of thing going on with my company. Who's gonna hire you if word gets out that your guys can't be trusted around the wives."

I nod. I'm thinking this is an honorable guy I've got here. Then I change the subject, because it's reminding me that certain close family members of mine aren't so honorable.

But in my rush to move on from that loaded topic, I jump right into another one. I tell Fred about Beth's death from leukemia, and the two nervous breakdowns or psych emergencies or whatever you'd call them, that she had prior to her leukemia diagnosis.

Fred watches my face, like he's seriously listening, so I go on. I say, "I know it doesn't really matter now, but it bugs me to no end that I don't know if the psych episodes were somehow related to the leukemia. That seems like a big coincidence for one girl to have both those problems, especially when she was so young. I don't know, it just weighs on my mind, you know?"

I look down and realize the waitress has brought our meals and we haven't even touched them. "Oh, I'm so sorry. Here I am blabbing on about sad things and our food's getting cold. Please eat."

We eat in silence for a while. Then he says, "I'm really sorry about your sister."

"Thanks," I say, thinking gee, aren't I just a barrel of laughs on a date. Meg's eyebrows would be up to her hairline.

He says, "So, having that answer would put your mind at rest a little more?

"Yes." I don't hesitate with my answer. "It would just make more sense, in my mind, if they were related. And even if they're not, at least I could stop wondering about it. You know?"

"To tell you the truth, not exactly, really. But I don't really have to understand. If that's what you want to know, let's find out."

He holds my hand across the table.

After I get home from my class the next day, I call the hospital from Mr. Vaughn's study. I don't want to seem too needy to Fred, but talking to him about it boosted my resolve to try to find out. I speak to the old nurse who tended to Beth the most. I feel more at ease talking to her than I would be asking the doctor a weird question that he probably thinks doesn't even matter. I tell the nurse I just wanted to know if she thinks it's possible that Beth's mental episodes had anything to do with her leukemia, that the question was weighing on my mind for some reason.

She says, "Oh yes, hon, they can definitely be related. And in her case, I'd be surprised if they weren't. After all, the brain is part of the body and when the body's in trouble, well, it's just all connected."

I thank her and she tells me to call her anytime, if there are any other questions she can help me with. She says, "The death of a loved one, especially a young loved one, is very difficult to comprehend. Many people do have questions that might help them be able to make some kind of sense out of it." I don't know why it makes me feel better, but it does.

I feel like Fred's already filling in a place for me that Larry used to fill, back when Larry and I were so close. Reality check giver or backbone bracer or something. Well, Larry and I are still close but not close like being each other's number one person anymore, and I doubt we ever will be again. It just seems like the number one spot is reserved for the love interest and that's just the way the cookie crumbles.

One thing I don't like about having an almost-boyfriend now is all the worry. Worrying if I said something wrong or came across too this or too that. I don't recall that with Larry. But Larry and I were only a fake couple.

Chapter 42

Mooms and Mr. Vaughn are barely back from tying the knot in Las Vegas, when Daddy and Kay announce their own wedding plans. They make the announcement at Sunday dinner, just as Mooms and Meg are about to start clearing away the dinner plates. They announce it in front of Mooms and Mr. Vaughn, who are, apparently, also invited. If you ask me, that's just weird.

Kay says it's just going to be a barbecue in their backyard, nothing fancy. She says we don't need to get dressed up, jeans or shorts are just fine.

Everyone congratulates them. Mooms speaks in that high, chipper tone she uses when she's being phony for social purposes. I wonder if everyone notices it or just me. At least Mooms and Mr. Vaughn had the sense to slither off and get married alone, keeping that indecency to themselves.

I doubt the plans my sisters and I already made for next weekend will be enough to get us off the hook. My best bet is probably to pretend I'm sick.

Having to watch my father take vows to the woman he cheated on my mother with, that's already too much. But having to also watch my mother watch my father take those vows, well that is just going nuclear on the corruption scale.

I mean, it wouldn't be much grosser if Mooms and Daddy had swinger party friends and invited them to come meet the entire family, all four generations! Now I remember hearing something about how a pineapple is supposed to be a symbol for swingers. Putting a pineapple prominently on display is how swingers let other swingers know they're into it and ready to get icky. I almost blurt out "Will there be pineapple?" but Fred's here, so I have to contain myself.

Now I regret inviting Fred to meet my family. It's bad enough that both of my parents are with someone else and all having a great big weirdo Sunday dinner together. But now Fred's sitting right here next to me while Daddy and Kay make this bonus display of family corruption. I feel like crawling under the table.

Fred acts like everything's normal, though. I hope to glob he isn't just being polite. I hope he's not thinking that he and I will be over as soon as this highly abnormal dinner is over.

But we finish dinner at Mr. Vaughn and Mooms's house. Now we're about to leave Mr. Vaughn, Daddy, Larry, John Brooke and Fred over here to drink beer and watch a ball game on Mr. Vaughn's big color TV, while the ladies and I all go over to Daddy's house.

I take Fred aside, and say, "You don't have to stay here with these guys. You and I can go somewhere else by ourselves, if you want." I'm kind of expecting him to come up with an excuse of why he has to go home right this minute, alone.

But he says he's having a good time and wants to stay and hang out with the guys. I can't be sure, of course, but I take that as a good sign. I mean, who would want to bother hanging out with someone's family if they were planning to get rid of that person?

See, this is what I mean, this part that I don't like, this feeling that this might be the start of something wonderful but on the other hand, it could all disappear at any time. But I guess that's just the way it goes.

I leave Fred with the guys and come over to Daddy's house with the women. Mooms and Aunt March always seem just thrilled to help Kay sort out the big Avon order and bag up the individual orders up for the customers. In fact, they just wouldn't keep their paws out of it. Kay finally gave up and started leaving the big boxes she gets from the Avon company twice a month unopened, until we're all here.

After that's done, we'll all sit down at the dining room table to play with the Avon samples and get first peek at the new products. I'm thinking about getting the men's cologne in the cool bottle that's shaped like a car, for Fred's birthday. I might get one for myself, too.

Meg, Amy and I are in the living room, watching the little ones while the older ladies finish sorting out the Avon orders for Kay's other customers. I bring up the sewer tunnels and abandoned farmer's house to Meg, telling her that Amy's taking me to check them out and that Fred wants to come, too.

Now Meg wants to come and she wants to bring John Brooke. She says, "Yeah, we should bring the guys. You never know what kind of weirdos might be hiding out in places like those."

I agree with her. But I say, "And those weirdos are probably worried about running into weirdos like us," which cracks Amy up. Our little Miss Tag-Along, already tickled pink to be the adventuress her big sisters want to follow, is positively beaming now that we think it merits bringing two grown men along, too.

Amy says, "Fred's a fox."

"He seems to be crazy about you too, Jo," Meg says, as she gets up to disentangle the twins, who are having an adorable tug-of-war over the stuffed bear Aunt March just gave them. I'm pleased that my sisters approve of Fred. I mean, I'd go out with him anyway but who doesn't want to be thought worthy of snagging a good catch.

I feel my face heat up though, so I change the subject. The babies are both screeching now because Meg snatched the toy away from them both. I say, "I wonder if you and I ever did that."

Amy says, "Whatchoo talking 'bout, Willis? You two still do that. You two never stopped doing that." I laugh at the certainty in her voice.

Meg says, "No, that would be the two of *you*," meaning Amy and me.

"Then you'd be little Robbie, coming along to snatch the toys away from us both. You know, like you just did to those poor little ducklings," I say to Meg, earning Amy's approval.

Meg says, "So, Daddy and Kay are getting married here next Saturday. In six days. Wow, they're going to have a busy week."

Meg, Amy and I had already bought tickets for us three, plus Fred and John, to go see the Doobie Brothers at the Mississippi River Festival in Illinois next Friday night. Meg says, "Yeah, we're gonna have to cancel the concert plans. I think Kay said about three dozen people would be here. She could use our help, guys. And from a couple of things she said while we were cleaning up, I'm pretty sure she's more or less expecting it."

It is disappointing but I kind of figured that. She could have asked first or at least given us more warning, globdammit.

Meg leans forward and lowers her voice. She says, "I was surprised they invited Mooms and Mr. Vaughn. Did you guys think that was kind of strange?"

Amy, too aware for her age as usual, says, "Oh, I know. I don't think Mooms expected *that* announcement at the dinner table. Did you see the look on her face? I thought she was gonna shit."

Meg says, "Amy!" Her shocked disapproval seems to make Amy happy.

"It's highly corrupt," I say, shaking my head while my sisters laugh at me.

"You think everything is corrupt," Amy says.

"Well, many things are corrupt, Miss Smarty-Pants. Many, many things."

Meg says, "Ugh. John really wanted to go to that concert." She's trying to be a good sport but I know she was looking forward to it even more than Amy and I were. Meg has a heavy load, with her secretarial course and the babies, too.

She's also told me she worries that a ready-made family will be too much for John, that he might bolt, and find a girl who doesn't come with all that extra responsibility from the get-go.

I don't tell her this but I think she's right. If I was John, I sure as hell wouldn't want that deal. What I tell her, though, is that she'll do fine because she's gorgeous. Well, she is still pleasing looking, if not as much as she was before a year and a half of living life on the edge, then having twins. At least Mr. Vaughn paid for her to get a new tooth, to replace the one the vicious animal, Edward Moffat, knocked out.

Amy says, "Hmm. Let me just talk to Aunt March, before we cancel the tickets. I'm pretty sure she likes me again. Maybe we can still go to the concert."

Aunt March got super mad when Amy moved out, as mad as she was at Mooms, back when Mooms wouldn't give one of us to her. The thing I've learned about Aunt March though, is she gets super mad, but she doesn't stay mad. We girls have decided that she's just lonesome. What she really wants, it seems, is simply to be included. Which you'd never guess, since she talks to people in a way that runs them off. But she also seems to especially like playing the hero.

When Meg doesn't object, Amy goes into the dining room and asks Aunt March if she can speak to her alone. After a stop in the living room to coo at the babies again, Aunt March follows Amy up the stairs for a private discussion. Aunt March looks pretty delighted to be required for a private conference.

#

We do get to go to the Mississippi River Festival on Friday night, after all. Aunt March swooped right in with her live-in maid and a couple of extra maids, and they got everything bought, set up and ready to go for the backyard ceremony and barbecue. Aunt March grandly waved us girls away. "You kids go on and let the pros handle this. You'll just be in the way."

It's great to be with Fred, who I'd say is probably my actual real boyfriend now, oh my glob. It's also great to hang out with my sisters and do that whole sister-friend, partners-in-crime thing. Meg seems like a different girl now, from the one who left us and stayed away.

Afterwards, I have Amy ride home with John and Meg because I want to talk to Fred alone. In the car, I tell him about my call to the hospital and how the nurse said it's very likely Beth's leukemia and mental problems were related.

He seems a bit surprised but interested, as much as he can show when he's trying to drive anyway. I thank him for his input on that. Then I say, "I was wondering if I could run something else by you. You know, on the same theory, that two heads are better than one. I hope I'm not overloading you with my problems, though."

"No, babe. Not at all. Whatcha got?"

Babe, huh? I think I like it. I say, "Okay, but I'll have to spill some family dirt here." Fred has already met my family so he must have a clue about the parental situation anyway.

He says, "Family dirt, yay. Spill it, sister!" which cracks me up. I almost tell him to call me "brother" instead but then I decide to hold on to that for another day. I don't want to overload him with too much at once.

I say, "Okay, first, I like Kay well enough and I like Mr. Vaughn well enough. But they both started out as affairs, while my parents were married." I decide to save the part about Daddy being in prison for another day, too.

He says, "Uh-oh!" in a kind of funny way.

"Yeah. I know! I never expected anything like that to happen in my family. And to be honest, I'm not completely over it."

He says, "Oh, I understand. My father did the same. I don't know if it's something you ever get completely over, really. For me, anyway. I mean, I guess they must have had their reasons. But still, they did kinda screw up your childhood, right?"

"Right. I'm sorry you had to deal with it, too. It sucks." He gets it. I had planned to just change the subject if he said any variant of me just needing to get over it, or grow up, or if he'd seemed overly horrified, or whatever.

I say, "So, Mooms and Mr. Vaughn just got married. They got married in Las Vegas, just the two of them, so we girls didn't have to deal with it. Are either of your parents remarried?"

"Nope."

"Ah, okay. Anyway, I really, really don't want to watch one of my parents marry their affair partner, who they broke up our family with. I just can't do it. But saying so would probably turn into a Big Thing. So, all I can think of is to get out of it by lying, basically, like by pretending I'm sick. But the wedding is right next door, and everybody will be in and out of both houses. So, I'm expecting people to want to take my temperature, people nagging me to just go for the ceremony at least, and all that. I feel like I'm about to spaz out over it, to tell you the truth. Any ideas?"

He says, "It starts at noon tomorrow, right?" He's expected to attend it with me. I say yes, and he says, "Let's go to my place and hash it out. Don't worry. We'll figure something out."

I fall back into the car's seat, feeling my anxiety lift a little. It's a good feeling when someone has your back. And if it was any other guy, I'd have to worry that he was only acting concerned so he could get me to his place and try something on me.

We get to Fred's house about forty-five minutes later. His place seems about as old as Daddy's, I mean Aunt March's, house. But Fred's is smaller, just two bedrooms. It's basic housing, plain but tidy.

He kind of laughs and says, "As you can see, I work my magic on other people's houses. I figure I'll care more about my own home when it's not just me living in it."

My heart leaps. Did he mean he was thinking about not living alone anymore? *Was* it possibly a hint? Just in case he can read my thoughts, I change them. I'm being a twit anyway. I say, "So, where are we, exactly? I mean, what city or suburb or whatever?" I have an awful sense of direction. I never know where I am.

He says, "We're in Overland. Hey, you know I was talking to John and his house is just a couple of blocks from here. Small world, huh?"

"It sure is."

He gets out some saltines and a package of individually wrapped American cheese slices. Not government cheese. I take that as a good sign. He shows me a bunch of canned beverages in the icebox. He says, "Do you want a beer? Oh, right. You don't drink. Vess soda? Let's see, I have orange, cream soda, cola and root beer."

"Cream soda, please. I haven't had one of those in ages."

He heads for the living room with the snacks and drinks and I follow. After we get seated and get started on our snack, he says, "Now, about the wedding. I think… You'd want to be far enough away that they'll have no choice but to just get on with the wedding and leave you alone. And you need a believable excuse for being in that out of reach place. Yes?"

"Yes. Exactly. But how in the world can I do that?"

He says, "Okay, how's this? We'll say were on our way home from the concert, which remember, was all the way across the river in Illinois. I suddenly got violently ill, so we switched seats and you drove me to St. Elizabeth's Hospital in Granite City.

So, we're there right now and you're waiting with me. So then you tell them you'll let them know more as soon as you know more. If your mother starts asking a bunch of questions, just say "Oh, the doctor's here. I have to go. I'll call you back."

"Whoa. That's brilliant! I'll tell her you probably got sick from drinking the water in Illinois."

He says, "Huh?"

"Never mind. All right, so far, so good. But, then what?"

He says, "Let's see, it's about one in the morning now. So, you call her now. Then you call her again at, say, five or six in the morning and tell her they're still running tests, which won't be back for at least twenty-four hours. Oh, and the doctor's put you on quarantine until then, because they suspect whatever I have is contagious. Until then, he's advised you to stay here in my hospital room. Besides, you don't want to leave me alone, with me being so ill and everything. Yeah?"

"Oh, wow. This is perfect. Do you think it will fly, though? I am not a good liar."

"Well, I'm very happy to hear that, Jo." He makes a funny face.

I laugh, then get serious again. "I mean, I don't know, though. It sounds like a lot."

He says, "I'll tell you what. You make the first call now, and I'll make the second call, in a few hours. At that time, I'll tell them they took *you* down to the lab for testing."

"Yes. Perfect!" We rehearse my lines a couple of times, standing in front of the wall phone in his kitchen. Then I make the call.

Meg answers. She says Mooms isn't home. She and Mr. Vaughn went the Tan-Tar-A resort in the

Ozarks. Meg says they claimed a sudden thing came up with some people Mr. Vaughn did some business with, and they just couldn't miss it.

In other words, it sounds like Mooms found a way to bail out on their wedding, too. I feel the tension lift from my shoulders. This is wonderful!

Since I only have Meg to deal with now, I go ahead and give her the whole pretend spiel at once. I tell her we're at the hospital and the doctor put Fred and me on quarantine, so we won't be able to make it to the wedding.

After I hang up, Fred says, "You did great, babe. Now we don't even have to get up for an early morning phone call. We can sleep in." He says he'll sleep on the couch, no problem.

But I want him to sleep with me. And it's just luscious, cuddling up with him in his waterbed. Especially now that I don't have to worry about Daddy and Kay's wedding anymore. All I have to do is stay here with Fred until late tomorrow night or Sunday morning, when it will all be over. The gentle waves lull me into a deep, untroubled sleep.

Chapter 43

I didn't hear much at all about missing the wedding. Just a couple of polite comments, like "Sorry you couldn't make it" and "Does Fred feel better now?" It sort of cracks me up in a weird way to realize maybe I wasn't nearly as important as I thought I'd be in that whole scene, in the first place.

The following Saturday, Meg and I, and Fred and John Brookes, follow Amy down the storm sewer. We all slip down the street access thing one at a time, without even having to pry off the big round metal lid. There's a metal ladder thingie attached inside, that you can climb down on.

Then we're in the concrete tunnel. We trudge along, single file. When we pass by more of the street access places, they seem like basement windows, up high, with light streaming in.

It's nice and cool down here. There's just a trickle of water at the bottom, with little snails in it. It's easy to avoid the water, you just walk with your feet spread out a bit, on either side of the little stream.

If you talk down here, it echoes, which is kind of neat too. After a while, we come to a larger, central tunnel.

It's a surreal way to pass some time, playing follow the leader in the drainage sewer system with Amy. I had no idea all this was down here.

Finally, after tramping all over town, or I guess I should say, all under town, we climb up an attached metal ladder at a random street access. I don't know where we are, back on street level, but somebody figures it out.

"Wow, that was something else," Fred says. "Man, if any of us ever needs to escape from the law or anybody else, now we know how to travel." I was thinking the same thing. I mean, I can't think of a situation where I'd need to get around underneath Black Jack, but I guess you never know.

We all pile into John Brooke's car and the guys treat us to a quick lunch at McDonald's. An employee left a stack of their little metal ashtrays on top of the trash receptacle, apparently ready to be placed on the tables. Amy snatches them, about a dozen ashtrays, on the way out. I swear, the girl just gets a kick out of doing bad things. I mean, when I do something I'm not supposed to do, at least I have a reason. Amy does not need those stupid disposable ashtrays.

Then we're on to the deceased old farmer's house. There's a collapsed barn in the side yard with a giant rodent sitting on it, which Fred assures me is a rat. I'm surprised. I think of rats as being dirty, greasy little things but this guy is large and actually pretty beautiful. I'd have guessed he was a woodchuck or something.

Inside, the house has definitely been ransacked. There's junk everywhere and the place smells like urine. The guys lead the way. John Brooke's carries a tire tool and Fred carries a tree limb he picked up in the front yard. It's pretty exciting. But it doesn't look like anybody's here.

There's a small storage room with built-in wooden shelves that hold Mason jars full of home-canned food. Upstairs, John Brooke finds an old dirty magazine with a couple of pages missing. The writing's in German. The ladies aren't naked though. They're only in lingerie. He says, "Oh man. I'm keeping this." Fred kind of laughs and Meg rolls her eyes.

We finish our tour and get into a discussion on the way out about what we think will happen to the place. I'd guess the old man didn't have any relatives, since people have been partying in here for months now and nobody seems to care. Are they just going to leave the house like this until it falls down? And then, what happens to the dead farmer's bank account, assuming he had one? Nobody seems to know.

Back in the car, Amy brings up us all going to the 270 Drive-In next weekend. She says she has a boyfriend now. And she wants to bring him along, too.

John says, "I haven't been to a drive-in in ages. What's playing?"

I'm thinking Oh, no. No way. First of all, Amy just loves to make out with boys, so I doubt actually watching the movie is what she has in mind. And then, Meg and John Brooke would probably start smooching, too. I've heard about what goes on at drive-ins.

And where would that leave Fred and I? Sitting there conspicuously not making out when everybody else is? How mortifying! Fred and I have discussed our unique circumstances and have decided to just keep it to ourselves. It's nobody's business. But I could do without being put into any super awkward situations.

Fred says, "The drive-in. Yeah!"

I glare at him. He looks hurt and confused. He doesn't get it.

I say, "Good Lard. No thanks."

Fred snaps, loud enough that everyone in the car hears it. He says, "Stop that."

I feel like he slapped me, speaking to me with that tone. I say, "Stop what?"

"Using the lord's name in vain. You know, Good Lard, globdammit, and that Jesus penis thing you say." His tone is sharp, annoyed.

Oh, no. I'm not putting up with this bullshit. I say, "Yeah, thanks but I'll say whatever the fuck I feel like saying."

"Yeah, you can say whatever you want but you won't necessarily be saying it around me anymore, then."

It's dead quiet in the car. I'm so embarrassed. I try not to cry. How dare he talk to me like that. I snap, "Well, maybe I don't need to listen to your girlie hyena laugh, then."

Nobody talks the rest of the ride home. Then Fred gets out of John's car and goes straight to his car, without a word. He drives away.

I go to my bedroom at Mr. Vaughn and Moom's house and lock the door. I don't know what the hell just happened. How did it all fall apart so quick? I just lay on my bed, staring at the ceiling.

#

I go next door after dinner, to hang out with Meg for a while and get my mind off the catastrophe that Fred and I turned into. I help her bathe the babies and put them to bed. Then I ride along with her to pick up a couple of things at the grocery store.

We don't get around to discussing the big ugly topic until we're back at Daddy's house and in Meg's room, where she's doing her nightly ritual of greasing herself up. She puts Noxzema on her face and Jergen's lotion all over the rest of her. She says, "You know, you really ought to get on a beauty regimen. I'm going to do a hot oil treatment on my hair. You want some?"

"Hell no."

She says, "You know, I've always heard that you're not a real couple until you've had your first fight."

That's a very positive outlook. I like it. But it seemed far more final than that to me. I say, "I think it's over."

"Oh, I don't know about that. I think he really likes you. There was just some kind of misunderstanding in there somewhere, then one thing led to another. That's my take on it. Honestly, I'd just give him a couple of days, and if he doesn't call you before then, give him a call. But make him wait. Don't make it too easy for him, you know?"

I don't say anything because I don't know what to say.

She says, "What happened, anyway? I mean, what started it?"

"Your guess is as good as mine. It started over the drive-in plans, I think. I don't know what that 'Don't say the lord's name in vain' bullshit was, though. I didn't even know he was religious. I still don't know if he's religious. It was probably just an excuse to get rid of me."

"Hmm. Well, let me do your nails, at least. A little pampering always makes me feel better. Want a drink?"

"Hell no, on the nails. I'll take a soda though."

"You got it." She doesn't try to correct my language for a change. She comes back with two glasses of cola on ice. She gets out her manicure supplies and starts filing her fingernails.

I say, "You really seem to like all this frou-frou stuff. Have you ever thought about going to beauty school instead of secretarial school?"

She says, "I don't know. I mean, I'm not sure I'd want to do this stuff on strangers, day after day. You know?"

I ask her if she and John have had their first fight yet. She says, "No. But I'm sure our turn is coming."

After that, I help her make a potato casserole thing to take next door for Sunday dinner tomorrow. Then it's getting late. I go next door to sleep because most of my stuff's over there now.

#

Fred doesn't come to Sunday dinner. Mooms says, "Where's Fred?" I don't want to get everybody involved, in case by some chance this really is just a passing fight like Meg said. I just say, "Oh, he couldn't make it today." That seems to be enough to satisfy whatever curiosity there is.

I bring down two identical, belated wedding gifts. I found them at Venture. I couldn't resist. They're beautifully wrapped in gold paper with gold bows. After dinner, I hand one to Mooms and one to Kay.

Everybody quiets down while they open them. They both start exclaiming at the same time, and then others join in.

"Oh look, a covered ceramic pineapple dish!"

"How sweet!"

"Oh Jo, you didn't have to do that."

"A pineapple is the symbol of hospitality, you know."

I know they're making a bigger deal out of me getting them wedding gifts than it really warrants. They're just being nice to me.

I laughed my head off all the way home from the store with these two pineapples-for-swingers presents, my private hilarious joke. But everybody was so nice that now I feel pretty lousy about it.

#

On Monday, I make myself go to school and then I come home and make myself study. I do the Algebra first because it's the hardest and the most boring. I save my English homework for later in the evening, because it's easier and I don't really mind it.

After dinner, I'm thinking I might call Fred, even though Meg advised waiting until at least Tuesday. She said something about how you don't want to start the habit where you're that doggie, chasing some guy's car down the road. So, there's another cringe for me. It dawns on me that I might actually be a shitty person in general, when you think about it. Who knows, maybe Meg would have listened to me more back then if I had talked to her in a caring way instead of mocking her. You never know.

As far as calling Fred, there's really nothing to lose. I mean, as it is, I'm a doggie who doesn't even have a car to consider chasing.

I go into Mr. Vaughn's office for privacy, and shut the door. I pick up the phone receiver, then put it back in its cradle. Then I pick it up again. Just as I'm about to start dialing, I hear, "Hello? Hello?" It's Fred.

I say, "How did you answer already? I just picked up the phone to call you, but I didn't even dial yet."

He says, "I just called you, and you picked up before it rang."

"Great minds think alike?"

He laughs. I notice it's a short, controlled, deep laugh though, and I feel terrible. I know it's because I said he had girlie hyena laugh. Me and my big mouth.

I wonder if he's calling to officially break up with me. Even if he does, I still want to apologize. I cringe every time I think of what I said to him, in a car full of other people, no less. I say, "I'm really sorry I snapped at you. I love your laugh. I just felt embarrassed about what you said to me And, in that moment, I wanted to hit back." He really does have a kind of girlie hyena laugh. But I sure hope I can keep hearing it.

He says, "I'm sorry too. I should never have talked to you like that, especially not in front of other people. There's no excuse. But that look you gave me, it seemed like you suddenly hated me. I just wanted to hit back in the moment too, I guess."

I said, "I forgive you. What dirty look are you talking about, though?"

"When we were all talking about going to the drive-in."

"Oh Okay, I think I get it now." I explained to him that the look I thought I was giving him was not trying to be mean, it was trying to show urgency, like "Please don't make plans for us to go to the drive-in." I told him the drive-in talk freaked me out at the time, and why.

He says, "Wow. That was all just a big misunderstanding. I'll tell you what. Let's make a pact to always keep it nice around other people, both of us. Let's do the same thing we've agreed on as far as any talk about sex, or the lack thereof. Just keep it between ourselves."

I say, "Deal."

Then I tell him that Meg says you're not a real couple until you have your first fight. We both kind of laugh about that.

He says, "I've felt so horrible without you. I read your whole story collection. I love it. You're super talented. And I'm not just saying that either, babe."

Feeling so great after feeling so low makes me kind of dizzy.

Finally, we hang up and I get my English homework done but it takes me a while, since my mind keeps wandering off to thoughts of Fred.

Chapter 44

Aunt March is dead. I had just come home from taking my Algebra final, which I'm pretty sure I did okay on. I was getting ready for one more quick review of my notes for my English final tomorrow, and wondering if I could switch my Fall class schedule around so I wouldn't have to take a damn night class, when Mooms called me on that damn room intercom and made me jump three feet in the air.

I go down to the kitchen as Mooms requested and Amy was there, too. Mooms tells us that Aunt March's maid called Daddy this morning. She'd apparently had an "event" as those in the medical profession call it, a stroke or a heart attack or something, and she fell down that big staircase in her house. She was deceased when the maid found her. Mooms said Daddy's over there now, handling whatever has to be done.

Daddy told Mooms that Aunt March had already given him a copy of her will, just a few weeks ago. Daddy gets the house he's living in and most everything else. But he asked Mooms to tell us that we're each getting a special keepsake, along with $75,000 apiece.

Seventy-five thousand dollars. PG! (Penis guacamole!)

Amy and I join hands and begin bouncing up and down, squealing with joy. Mooms lets it go on for a minute, then reminds us that it's very sad when a family member passes.

It is sad. I say, "She was definitely a force to be reckoned with. I'm glad I got to know the good side of her more before she went."

Amy says, "Me too. She was a tough lady."

Mooms says, "All true. You know, I've wondered sometimes if you two got your strength from her, if there's a genetic component to it. You both have that brave, independent streak that I've always admired so."

I catch Amy's eye. It always surprises me when I get a compliment from Mooms, for some reason.

Mooms says, "I was close to Aunt March at one time, you know. Back when Daddy and I were just dating."

I say, "Really? I didn't know that."

Mooms says, "Well, then we had our differences. You know." She suggests we check our closets for something appropriate to wear to the funeral. "Black, gray or navy blue is best," she says. "Or any dark color."

I think of the black jumpsuit Mooms made me from her death tent fabric. It seems like that was half a lifetime ago. I think it will do, though. I go over to my garret at Daddy's to get it, while I'm thinking about it. It will need to be washed, after hanging in my armoire for so long.

#

Aunt March's funeral is pretty small and plain, considering how wealthy she was and everything. It was mainly just everybody who comes to our Sunday dinners, plus a few of our friends, and people who had worked for Aunt March at some point.

Oh, and some kooky old woman showed up, with eyebrows drawn on in such pronounced upside-down letter U's that they looked like the St. Louis arch times two. She also had highly unnatural looking hair, pastel pinky-orangey. Meg said that can occur when you try to cover gray or white hair with red dye and don't follow the instructions on the box.

The woman, who called herself Lulu, sobbed conspicuously at the wake, service and burial. Then she showed up at the buffet lunch over at Aunt March's house afterwards. I saw her wrap up some bundt cake slices and a sandwich in napkins, and dropped them into her large straw purse. Then she went about telling people that "Jo" wanted her to have the mink stole and the Waterford crystal fruit bowl and a few other pricey items, some of which weren't in plain sight. So she didn't just wander in off the street. It led to a big discussion later, about who the woman might have been.

Kay finally gave the Lulu person a couple of pieces of Aunt March's costume jewelry, as she ushered Lulu out the door. It was kind of funny. Kay held the jewelry out in front of Lulu, who followed along after it. It was like luring a cat with a piece of fish. After Kay lured Lulu out the door, Kay handed over the goodies, with a cheerful, "Be careful on the way home, now." Then Kay shut and locked the door real quick. I guess Kay's had lots of practice getting rid of problem people, from her bartending job.

Then Mooms and Kay got into a nice-nasty tiff about who would get stuck with Mop the dog, who cowered under a corner table in the living room. He wouldn't come out, even when Party began batting at him. The poor thing was seriously sulking.

Kay said, "Well, you know, we have the three little ones at our place, who might hurt the dog or get bitten. Oh, and come to think of it, I'm pretty sure Little Robbie is allergic. I swear, he get sniffly whenever that dog's around." Kay hates dogs.

Mooms, tight-jawed, says, "Well, I think you'll want to take this up with Robert. After all, Aunt March did leave *everything* to Robert, aside from what she specifically mentioned for the girls." Mooms isn't happy about losing out on the windfall, especially when Kay stands to benefit so handsomely from it. Which really doesn't seem fair at all, if you ask me.

So I'm on Mooms's side with the dog issue too, on the grounds that I don't see how it could be considered Mooms's problem. But then, to be completely fair, both of them seem to have missed some early childhood home training on what belongs to them and what doesn't.

Kay starts to nice-argue some more, when the maid, the older one who Mooms hired herself, says, "I'll take Mop." It's a little disappointing though, to be honest. This could have turned into something interesting. Possibly even a slap fight.

Sally Gardiner attends the whole ordeal from start to finish and so does Steve, who has settled in to being "just friends" with Larry. I remember that they both showed up for Beth's funeral too. But I have to say, there's something about the people who show up for your family members' funerals that makes it hard not to like them. I decide to consider both Sally and Steve friends from now on. I mean, if they want to be friends with me. They've paid their dues to our family.

Fred looks handsome in his dark gray suit, which he bought especially for the occasion.

The Lulu woman had called Aunt March "Jo," which I remember after we're back home. I ask Mooms about it. "Did you name me after Aunt March?"

Mooms looks surprised, then she says "Oh, you mean her going by "Jo?" No, dear. The nicknames are just a coincidence. Her first name is "Joella."

"Like Cruella! Cruella de Vil."

Mooms says, "Jo." Doing that thing where she says my name in a tone you'd use for a curse word. Well okay, maybe I deserve it this time, but still.

I say, "Hmm. Why did we always just call her "Aunt March? I mean, don't you think it's strange that I didn't know her first name, even when I used to work for her and everything?"

Mooms says, "I suppose so. I don't have an answer for you, though. We've all just always called her 'Aunt March.' Though I suppose it's possible she wanted to keep little devil children from calling her Joella de Vil."

"Ah. Good one."

Mooms says, "Oh, I almost forgot. Daddy said Aunt March wanted you to have this." She goes to her bedroom and comes back with a small red box, the kind jewelry comes in. I open the lid and it's a simple diamond necklace. Simple, in that it's a plain solitaire diamond pendant on a plain gold chain. But the diamond is big. Bigger than the tiny diamond that rodent Edward Moffat gave to Meg way back when, and bigger than Mooms's engagement ring from Daddy. It's not bigger than the rock on Moom's finger now, though.

Mooms said, "That's a good quality diamond. And it's a full carat."

I say, "Thanks. I hate it."

Mooms laughs and ruffles my hair like I'm little Robbie or one of Meg's ducklings.

Chapter 45

My summer grades come in the mail on the same day my check from the Red Lion Press arrives. The two envelopes are waiting for me, stacked on my dresser at Mooms's house. It's the first time I recall ever getting two pieces of mail in one day. It makes me feel important, like it's proof that I'm a real grown-up now or something.

I get a B in Algebra and an A in English 101, both of which I expected. My advance for the short story collection is $500, which seemed like a lot when I signed the contract but doesn't seem like much at all now that I have that big inheritance coming to me. Not that my writing is about the money anyway. It's more than that, to me.

Meg has completed her basic secretarial course and is all jazzed because she ranked second highest in the class. She has also snagged an interview at McDonnell Douglas. Mooms and I agree that she'd never have bothered with her studies enough to score that highly, before she had the ducklings to consider.

I say, "Well she *was* valedictorian at the school of hard knocks."

Mooms laughs her head off, which I appreciate, though it wasn't really that funny. It was probably more like hysterical laughter over everything Meg put Mooms through, and Mooms being eager to think Meg will stay on this better path now. I think Meg is still Mooms's favorite though, in spite of it all.

Larry said the kids at the tents are getting big-time harassment from the cops now. Some officers nabbed a girl who was staying there and dragged her off, kicking and screaming, to foster care. Another time, they pulled down a tent and took it away, and we never found out why.

Larry's grabbing snacks and drinks from downstairs for a meeting in his room. He's decided we need an organized tents committee, which will consist of Larry, me, Steve and Fred. I hear Larry talking to Fred out in the hallway now. We were waiting for Fred to get off work before getting started.

The first tents committee meeting goes on for two hours. By the end, we've agreed that the tents camp will be completely moved within the next couple of weeks, to a new temporary site. The site is still to be determined, but two possibilities have been mentioned so far. It will be out of the Black Jack city limits, to get away from the local campaign against it.

Also, a parcel of land will be located, agreed on and purchased by the committee for a more permanent tent camp. We've left the details open for now, since none of us have any idea what a piece of land might cost or which locations are less likely to encounter resistance from the locals.

Then we toss around ideas about setting up a self-governing body at the permanent camp, when we get it. But the guys are drinking, along with smoking weed and then they're just getting stupid. After the third dirty joke about camping and "getting s'mores," I drag Fred away and make him take me to Arthur Treacher's for fried clams, as punishment for getting on my nerves.

#

I start a fight at Sunday dinner, or rather everyone here who is a pinhead starts a fight. It started when Meg asked me to watch her ducklings at Daddy's house, while she helped get ready for the dinner over at Mooms's.

I got the idea to switch the twins' clothes, because I was bored or something, I don't know. Like big deal, right? So, I showed up for dinner with Donald in a pink dress and a matching bow on his head, and Daisy in Donald's pastel blue overalls with the little truck embroidered across its bib and the light blue baby baseball cap. I thought it was kind of cute.

Well, penis guacamole, you'd think I gave them sex change operations right there on the dining room table. Of course, everyone who is stupid was mad about Donald being dressed up like a girl. They barely even mentioned Daisy being dressed like a boy. Now, what does that tell you? It's blatant, unexamined misogyny, pure and simple.

Meg and John snatch the babies up all sanctimoniously and started pulling their clothes off, with great vigor. If you ask me, they were just making it into a big overblown bonding moment, at my expense. Ooh, look at Meg and John everybody, they're super-duper coupled up against the big bad Jo, they're the morally superior crusaders against incorrect clothing colors! So dumb. And Kay and Daddy and Mooms all have the nerve to sit there, sadly shaking their heads at me. Glass houses, glass houses!

I didn't expect this crazy reaction and it makes me furious. I say, "Fine then. Fuck all of youse crazies." Just like that maid said to them when she walked out on Christmas. She knew they were nuts. It's not just me who thinks so.

I look back to see that Larry, Steve and Amy are laughing though, and Mr. Vaughn looks amused, too.

I'm on my way out because I can't take any more of Meg's stupidity and because everybody always takes her side. But I stop at the open front door, for some reason. I watch as they all settle back in and start passing around the fried chicken, the mashed potatoes and the wobbly pink Jello salad.

Fred comes up behind me, coming in from the porch. He was running late today. He puts his arms around me from behind, like he's bolstering me up to face whatever's in front of me, because that is what he does.

We just stand there watching my corrupt, crazy, stupid and beautiful family, forks clattering onto plates, until they notice Party, perched in the middle of the table like an exquisite centerpiece. Then there's a big communal intake of breath, before they start going crazy over that next, like they're frozen in time for a second.

It's like I'm watching a still life, just outside the frame of it but guarding the door, always guarding the door. And then of course they all start their damn squawking again, picking on Party this time, and the curtain falls on the March family.

The End

Dear Esteemed Reader,

I hope you enjoyed reading this retelling as much as I enjoyed writing it.

Also, Amazon book reviews help us authors out hugely and are most appreciated, if you feel so moved and can spare the time.

Best Regards,

Carly

www.ingramcontent.com/pod-product-compliance
Lightning Source LLC
Chambersburg PA
CBHW030558180626
46816CB00005B/1596